C000004185

Disclaimer (All characters and scenes within this novel are fictional. Although geographic places do exist, they are used as points of reference. Some of the content may be graphic and written for dramatic effect. It is not the authors wish or intention to offend or upset any victims of crimes portrayed within this novel)

Copyright © 2022 David Mayall

To request permissions, contact the publisher at d.mayallwriter@gmail.com.

Hardcover: ISBN 978-1-73961492-8
Paperback: ISBN 978-1-73961491-1
Ebook: ISBN 978-1-7396149-0-4

First publication produced July 2022

Acknowledgements

First I would like to thank my wife Eleanor Mayall for not giving up on my dream of writing a book. Without her support, encouragement, and belief; this would never have been completed.

Additionally, my special thanks to my friend Tracey Friel for her countless reading of the many early drafts. Her honest opinions and straight to the point advice has really helped bring this project to completion.

I thank my Editor Gina Fiserova for her superb help, guidance, tips, advice, and the countless other things she has done for me over the years. Gina's patience and perseverance, at times when I was ready to give up, were the encouragement needed to complete this project. Its her belief in me which gave me belief as a writer. I am truly indebted to Gina and cannot thank her enough.

I thank all alpha and beta readers who read this during its many drafts and I give a special thanks to Donna Morgan for her helpful tips and advice.

I'd also like to thank the many people who have helped me learn and practice the art of writing throughout the years.

A final thanks to my Mother and Father who have always stood by me even during my darkest hours.

To my children,
Ben, Matilda, Marcus, and Oliver.
Remember,
you can do anything you set your mind to.
Never give up on your dreams and always believe.

MR BLUE

EYES

By David Mayall

PART 1

Kirsty and Steve

Kirsty Edwards' lungs burned as her heart hammered. Only the noise of her trainers against pavement matched the thunder beating her ribs. It was 6am, and she loved these early June mornings. They helped her relax and think, both of which she needed to do. Steve had rattled her. He hadn't been himself, and Kirsty's insecurities were a ravenous beast which grew over the slightest of reasons. Her boyfriend's secretiveness made Kirsty nervous.

"You're being silly," she said between concerned gasps. "Steve loves you and you him. You have little reason to worry."

She smiled as the sun's warmth stole the chill from the dawn and the blackbirds twittered. *But what if he doesn't anymore?* She worried; the thoughts screamed as a banshee inside her head. *What if he wants to dump you? Perhaps that's why he's been so withdrawn.*

"Don't be so absurd," Kirsty said with a sharp retort, but the doubt had crept into her brain and the paranoia grew.

She jogged a little faster and reached her last mile. A modest cottage where the smell of lavender and rose bushes engulfed her. Intoxicated by the perfume, *you're being foolish*, she decided and smiled. She was an attractive nineteen-year-old girl with strawberry-blonde hair which would dance about her shoulders. This morning she had tied it back, and as she ran it swished like a horse's tail. Her aura of childlike wonderment shone within the turquoise of her eyes. She quelled her fears and pushed aside her insecurities. She loved Steve and to her, that's what mattered, but as her pace slowed, and she neared the meagre three-bed semi where she lived with her mother. A small part of her brain still wondered, *why was he being so strange?*

— ☐ —

Steve hated keeping secrets. Especially ones as damaging as the one which had him awake most of the night. He hid two secrets and glanced over at the ring box placed on his cabinet. This was Steve's master plan, the one he and Abigail, Kirsty's best friend, had taken months to organize and arrange. The hidden messaging, and phone calls, his flimsy excuses not to meet up on various nights. The holiday arrangements, the practised speech. These activities Steve had been doing without Kirsty's knowledge. He just hoped it was adequate.

Something darker dwelled on his mind, but Steve didn't know how to tell Kirsty. He still couldn't accept what the police officer had revealed to him or what she had disclosed. He was the last person to see the sixteen-year-old girl. The girl that the news articles were chuntering on about. She had been in that car when Steve had been visiting mom and dad at the cemetery. The young girl appeared fine to him, nothing special about her. They had shown her picture on every channel saying she was missing; it was possible she might have run away. So, he thought little about it until her body had been discovered, and now he battled his guilt. This is what led him to go into the police station and provide a statement. The officer hadn't let him leave until 9pm the night before. Asking the same questions over and over, "Where were you?" they inquired. "What time was it?" and, "Why didn't you come forward earlier?"

Truth be known, Steve hadn't granted it much attention. He'd seen her in the car, and that was about as significant as it went. He asked why she was there, but didn't pry any further. Now she was dead, and the police suspected Steve was in some fashion connected.

They were going on holiday today and he'd lain awake since the early hours trying to fathom what to say to

Kirsty. He didn't know how, or when, he should tell her? *What would she think of him? Would she still feel the same towards him as he did toward her?* Steve looked at the small box. *Would she give him the answer he hoped for?* These questions and more were hornets buzzing inside his head. This is what had kept him up for half the night.

A knock on his bedroom door interrupted his thoughts.

Lost Dignity

Madrid, Spain

Standing on the bank of Madrid's Manzanares river, Detective Baldomero spread his magnificent eagle winged moustache between thumb and forefinger. He watched the policia underwater search unit as they swam out to the corpse pinned against the footings of Puente de los Franceses (Bridge of the French). The railway bridge had been named after the French engineers who built it, comprising five semi-circular brick skew arches. The second most significant arch was where the body of a woman had been snagged. Its exposed torso whose bleached appendages waved white cotton flags of truce in death's ultimate surrender. Baldomero waited as the three frogmen worked to retrieve the body.

He wondered, *what's your story?*

48 hours earlier... 5:45 am.

Celia's face burned crimson as she snatched the bottle off her desk. In a scramble to reach its contents, her hand twisted off the cap and it fell to the floor to give a metallic clink. Already lost beneath blankets of grime that sheltered from the shafts of dawn sunlight. In her shaking hands, the bottleneck rattled against the glass, so she fore-went the tumbler and slugged liquor non-stop before banging the bottle down upon the counter. A spatter of the cheap vodka jumped from the neck and puddled around the base. She was positive that Marco would blame her because Stefania had been missing for days. She hoped the foolish girl hadn't got herself a regular client. This sort of arrangement was the last thing Celia or Marco wanted.

Was it the vodka that caused her to tremble, she considered, or Marco, she couldn't be sure? He wouldn't tolerate their best girl entertaining clients without his authorisation. Celia chewed on her lower lip before gulping more vodka and sucking from a lipstick-smeared cigarette. She allowed it to dangle from the corner of her mouth as bluish smoke gushed, dragon style, from each nostril. Watching their tendril's hypnotic dance, she thought for a moment, then emptied the contents of the bottle to savour its intensity. The liquor's harshness did little to warm her mood, and she sagged with a groan against her office chair until a knock at the door disturbed her brooding. Chantelle, one of the business's newest girls, appeared at its threshold. Marco and Drulovic had spent the previous few weeks forcing her drug addiction. It didn't take long before she accepted her role as a whore.

"Well?" Celia barked. "Don't stand there gawking. What do you want?"

"We... Well..." Chantelle spluttered. "I couldn't help but notice, Stefania hasn't worked for the past few days?"

"Huh," Celia shrugged. "Do you know where she is?" her words slurred. "Is somebody with her?" Celia answered the question. "I know there is." Scrunching her hands into tight fists, "So? Tell me who it is?"

"Honest, I haven't seen or heard anything," Chantelle protested. "But I never get the good-paying clients when Stefania works. I'm making decent money, could I keep her spot?"

"Find out if Stefania is entertaining a client," Celia said with a snarl. "She's our best earner but if there's no sign of her working by tonight, then it's yours."

— ☐ —

Stefania's belch broke the silence inside the bathroom of room 61. Her vacant eyes had lost their sparkle as she stared at the white tiled walls. Her stomach lurched a noxious odour, like putrefied cabbage, fouled the air. A rubber tourniquet strapped around her emaciated forearm; a needle dangled from the open scars of tracked veins. She sighed, a long-drawn-out sigh that could almost be mistaken for one of passion. But the wet gurgling erupting from deep within her revealed a different story.

Nothing mattered any more. Not even the chill coming from the tiled bathroom floor gave her any concern. She didn't care about this indignant display. The drugs had whisked her away to peaceful tranquillity.

— ▢ —

Madrid, Spain, 4:00 pm.

Celia slugged more vodka, but her shudder this time was more hesitation to call Marco than the effects of alcohol. Tapping a Lucky Strike cigarette from a new carton, she lit it as the silhouette of Chantelle shrouded the light from the open doorway.

"Have you found her?" Celia snapped.

"No, ma'am, she wouldn't answer me," replied Chantelle, "but she's in the room. I heard sighing. You know…" She grabbed an invisible person and pumped her hips to simulate sex. "That kind of sigh." She grinned at her act, then shrugged. "But none of the other girls have seen her — either. So, she must be there."

Celia forgot about Chantelle for the moment, and spoke aloud, "I know she's there." Pulling hard on the cigarette, vaporous smoke hovered in the air. Her eyes locked with Chantelle's.

"Stefania must think she's too good for work." The cigarette's glowing red tip crackled as it smouldered. "It's time she came back down to earth." Celia swayed when she stood. "Get yourself ready, we're opening soon; it looks like you have your wish." She chewed away at the cigarette. *Sometimes the girls need to be put in their place, she thought.*

They'd allow popularity to go to their head. Believed they could do as they pleased. If Stefania didn't answer this very second, then God damn it. She slammed her fist on the desk. *I have little choice other than to call Marco.* A chill as intense as the arctic wind froze her heart.

Like a sailor in rough seas, Celia weaved from left to right. Drunkenness exaggerated each small stagger. At Stefania's room, she was panting. Sweat slicked her brow and dripped from her nose. Celia rapped her knuckles against Stefania's door and caused the girls from other rooms to peer into the corridor. They soon vanished when they saw Celia's glowering face as they listened to her ranted profanities. Her fists made loud thumps upon the wooden surface, but still, she gained no response.

Celia screamed, "Marco will not be happy with you, Stefania. Or the client you're hiding in there!" Flecks of white spittle sprayed on the bedroom door. There was a noise from within. *What was that?* She quizzed. *Was that a shuffle of movement, or was it a groan?* Celia couldn't be certain. Then another sound, this one a whispered cry, like distant pan-pipes carried on a breeze. The cries of a woman during the heightened throes of pleasure.

Anger swelled, and Celia pressed her ear flat against the cool surface of the door. Another faint murmur came from inside. A soft bubbling gurgle, followed by a long whistling gasp. The sound lingered, as if mocking her. "Are you listening to me?"

Celia changed tack. Aiming her threats toward the man, who must be in the room, to make Stefania groan that way. "Hey?" she shrieked, "You had best take your things and get the hell out." No response. "You want to avoid being in there when Marco arrives."

— ☐ —

Celia's hands shook from anger and the effort of clambering up and down the stairs. She lit a fresh cigarette, sucking in hard. Then reached for the vodka as she exhaled.

Slugging the bottle's contents and embracing its warming relief. Celia loathed involvement with Marco, but knew there wasn't any other option. If she left the situation any longer, he would kill her. He would beat her anyway.

A good-looking Englishman would sometimes accompany Marco. He had the brightest of blue eyes. The bluest Celia had ever seen. Vast oceans of intoxicating confidence showing he was the Alpha male and the man in charge. This mysterious Englishman with his deep sapphire pools petrified her almost as much as Marco. But the Englishman always thwarted the beatings so she prayed Marco wouldn't show up alone. She picked up the phone. It was time to carry out the dreaded call.

— □ —

Marco Brancho was a goliath. Two hundred and fifty pounds of serious muscle. His mahogany eyes pierced deep into a person's soul. A natural slope to his forehead and heavy-set brow was common of Eastern European men. Spreading across the jawline of his left cheek, ending a little below Marco's left eye was a savage scar. Born in 1984 in Sarajevo and orphaned at a young age, he suffered but survived the Bosnian — Serbian war. His upbringing had changed him into an emotional cripple without empathy or value for life. His boss, who Marco had nicknamed Mr Blue Eyes, was the sole person he'd show any understanding toward. Exercising out of a necessity to complete his duties meant Marco was ready whenever Mr Blue Eyes ordered. To Marco, this was his gratification.

— □ —

The business opened for work at 5 pm; it was now 5:20. Marco entered through the rear and followed the stench of cheap perfume and stale cigarette smoke. Barging into Celia's office and grinning when she flinched to divert her gaze away from his mutilated face. He didn't appreciate people who stared at his brutal scar.

With a growl, he made his demands and said, "Take me to her."

Celia shuffled past him in silence and headed towards the rear stairwell. Ignoring Jonas, one of the club's security personnel who they passed on the stairs. Marco followed Celia, who was now hammering her fist upon the door of room 61.

— ☐ —

He became impatient after Celia's third attempt, and Marco threw her out of his way. She pirouetted across the corridor before striking, dazed, against the adjacent wall. Bracing against the door's frame, he booted the lock. The framework rattled, but remained locked. He kicked and was rewarded by a splintering noise. After another kick and shoulder barge, he crashed inside with sufficient force to shower plaster dust and wooden shrapnel.

The room's off-white walls were a typical Spanish design. A double bed against the far wall and a small bedside dresser with a lamp stood next to the bed. The place itself appeared harmless enough but Marco hesitated. He realized all was not good inside. A slight, but pungent stink of vomit lingered but was overpowered by a more disagreeable odour. It was this foulness which caused Marco's hesitancy. He eased the wrecked bedroom door further to see inside the room.

Marco already knew the tenant had departed from this earth. It stank like raw sewage at an abattoir. The air seemed cloying somewhat, as if thickened by a loathsome pestilence, and he headed toward the bathroom.

And there Stefania lay.

— ☐ —

Stefania's nightdress pulled half up above the knee to expose her left thigh. Her skin veined like blue cheese with mottled purplish bruising. Her shoulders propped between the sink and lavatory bowl, body sagged with limbs bent, and her knee curled up. The last stage of Rigor Mortis leaving her. One foot, resting against the bath panel, had swollen, and turned black from blood's lividity.

Head tilted backwards with dried vomit which crusted Stefania's mouth. Her once radiant hair was lank and flat as it hung over her right shoulder. Burnt ochre eyes were half closed and rolled back, staring at a point beyond this life. Her skin was a slackened wax of greyish-white and held a lustrous appearance. Lips were dirty-black and swollen as was her protruding tongue. Stefania's arms were at her sides. These displayed the same blue-cheese effect and pooled on the floor was a tarry puddle of viscous blood.

Stefania's corpse seemed to breathe. A deep grumbling sigh which startled Marco into thinking she had come back from the dead. Built up gas passing vocal cords as internal organs putrefied. A lone black fly crept across her face searching for a place to lay its eggs. It settled at the corner of Stefania's once pretty eye, and in death as she had in life, Stefania lost her dignity.

First Holiday

"Steve?" cooed Ruth. "Steve, darling, wake up?"

Ruth rattled a woodpecker knock on his bedroom door, then tutted disapproval from his lack of reply.

From the bottom of the stairs, Mark shouted up, "The kettle's on."

"Okay, love," she replied. "I'll be down once I've woken him up."

Her knock turned into a flat palm bass drum thud.

She called to Mark and added, "Be a darling and start setting for breakfast." Ruth grinned as she listened to him moan. Her attention shifted back to the adjacent bedroom door.

"It's time you were up, Hun. You awake?"

From further down inside the house, "If he's too bone idle," Mark said, his remarks a dull mumble, "to get out of bed, by himself, at his age — then leave him."

"I'm alive," Steve murmured from inside the room. Trying to ignore his foster mum. He'd been up for hours mulling things over, but didn't wish for them to know. They'd only worry.

But Ruth knocked again and said, "Come on darling, if you want to avoid being late for the airport. I assume you've packed everything."

Steve knew she'd never go away unless she'd seen he was up and out of bed. *God, I hate mornings,* he concluded.

Wishing Ruth would leave him in peace, but it wouldn't happen.

Steve opened the door. "Morning mum."

"Are you getting up, sweetie?" Ruth inquired.

"I'm up," he declared. "Be down in a mo."

"I'll make you breakfast." she answered. "You need to hurry, or you'll be late."

Head thick with sleep, his mouth parched like a cat's sandbox. "On my way," Steve responded, "Down in a minute."

— □ —

Kirsty slipped both arms around "Snuggles," a toy stuffed Panda Steve had given to her on last Valentine's Day. She had called it Snuggles because it reminded her of Steve and how she enjoyed their cuddles so, she squeezed it tight.

"Aw, I'm going to miss you," she said in childlike fashion, "But I have my Steve to cuddle... You'll have to keep Flopsy company." Flopsy was another stuffed toy, this one a bunny.

Kirsty picked up her mobile and messaged.

"Morning darling. OMG. G. G. Today's the day we go on holiday. So excited. LOL. H&K. LUVYA XX,"

— □ —

Kirsty gave Steve a squeeze as they booked in for their flight. Then she tugged his hand and dragged him with her. "Come on!" She giggled.

They rushed towards the cavernous departure lounge. Releasing her grip enough to allow him to pass security but once through, she hugged into his bicep. This was a welcome distraction from the recent stress he'd been under. His visit with the police inspector raced a rollercoaster through his belly. He hadn't told Kirsty about the encounter in fear she would worry, but knew keeping it secret wasn't a choice, he would tell her, but couldn't determine when to have that discussion. Anyway, he had another happier secret to see through first, so thought best not to dwell on the inspector's ludicrous ideas. Steve grinned as he watched Kirsty become like a child at Christmas.

Nearby a mom with a pushchair stopped to manage the needs of her toddler. The infant cried, and its damp face was a vivid crimson. Behind the mother, two other children followed. It was clear they were brother and sister, as they looked like each other. The boy was about eight and sported a shock of ginger hair combed to a side parting. Plump plum cheeks under a smudge of freckles which puffed exertion as he raced after the girl. He kicked out but missed her, and the boisterous pair ploughed into Kirsty and Steve.

A volcanic outburst of anger bellowed from the mom who shrieked, "Will you little shits pack it in?"

"But she started it," moaned the boy. "She's spitting at me, Ma," he grumbled. "Tell her to stop spitting."

Their mother's face scowled, hot embers behind hazel eyes. "I don't care who started it," she said and jabbed a finger at them both. "You two better start behaving, or else." She flicked her chestnut hair and searched the surrounding area for someone. "Where has your dad got to?"

A man with receding copper hair and a ghost white complexion with sallow cheeks and empty eyes appeared. He sounded disinterested in the pandemonium and averted eye contact with the mom. "Please children, do as your mom asks."

Leaning close to Steve, Kirsty giggled and pointed at them. "I hope the family from hell aren't on our flight."

A tin-can announcement informed them their plane was ready to board, so Kirsty and Steve headed towards their gate. The disruptive family followed, and Kirsty groaned as she clutched Steve's arm and leant into his shoulder. The children who were creating chaos, unconcerned by the disapproving glares from other passengers, plus their mother and toddler, were seated in the row behind Kirsty and Steve.

Steve leant in and pecked a kiss on top of Kirsty's braided hair and spoke in a whisper, "This is going to be an eventful trip."

"Mom, you promised I could sit by the window?" Squealed the little boy, who was busy tugging his sister's pigtails. He kicked into the rear of Steve's seat.

"No, she didn't... she said I could... aargh, get off my hair." Said the girl who squealed more than spoke.

"For God's sake. Can you pack it in?" yelled the mom who was bumping the toddler upon her knee like she was a basketball player about to start the last quarter.

Another clonk hit into the chair, and Steve gave Kirsty a sideways glance. He peered out of the window and watched the wings of the aircraft slice through cotton clouds.

The aircraft's rhythmic motion lulled Steve toward slumber, added to his terrible night and it wasn't long before he'd given up the battle. Sleep was unsettled, tormented with images of a juvenile face. The sixteen-year-old was speaking to the blue-eyed man. Steve quizzed him on why she was in his car, but the vinyl record of his dreams skipped the needle. Steve now witnessed the anguish of her parents, who pleaded for their daughter's safe return.

The girl's name had been Kerry Wells. A troubled teen who had run-away. Kerry was front page news and had been for the previous three weeks. Steve's dream skipped again. He was crunching along a gravel path; he recalled the rain was a frigid mist of ice needles that chilled his face. The man's blue eyes averted Steve's questioning stare and Steve asked, "Why is she in your car?"

The guy explained he was helping the girl and would take excellent care of her. That Steve needn't be concerned. Another dream skip and developments of recent days replayed. The girl's image flashed before him once again, but Kerry hadn't received excellent care, like the man had promised she hadn't been, "Looked after." They had discovered her; part concealed within the undergrowth on a West Midlands canal towpath.

— ☐ —

Steve's dream shifted to Inspector Collins. Her voice was as gentle as duck-down feathers. "Steeeve…" she murmured. Her tone puzzled him. The police officer in his dream opened her mouth and spoke again. Only it came with more urgency, a louder, more familiar tone.

"Steve, wake up darling, you're snoring." The police officer spoke in Kirsty's voice. "Steve," Kirsty said with a shout and shook him by the shoulders.

Like a strike of lightning, he was awake. "Wha… what?"

Kirsty giggled and added, "You're snoring — so loud, you're going to bring the plane down."

His cheeks flushed, "Was I?" He yawned and wiped his mouth as he realized he'd been drooling too, "Sorry," and looked out of the window, "Are we there?"

"I think so," Kirsty said.

"You think so? What?" He quizzed, already forgetting his question.

"I think we're there, silly," Kirsty replied with a disapproving tut.

Like flotsam on a languid shore, the dream drifted around his thoughts. Inspector Collins, the leading investigator, pleaded with the public to come forward. Steve had plucked up the courage to ring the Police officer and had seen her the previous night. Unable to believe what she disclosed to him. It just couldn't be right. However, Collins had presented a solid argument. She was also certain that Steve was a key witness, and he had agreed to help.

The plane descended, buffeted by dense cumulus clouds which rocked Steve from his thoughts. He glanced over at Kirsty. I'll tell her everything as soon as we return home, he decided, but for now, let's enjoy our first holiday.

Preparations

Marco called Doctor Drulovic knowing he would set in motion the disposal of the corpse. The next person Marco called was Mr Blue Eyes to update his boss about the corporation's loss. Mr Blue Eyes had a replacement in mind.

"Don't fret," he assured Marco. "Stefania's replacement will visit Spain soon. Get everything cleaned up and make sure they can trace nothing back to us." Blue Eyes paused, then added, "When you're happy, Marco, you'll need to go hunting."

Marco felt hot shivers of excitement electrify the hairs of his neck. He smirked at his next series of instructions. His scarred face sneered hatred as his concern shifted to Celia who trembled as if an animal awaiting slaughter.

Spittle sprayed through clenched teeth. "One job," came his contemptuous roar, "That's all you have, just one simple task," his viperous eyes narrowed.

"I'm sorry ..." Celia began.

Marco slammed his left boot between her legs,

She was washed away in a storm-surge of pain and crumpled onto hand and knee. A cry, like a scared dog, pushed from her lungs as she squirmed around on the corridor floor. Her tears blinded beneath a mask of smudged mascara, and she choked at his feet. Gripping her hair, Marco twisted into his bunched-up fist, then yanked her up. A million stars from a clear midnight sky danced at the back of her eyes when Marco's knuckles exploded her nose. The bone crunching crack echoed before a swathe of black oblivion welcomed Celia.

— ☐ —

The next morning Celia woke in a crumpled heap upon her bathroom floor. She couldn't recall how she'd got there. Clutched in her grip was a half-drained bottle of vodka. She sobbed and stood, bringing the booze to her lips. Peering at herself in a narrow, wall-mounted mirror. Looking at the grim spectre, who gazed back. An oval-shaped lump like an intense bluish plum protruded over her left eye. Her crooked nose was inflamed and leached, purplish bruising underneath each orbital socket. She whimpered and said, "How have I let myself get to this?"

Gripping the vodka, she was intent on pouring it into the sink. To be done with its evilness but, something compelled her to stop. Her willpower was weak, and she couldn't force herself to dispose of its precious contents. Another big glug of the booze made her flinch, and she sagged down on the bath. A self-pitying sob juddered from her. This is no way to act, she instructed herself, and stood up. Looking back at her reflection, In defiance, "I won't give that bastard." referring to Marco. "The satisfaction."

Celia staggered to Stefania's bedroom. She couldn't believe the girl was gone. If only I had checked sooner, perhaps I could have saved her. Guilt tore into her like sharp talons ripping carrion. "I'm so sorry, Stefania," she whispered. The sickly perfume of decay still lingered in the air. A token reminder of Stefania's demise.

— ☐ —

Celia had overheard Marco's conversation about the replacement which was on its way. That was how simple this had been for him. One young woman's memory washed away like soiled laundry. An alternative had been chosen, and he had left to secure her from Salou.

Picking up a small photograph, Celia stared into Stefania's pretty face and vowed, "This unknown girl, whoever she may be, I guarantee I will take care of her." The image shook in Celia's hands. "I will not allow the same to happen to her." She patted the sign of the cross on herself. "As God is my witness. I promise this to you." Her words slurred, part through her injuries and part from alcohol. Glancing one last time at Stefania's face before throwing the photo into the sack of Stefania's clothes.

Somebody outside the room coughed. A wiry fellow in khaki coveralls said, "Sorry miss, I didn't mean…"

"Who are you?" Celia answered, her words sounding stern. "What do you want?" Then stared at the bag of woodworking tools.

He tried not to gawk at Celia's battered face, but found it hard to avert his stare.

Holding up the bottle of vodka and giving it a slight jiggle. "Had a little too much the other night and took a tumble," she lied then inquired, "Have you come to secure the door?"

"Yes ma'am, it shouldn't take long."

Looking around the room, happy it was now ready for a fresh tenant. "Ignore the stink. I discovered a dead rat," she said in a way of explanation. "Shut the door when you're done," she directed, "I'll be in my office," and lurched past. "The ladies will show you where."

— ☐ —

Detective Baldomero rubbed at his temple as he referred to the medical examiner's report. He slurped tepid pond water coffee, its bitter taste doing little to stave off fatigue. He gripped clumps of dense coal-black hair and flexed his muscular shoulders before stretching out his creaking back. The cause of death recorded for the Jane Doe they pulled from the river was an overdose. The toxicology report showed respiratory depression, from the combined effect of opioid (heroin), alcohol and benzodiazepines (Valium). The individual also revealed recent traces of sexual activity but no evidence of force, so was most likely consensual. However, someone had gone to considerable lengths to dispose of her. Why? This was a question which baffled Baldomero. He read further into the detail and scoured the database for related deaths. There were several overdose deaths, all within the last month. Only one of these became of interest because of the chemical screening on the barbiturates being the exact same composition. This death happened a fortnight ago. They found the remains of Sebastián Garcia, who was a petty crook in the Bravo Murillo District. Discovered in the early hours, lying with the gnawing rats which had nested in the cardboard, discarded behind a side street café dumpster. Garcia, to the detective, was a small-time opportunist who associated with a fellow addict and dealer called "Curly." All local law enforcement recognized Curly as another scourge of Madrid's populace. Well, it's a lead, I suppose, thought Baldomero as he prepared to leave. It may amount to nothing, but all leads are worth investigating.

— ☐ —

The S.F.A. Corporation (Sustainable Fungicides for Agriculture Corporation) was owned by Mr Blue Eyes. The firm ran several plants in the Tarragona area of Spain, Spain's main centre for the petrochemical industry. Out of the three S.F.A. facilities in Tarragona, only two of them produced sustainable fungicides. The third location was under development. A discreet facility of abandoned storage depots and a warehouse. The building was manned when safety inspections were required. Marco would oversee their care whenever the inspectors visited. High-profile individuals also utilized the place to satisfy their carnal tastes which were of the more demanding kind and discretion was paramount. The prostitutes would take care of the desires of the clients in the areas beneath the warehouse. The construction's main activity was a cover-up which concealed the basic purpose for the import and export of girls around Europe. Four days after Celia called him to the club, and after dealing with other issues, Marco had driven to this location.

— ☐ —

Marco entered the chill of the warehouse basement. A playroom for those with a sadomasochistic desire. Bondage, domination and similar fetishism whatever were the clients specific tastes. The smell of the maroon leather walls did nothing to arouse Marco, nor the sight of all the hand and feet chains and locks. A black PVC bench with several handcuff and leg cuff restraints stood central to the room as if it were an art gallery exhibit. Marco, being an asexual man, never sought gratification of the flesh, and these practices were foreign to him. However, the ceiling restraints, where an individual could be suspended from the roof and off the floor, plus the iron shackles to avoid escape did. Together with the gags, hoods, whips, floggers and many other torturous devices, they were perfect for his demands. He made the area ready for his intended victims before returning upstairs. Marco switched on his smartphone and scrolled his messages. He opened the most recent from Mr Blue Eyes- it showed:

Marco.

The package will arrive next week.

Landing at Reus airport at 2.20pm.

You know what you must do.

— ☐ —

At Reus Airport, Marco read the monitor for the scheduled inbound flights. Armed with a picture of his victims, he waited until Kirsty and Steve walked past. He saw them leave and head for their transfer coach. Unaware of the menace presented by Marco who pursued with rigid concentration, a prowling cheetah who had singled out its destined prey.

He watched, scorched under the mid-afternoon sunlight, and observed them climb aboard a sky-blue coach. "Holiday Sun," was its brand and a picture of the glowing sun was along its side. Marco made a mental note of the coach company and returned to his vehicle, a white Range Rover Evoque.

"Don't worry." He glanced at the shrivelled car ornament dangling from his rear-view mirror. "We will catch them."

He cleared the busy airport traffic and headed south. There was only one way for the bus to travel, and Marco followed the sign to get him onto the C-14 highway.

Sure enough, he quickly caught up as they approached the T-11 to Falset/Alcañiz/C-14/Salou. The route would take twenty minutes, but with regular stops at various locations, the trip would last an hour. Marco settled into the soft leather of his seat and said, "It's going to be hot again."

— □ —

Marco had taken care of one complication. The junkie known as Curly who supplied the heroin that resulted in Stefania's death. Marco visited him the day after being called into the club. He glanced at the tablets he had been given.

"Rohypnol. This'll work, Eh? Curly." He spoke with a smirk. A pulse of satisfaction ran the length of his spine. Marco laughed as he listened to the comments of Mr Blue Eyes echoing inside his skull. Mr Blue Eyes' military background had taught Marco well. It's best to be versatile; to accomplish the objectives involved, Blue Eyes instructed.

"And what if it breaks down?" replied Marco aloud.

The voice echoed again. You should have a plan A, B and C, too many factors can generate complications and influence the result.

"I have my agenda, trust me. I'll get the job completed." Marco spoke as if the empty air would answer him. He looked across toward his gruesome ornament and grinned. "We have our strategy. Haven't we, Curly?"

Red Handed

Kirsty walked onto the terrace, leaving Steve to grapple with the bags.

"Come on out darling, it's stunning," proclaimed a delighted Kirsty

Steve was already rummaging in one of the suitcases. He hunted for his secret package. "I'll be out in a min," he said with an edge of desperation. *Christ, where's it gone,* he panicked. *I remember sneaking it into this one.* "Err, I'm just unpacking the cases, darling," he explained as he found what he sought. *Thank God,* Steve thanked as he stashed it in a shoe. Then placed both shoes into a shabby-looking closet.

With a breathless whisper, Kirsty peered out at the vapour trailed, cerulean sky. Aircraft criss-crossed the heavens like an ethereal game of tic-tac-toe, marred only by the occasional cotton ball of cloud, which sailed on a lazy breeze. Closing her eyes against the sun's warmth, which caressed her porcelain skin. "This is divine," she declared with a wistful sigh. *How sweet of Steve to unpack*, thought Kirsty. Then recalled the nights of continual nagging for him to pack before the holiday. It had been as prosperous as requesting cash from a miser. Accepting defeat, she'd packed both cases. Steve's input was a few last-minute items. *Perhaps Steve felt guilty*, she surmised. But her suspicions grew the more she thought about it. *After moaning about carrying the luggage, why his sudden change of heart?* She contemplated. A grin of intrigue dimpled her face. *What's he up to?*

She tip-toed across the terracotta tiles and drew back the net curtain which divided the balcony from the room and spied on Steve. He collected something from out of the suitcase, then hid it in one of his shoes. Kirsty's stealth matched that of a ninja assassin as she trod in silence and crept up until she was right behind him.

As buoyant as a delighted child and with thunder in her tone, Kirsty said, "What are you doing?"

It was as if a thousand volts had passed through Steve. He shrieked in fright. "Eeeeeraugggh?" Spinning to confront her with shocked surprise, he gasped, "Don't do that." Clutching a melodramatic hand against his heart to quell the war drums inside. "You scared the hell out of me."

Kirsty flinched at his reaction, concerned she'd gone too far, and grinned as the trace of a smile crept onto his lips.

Steve chuckled. His chuckle grew into a snigger, and they both burst into uncontrollable, gut fluttering laughter.

Kirsty taunted, "You screamed like a schoolgirl."

The warmth of his embarrassment made Steve's face burn scarlet. He responded, "What did you expect?" he added in a light-hearted fashion. "You scared me half to death."

"Well?" She raised her eyebrows. "What are you up to?"

"It's a surprise," he answered.

"For me?" Now it was her turn to be shocked. "A surprise? For me?" she asked a second time. "But?" Placing her fists on her hips, as if scolding a small child, as she feigned to be upset. "We agreed we wouldn't get each other anniversary gifts."

Steve laughed again, "It isn't an anniversary gift." He slipped his arms around her waistline and brushed her forehead with his lips, and said with a whisper, "It's just a surprise."

Kirsty pouted like a spoiled child and nudged him away. She professed to be displeased and folded her arms with a huff and kept them across her chest. "We don't keep secrets from each other." She argued with a disapproving glare. "And I don't like surprises."

Seeing through Kirsty's charade, knowing it didn't upset her, Steve replied, "You'll want this surprise." He pushed a wisp of strawberry-blonde hair from her eyes then cupped her chin within his palm. "But you have to promise me?" He angled her head, so she stared at him. "Swear to me, you won't spoil it; don't you sneak a peek?"

"Tell me what it is then?" She tried hard to lose her smile. "I won't have to sneak a peek if you tell me what it is?" Fluttering her long eyelashes at him, hoping to look cute, but it didn't work. "Go on please?"

"No, uh huh," he shook his head in defiance. "I told you it's a surprise. Now promise me?"

She turned to one side and gave a disgruntled, "humph."

"Promise?" Steve repeated.

Kirsty smiled, "Okay, fine; I promise, jeez."

He drew her into him. "Now what are you going to do to make up for scaring me?" A playful glint danced across his eyes. The heat of their kiss unlocked their passion, and she tugged him towards the bed.

Later that evening Steve woke and eased his arm out from under Kirsty's waist, but froze when she murmured. He relaxed when her soft snore returned. Satisfied she remained asleep, he slithered his leg from beneath her own and got out of bed. This was the ideal moment to organize his plan and play a trick on her. It was an amusing idea, Steve thought as he tiptoed over to the closet and removed the parcel from his shoe. He found a clean bin liner in the wastebasket and used it to wrap a second package. Returning this fake gift to the shoe and placing this back inside the wardrobe.

"Darling?" he said, voice hushed but cheerful and not wanting to wake her. He threw on his jeans and a plain t-shirt and listened to her gentle, rhythmic snore. "You awake, beautiful?"

Satisfied Kirsty was still in a blissful sleep, Steve slipped as quiet as a mouse from the room.

— ☐ —

Josephine sat behind the welcome desk, her fingernails chattering on the computer keyboard. She glanced up and beamed at Steve's blithe approach. Jovial as normal, she inquired, "Is everything okay?" leaning forward to prop her elbows on the cool marble counter. "How can I help?"

Steve returned her smile. "All is fine. But perhaps you can help me out." He revealed how it was Kirsty and his first year's anniversary, he told her about the ring and his honourable intentions for the holiday.

Josephine, who was whisked away on the romance, was exhilarated to be involved and before long she'd taken control. Making several phone calls. The first being to a local florist, and she ordered Steve a bouquet. "Every girl loves flowers," Josephine said, full of exuberance. Her next call reserved a dinner table at a favoured restaurant. She muted the call but still whispered, "The view is breath-taking."

Josephine's masterpiece was to organize a chauffeur-driven limo to take Kirsty and Steve to the restaurant. The limousine would collect them from the hotel at 7pm the following evening.

"I don't know what to say," Steve responded, both amused and stunned by her benevolence, "You needn't have gone to all this trouble."

His praise gave her a cheerful hue. "Nonsense!" she quipped, and beamed. "Your night must be perfect!"

"I'm confident it'll be fantastic," Steve laughed.

"This is a joy, not an effort, and you're the one doing all the work. Make certain you do things properly." She clapped her hands together, "She is such a lucky lady."

— ▢ —

Kirsty patted the empty mattress beside her, then rolled over and opened her eyes and groaned. "Steve...?"

No answer.

Sitting up, "Darling? You in the bathroom?" she called. Only silence replied. "Weird," she said aloud. "Where has he got to?"

A devilish idea entered her thoughts. "I couldn't," she considered. "Or could I?" she grinned; her mood became playful. "Well?" She chuckled, "Only one way to find out for sure, Kirsty, darling," giggling at her childishness. She bounded out of bed and over to the closet. Her actions were laughable. "If I'm quick… he'll never know."

She was a child again, searching for presents at Christmas. Sidling up to the wardrobe in a farcical manner, "Well?" she tutted, "Fancy leaving me in a room with a surprise gift hidden." Feigning her innocence, "What's a girl supposed to do?" Stepping closer to the closet. "Now, it's not my fault. Is it?" she clucked her tongue and took another step. "He ought to know better?" and yanked the doors wide. "And fancy having it open." the pine doors creaked as if in agreement. "I mean- tch-, please. How careless of him." Looking once over her shoulder, before delving deeper into the closet.

"Oh, what the heck, he won't find out," she said with joyful glee. "I'll only have one little peek... Just one." She giggled. "What harm could it do?"

The shoes, with their hidden surprise, were right there, as if asking to be picked up. Kirsty could see the parcel poking out of one shoe and pulled. It was small and oblong, wrapped in a white plastic bag.

— ☐ —

Steve held the key card up and unlocked the door to find a guilty looking Kirsty with the shoe in one hand and package in the other.

"Kirsty Edwards?" boomed his stern voice.

Kirsty threw everything into the air and slammed the doors pressing her back against them as she turned to meet Steve. A furnace blast of guilt caused her face to run scarlet. She tried to look innocent and twisted her finger through a lock of hair whilst giving a doe-eyed look, "I wasn't looking at anything." But her satirical protest didn't work.

"I caught you red-handed." Steve stated, and his grave expression made Kirsty think it upset him, but then he smiled.

Mischief in her voice, "But I wasn't doing anything, I promise."

"Go on," he walked up to her. "It's clear you can't wait. So — go on. Look."

"But you told me I couldn't." Her bewilderment was genuine. "You said it would spoil the surprise."

Easing Kirsty aside, Steve opened the wardrobe doors. Finding the package, he gave it to her. "Have a look before I change my mind."

She inspected the parcel by turning it over. Both its size and shape reminded Kirsty of a mobile phone. Has he got me a new phone? She wondered, somewhat disgruntled, and unwrapped the package. It was just a mobile phone, and it wasn't even a different mobile phone, but was Kirsty's tatty and out-dated mobile. She was puzzled, and then she realized it had been a trick.

"Uh?" looking at Steve. "I don't get it?"

He tutted. "Do you think I'm that stupid?" and he started chuckling. "I knew you'd look.,"

"You — sneaky bugger," the penny dropped, and she gave him a playful whack on his chest.

"The minute I knew you were sleeping; I hid my surprise somewhere else." His laugh was riotous. "I realized you wouldn't be able to help yourself."

Kirsty felt foolish, but her laughter quaked from deep inside. She realized it was pointless, but pleaded all the same, "Oh go on? Tell me — Pleeease?"

"Nope," he grinned, "You will have to wait and see." He walked out onto the balcony. "I want to explore. Get yourself ready. I'm famished."

Kirsty watched him. She adored Steve's sense of humour, but felt a twang of guilt at her insecurities as she headed toward the bathroom.

Curly

Detective Baldomero had picked up the call on his way to Curly's flat and chose to lead the investigation since he was on route anyway. Opting to ascend the stairs and evade the urine fragrant, ochre stained lift. He'd powered up the initial four flights, slowing to two treads at a time for the next four and walked the remaining floors. He was breathing like a climber on the summit of Everest and horse's hooves beat against his ribs. Despite his athleticism, he hadn't regained his composure by the time he found Doctor Luciana De León on the tenth floor. A plethora of odours tainted the air from decaying fruit, faeces, rotting eggs, and rotting cabbage, and all made Baldomero thankful to have skipped breakfast. De León held out a white boiler suit, cotton balls, vapour-rub, and a paper cup shaped mask.

"You better put these on," she suggested. "The hot weather has advanced things, be prepared, this one is vicious."

Baldomero nodded as he smeared vapour-rub around each nostril and packed both with the cotton balls. It gave him a mechanical sounding tone, but at least he'd be saved from the full brunt of obscene air. Boiler suit on and hooded, he zipped up. "Do we have a time frame yet?" inquired the Detective.

"Not exact sorry, but you need to look at him." De León said, thumbing over her shoulder towards the flat's entrance. "It's barbaric, so I won't be able to provide you specifics of death until I have him at the lab. Judging by the insect larvae being at a stage one infestation and absence of parasitic insects or flesh flies. Add this to the body condition from intestinal seepage and the extent of bloat," she said, with an assertive tone, "I would estimate death to have occurred between five and ten days ago, but it's been humid up here. I'll have a better result after further analyses."

She never failed to impress him; at 38 years she'd established her career working with the dead. She was at the top of her field and looked at death not as the end but the beginning for a whole new ecosystem which teemed with microbial, bacterial, and parasitic life. "As ever, it sounds delightful. Have you identified the cause of death?" he asked.

A humourless smile danced against the specks of her chestnut eyes, "Well I won't risk my career on this presumption but, I'd guess the removal of his facial epidermis and the large nail through the individuals' cranium has a lot to do with it."

"Ah..." nodded Baldomero, "I think I had better see for myself..."

— ☐ —

Six days prior to Curly's discovery:

Doctor Drulovic introduced Marco and Curly on the pretence of Marco needing a supply of Rohypnol. Little did the drug dealer realize this would be his last deal. They entered his squalid abode and trudged through built up magazines that cluttered the hallway. To their right was the kitchen, buried in filth where a miniature metropolis of greasy dishes towered upon the sink drainer. Gardens of bluish mould grew in fur mounds over left-over food, and toadstool forests edged these. It was strewn with dead fly and beetle carcasses together with their pupae casings beneath dust-yellowed cobwebs and black polka-dot rat dropping trailed around the dustbin.

Opposite the kitchen was a bathroom where soiled laundry piled up in the bathtub to aid a communal dwelling for roaches and silverfish which skittered throughout.

Marco followed the junkie into his living room, with every scrap of furniture covered in bundles of miscellaneous belongings.

"Have you got the pills?" Marco barked.

As if reading his mind, "Here ya go," Curly threw a small packet of pills toward him.

Snatching them from the air, Marco inspected the dozen green tablets. He took out two and placed them into his right palm and stepped with purpose toward the dealer. He grasped his left hand around the scrawnier man's throat and growled, "And how do I know they work?" squeezed tighter, cutting off his breathing. "How can I be certain you're not trying to rip me off?"

Curly retracted between the mountains of hoarded detritus and tugged at Marco's grasp. Desperate to free himself, but failed to loosen those vice-like fingers which smashed him against the far wall with such a ferocious thump it stunned him. "I wouldn't rip you off, bruv. Chill out," he croaked when Marco slackened his grip just enough to let him breathe. "Please." Curly said as his voice pitched to a squeal, "The pills work, you can have them for nothing. Please? Just... let... me... go..." But his words pinched off.

Marco clenched his hand tighter and picked the stickman up onto his tip-toes and squeezed even harder. Stopping, before he crushed the cartilage of vocal cords and enjoyed the swell of fear as the dealer's eyes bulged. Lines of blood spider-webbed into his jaundiced orbs, and Curly's mouth was forced open so that his large violet slug tongue distended, allowing drool to dribble upon the arm of his assailant. Marco pushed two pills of Rohypnol onto Curly's slime-coated tongue and then released him. The tablets shot back into the druggie's gulping mouth, and he choked them down when he swallowed gulps of air.

"What... did... you... do... that... for?" Curly wheezed.

From his trouser pocket, Marco got out his phone and checked the time, discounting the question. He moved through the passageways of knick-knacks and boxes and cleared a space, then dragged an old wooden chair to this den within the cardboard structure. Returning to Curly, who'd rammed two fingers, knuckles deep, into his own cavernous mouth and retched over the floor. Marco grabbed Curly's drool slick hand then relished the noise they created when he snapped both fingers like brittle twigs. The cardboard wall reverberated with the music of agonized shrieks.

In a cool tone which caused him to appear even more sinister, Marco said, "If you force yourself to puke." He pointed at Curly the way a mother points at a mischievous child. "I will have to start the process again." He smirked. "Now quit being a snivelling little runt."

"Why?" Curly whined. "What do you want?" he attempted. But, his words slurred into, "Shy, what do shou laaant?" Fog had slithered in from the shadows and the dealer shook his head to clear his wooziness. But the drugs' rip-tide, pulled him in.

Marco checked at the time on his phone. 15 minutes had passed by. *Okay, he* thought, *the pills are fast.* At 20 minutes Curly's eyes rolled. The junkie slumped in a heap upon the floor and was unconscious at 25 minutes his breaths whistled slow and shallow. Marco left him in place but returned ten minutes later with a brown canvas tool kit containing hardware tools. Curly hadn't moved, 45 minutes had now elapsed.

— ▢ —

It had been an uncomfortable night for Marco, who had remained to see how long the drug's effects would last. As dawn broke some 18 hours after Curly had been subdued, the druggie groaned as he woke. After giving his intended victims the Rohypnol, they'd be suppressed within 30 minutes and should remain in that state for a minimum of twelve hours. *More than long enough*, Marco grinned.

"What's happening?" Curly slurred when he found he was tied to the chair, "This ain't cool — bruv."

Marco stood and stretched away the oceans of fatigue which surfed a swell upon his senses. He yawned as he opened the canvas tool bag. Taking out the gas firing nail gun, he felt the thrill of anticipation invigorate him. He watched Curly tremble as if inside a deep freeze, and as he approached, the junkie shook his head.

"Na — man," Curly said and swayed on the chair. "There ain't the ne...ne...need f...f...for th...this."

Marco moved closer.

The chair legs produced a loud creak, as Curly lurched back and forth. The momentum built. If I tip the chair, thought the junkie, I may escape. He focused on this task and almost teetered backwards far enough to tumble; he believed his plan would work until Marco's granite hands steadied him.

As relaxed as a breathless day, Marco leant down and pressed the nail gun into the top of Curly's left Adidas clad foot. Firm pressure applied and an earth-shattering Thwack-hiss… whirr ruptured the silence of the dawn. A nail splintered the dope dealer's navicular bones as it traversed its way into Curly's left foot. It pinned him to the linoleum covered concrete. Curly's brain hadn't the chance to register the injury before another thunderous Thwack-hiss… whirr cracked the air and both feet became fixed to the floor.

A torrent of agony rushed over him as his screech became an injured cat wail. Marco took satisfaction from this suffering and, as if making repairs to the floorboards, he paced around him.

"There we are." Marco laughed a crazed hyena's cackle and went on, "That should stop your squirming," as he leant in close. "I can smell your fear." his demeanour became hostile as he continued, "It's an alluring aroma," he declared. The nail gun hovered over Curly's right hand before pushing the gripper into the bleached papery skin.

Curly shook his head from side to side and stammered, "Nnnnooo, pp-please dd-don't."

"You're the one who supplied Doctor Drulovic? Weren't you?" Marco whispered.

Curly's head shaking became frenzied. "Nnnnooo."

Thwack-hiss… whirr, ripped his world apart as the nail gun clattered another projectile into the right hand. This shattered metacarpals, which fastened the appendage into the top of his right knee.

"No, no, no, no. Pleeease," came a lugubrious squeal, "Pl...pl... please st...st...stop."

If Marco was enjoying himself, it didn't show. "You ripped off the doctor with your dope? Didn't you?" Marco's sinister tone defied his calmness. The hot coppery scent of Curly's blood excited him like it would a shoal of Piranha, and he battled to maintain control.

Curly nodded. "OK, yes." he would have admitted anything for the torment to end. "I'm sor…" but before he could finish.

Thwack-hiss… whirr.

Volcanoes erupted through his left hand, which was now fixed to his left knee.

Marco trailed the anti-slip gripper up Curly's left side. He allowed it to snag the skin, leaving small dewdrops of blood weeping with scarlet pearls. The dealer tried to flinch, but the nail gun rested in the soft depression behind his left collar bone.

Thwack-hiss… whirr cracked the gun.

Marco walked away but returned holding a butcher's knife, its blade honed to precision, fit for skinning meat. He grasped a fistful of Curly's black, wiry hair and jerked his head backwards, then sliced.

The drug dealer shrieked as Marco sliced and tugged until his reward was free. He offered one ultimate tribute to Curly by settling the nail gun upon the dealer's head.

Thwack-hiss… whirr... was the last sound before an everlasting darkness swallowed him.

— ☐ —

Baldomero had reached a brick wall with the investigation and now, to top matters off, he had two bodies. The Detective studied the picture of the young woman they'd dragged from the river. It had been two weeks since her discovery and they hadn't a name for her or a reason on how she'd ended up snagged in the Manzanares river. There was still the gruesome slaughter of the drug dealer to investigate. On the surface both looked like isolated incidents, but Baldomero's pragmatic intuition screamed they were linked. So, all he'd got to go on was the dumped naked corpse and a homicide. Both happened in the same area of town. It could be a coincidence, but he guessed not. And then there was the death of Sebastián Garcia, a known associate of the man found murdered earlier this morning. Baldomero considered for a moment, then whispered to his unoccupied office, "Three deaths. Two by overdose and one by murder. Two of them knew each other." He smoothed his moustache between thumb and forefinger. "I bet the woman knew them. Perhaps she's a street girl?" he contemplated, then thought; it's all conjecture, but the theory might carry some weight. He took a map of the city and taped each corner onto his office wall. Then placed a pin at the bridge over the Manzanares river, another at the Café where Sebastián had been discovered, and a third marked Curly's flat. He was in a pensive mood as he scanned the map and stated, "The Medianoche Exótica dance club isn't far from these three locations." He gave this some serious thought. "I wonder if the girl worked at the Dance Club.

The Package

The Inspector's accusatory tone outraged Mr Blue Eyes, and he paced out his frustration back and forth around his quaint Herefordshire countryside office. Staring out of the window toward the rolling meadows and lush fields did little to soothe his mood.

An acerbic tone, he said, "Stupid bloody police," referring to Inspector Collins, who had left only minutes ago.

He turned to Geoffrey, director of the Corporation's legal team. "What do you think?"

"Collins is tenacious," admitted Geoffrey, seeing how the officer had crawled under his boss's skin. He continued, "She hasn't any evidence to associate you with Kerry Wells' case, don't get so rattled." Geoffrey thought for a minute, "I wouldn't be concerned."

Mr Blue Eyes slumped into his office chair and exhaled. Lacing his fingers at the back of his head, he arched backward. "She's very tedious," he declared with an air of ambivalence. "What about this so-called witness? Collins seemed pretty sure about him." He slapped both palms down on the desk with sufficient force to cause the computer keyboard to clatter. "Shame I know the witness." He grinned. "Marco will take care of that complication."

Geoffrey's remarks became cautionary. "You shouldn't do anything to bring attention," he said. "The facts remain: when the girl's death occurred, you were out of the country. There isn't any evidence linking you to this girl." He shrugged. "This so-called witness is irrelevant, and the Inspector's grasping at straws. She's trying to get to you."

"She's making a good job of it." Blue Eyes conceded.

Geoffrey looked over at his notes. "Unless they have concrete evidence, which Collins doesn't, I can make sure I hold her investigation up in red tape. Leave it to me."

— ☐ —

A curious Mr Blue Eyes sat deep in thought. Geoffrey had departed a few hours earlier. Am I overlooking something? He deliberated. Something important? He knew Inspector Collins wouldn't let up. She was that type; a no nonsense can't be bought type. It's imperative I find out what Steve has said to them, He concluded. But I will discover nothing sitting behind my desk. Blue Eyes plucked up the phone and called through to the office reception.

"Jenny, sweetheart. I'm leaving on a trip. Could you call the airport?" he requested, "I'll be ready to leave in an hour?"

"Sir. Right away." Jenny replied.

— ☐ —

The phone rang twice before the indignant gruffness of Marco answered, "Hi boss."

"How's it going?" inquired Blue Eyes. "Is everything organized?"

"Business is smooth as glass. I have located the package. They're in a hotel called the Plaza."

The cryptic message made Blue Eyes smile. He realized, "The Package," was Kirsty and Steve. "How long?"

"Should be secured within the next couple of days," Marco assured. "I'm going to need Brodie's help."

He disapproved, "You know what Brodie can be like." Blue Eyes warned. "Make sure he keeps his mouth shut."

"You can depend on me, boss. Brodie will keep quiet," came Marco's belligerent reply.

"I don't want loose ends," Blue Eyes said with force. "Okay. Do what is required," he went on. "We have an excellent business arrangement with Brodie. I wouldn't wish it to be threatened."

"So long as Brodie does as I ask, he will be fine," replied Marco.

"I must talk to the package once you have it... there are a few questions I need answered. I'm flying to Madrid later this evening," informed Blue Eyes. "I'll check in at the club then meet you at the Tarragona site soon."

"Sure, OK Boss," Marco grunted.

"And Marco?"

"Yes Boss?"

"The package is to remain alive until I have seen it."

— □ —

The ash-blonde waitress beamed at Marco when he entered Brodie's bar. In his mind, her eyes lingered far too long over his scar, but he feigned a smile as he read her name badge.

"Hi, Sally. Is Brodie about? I'm a friend," he lied. He felt pretentious, and his smile awkward. "I was passing by and wondered if he's free?"

Sally relaxed, her cheerful laugh and polite attitude returned as she welcomed him. "Sure, who's asking?"

"I'm from the Corporation. He'll know who you mean," Marco answered.

Arctic rivers froze Brodie's core when Sally described the man who remained at the bar, the one who claimed he was from the Corporation.

"Are you okay — Brodie?" she inquired, worried, as the colour flowed from his face.

"What… oh. Erm." Brodie said and wiped sweat pearls off his brow. "Aye lassie aye, I'm okay." His Scottish slur brushed aside her concern. "Dinnae hae him waiting, bonnie lass, shaw him in."

He rose to greet his unwanted visitor as Marco entered, shaking hands with his usual over-enthusiastic jolliness. The bar owner said, "Marco?" He feigned surprise. "Bin far tae lang." As much as the Scotsman didn't wish to be alone with him, Brodie invited Marco to sit, then glanced at Sally. "We're nae tae be interrupted, is that clear?" he instructed. "Claise th' door."

As soon as they were alone, Brodie's charade changed. He gave up on the farcical display and didn't hide his indignant tone. "Whit brings ye — 'ere?"

Marco ignored the question and sat down.

— ☐ —

Brodie's squirming amused Marco. He sat back and watched with the deliberate fierceness of a jackal after its kill.

After what seemed an eternity, he shifted his gaze and scanned each of the office's upper corners to check for a CCTV system.

Marco's voice burst into the room. "Are there any cameras?"

Brodie jumped. "Na, nae a thing. Wur safe tae discuss whatever it's yi'll need. Althoogh ah ament tae too sure whit ye kin require?"

"You are not to talk to anyone about this visit." Marco glared at him. "I was never here. Do you understand? I can make things very beneficial for your business if you will assist me?" He became aggressive. "Or I can eradicate this little dump with you in it. It's your choice."

"Marco, please." An obsequious Brodie slithered. "O coorse ah wull hulp. Whit's it yi'll need?"

— □ —

Brodie picked up the photograph provided by Marco. The picture was of a happy-enough couple. The man was handsome, but the beauty of the girl outshone everything around her.

"Well?" a belligerent Marco snapped. "Will you do what I ask?"

Brodie spluttered, "O' coorse."

Marco got out the Rohypnol he had picked up from Curly and pushed the pack across the desk. "Okay, this is what you're to do..." he began.

"Woe," Brodie protested, "I dinni get heavy with gear any more."

Marco became aggressive at the interruption. "Stop your whining and listen. I'm certain you're familiar with Rohypnol?" he didn't expect an answer. "When those two," he pointed to the photograph of Kirsty and Steve. "When they're here, dissolve two tablets into their drinks. Two of them will be ample; I need the pair unconscious. Call me when it's completed."

Brodie became compliant. "I presume you dinni want the transaction happening in the middle o' the day?"

"The earlier you get my package into the club, the better. The rest we can sort in the early hours," finished Marco.

Proposal

It was a warm twilight evening and an elated Kirsty peered across the languishing harbour outside the restaurant. A shimmer yawn of a full silver moon crested across the infinite stars. These were blusher brushed against a velvet skyline. Kirsty was astonished and sighed, "this is perfect." The tepid night carried the hint of a breeze and provided a ballet of candlelight on each table. The soft plucked strings of a classical guitar accompanied their dance. Its melodious tune wove into the dusk and the waves crashed along the shore to add percussion for the street musician who sidled between the tables.

— ☐ —

Steve admired his handy work, or more correct the efforts Josephine had planned. The reception he gained from Kirsty when the limousine arrived was priceless. Her jaw almost hit the floor as the glimmering white vehicle drew up alongside. Only when the chauffeur climbed out and opened the door, did Kirsty realize the ride was for them. Several selfies and pictures taken, thanks also to Josephine, and they were on their way. Now Steve sat opposite, awestruck by her elegance, and feeling a little unworthy. He just hoped she would say, "yes." Flowers were to be his cue. This was when he'd organized to ask her. A mauling bear of nerves clawed his gut as he re-played the speech over and over inside his head. Toying in his pocket with the small ring box which contained the elegant, princess cut, diamond. Set in a modest four-claw setting, mounted upon a tapered shank. *Was it good enough for her?* Steve thought, *Am I good enough for her?* He didn't wish for the answer. Kirsty's sculpted face bloomed in the moonlight. She wore a cream, strapless linen dress, and Steve's heart leapt as he drank her in.

— ☐ —

Feeling his eyes adoring her, she smiled, a little self-conscious. Steve is plotting something I know he is. I'm certain he's going to ask me the question. Her thoughts fed insecurities into the turbulence of fear building inside. She prayed a silent prayer. Oh, please God, let it be true?

"All okay, darling?" Steve inquired.

"Oh... err... yes." Kirsty was timid in her response.

"You've not eaten a thing," He pointed out.

"Sorry, I'm a million miles away. I never imagined this place to be so..." Tears shone in her eyes. "Wonderful. So, romantic." a smile broadened her face, "Everything is gorgeous."

— ☐ —

Clearing the table, the waiter placed a magnificent floral bouquet in front of Kirsty. An excellent partnership of crimson-red and dusky-pink roses intertwined with delicate pink, fragrant lilies. A small card read, "I Love you."

"Happy anniversary, darling," Steve whispered.

Kirsty gasped and clasped her hand over her mouth. Now a tear spilled onto her cheek, a single pearl at risk of spoiling her makeup. Her cheeks glowed with the same pinkness of the lilies. "They're beautiful." She gasped in astonishment. "How on earth have you managed this?" More tears welled, and she blotted them away. "I feel bloody awful. I have nothing for you."

Steve reached for the wine, pouring them both a fresh glass and returned the bottle to the table. "I have another surprise. For that, you will need to close your eyes."

"But?"

"No peeking. Understand?"

"But Steve, this is too much. It is."

"Nonsense. Are they closed?" Steve stared hard into Kirsty's face, trying to see any gaps in her scrunched-up eyelids. "And remember, no peeking until I say you can look."

Kirsty's smile shone. Enjoying the romance and the wonderful gentleness of his tender touch. His words made her hesitant and a hornet's nest of nerves buzzed in her tummy. Kirsty gasped when she looked, and her other hand flew up to her mouth when she saw Steve, who was down on one knee. The world became tunnelled, like peering through opaque glass, and the sole contrast was Steve kneeling with an open ring box held up. She followed his lips and listened to every word.

With reverence, Steve said. "Kirsty. You make me so happy..." a dam of nervous anticipation stemmed his flow. He drew in a sharp gasp and started anew. "I wish to share the rest of my life with you." Candlelight bounced off the ring, it twinkled like the stars throughout the obsidian sky. "It would be an honour." his throat dried out, and he coughed to clear it. Why is this so difficult? He thought, and panicked. Concerned, it's all going wrong. "Would you spend yours with m...'m...me?" He sputtered. His eyes glistened as emotions almost stole his moment. Gulping breath, he spoke the four small words of the most significant sentence. "Will...you... marry... me?"

Kirsty watched, breathless, as Steve awaited his answer.

— ☐ —

Sat opposite were an elderly American couple who witnessed Steve's proposal. They had become spectators at a tennis match. Their heads flitted, first from Steve and then over to Kirsty, before coming back to Steve. It was the woman who spoke, with an ardent Californian twang, she said "Well? Come on? Are you going to say yes? Go on? Say yes?" She was benevolent, even if a little brash, but well-meaning. "You can't have him kneeling in the dirt..." pointing down at Steve. "Come on, honey. Say yes..." Excited, she clasped both hands in front of her pursed lips, and gave a delighted gasp, "Oh... Do Say yes."

Kirsty stifled a joyful sob as her bottom lip quivered, she battled with her emotions. It was all she could do but to nod. "Y... Y... Yes." she stammered. Then, her doubts took a grip, and she worried if Steve heard her. Kirsty repeated, "Yes — oh my God — yes, of course, I will marry you."

— ☐ —

Meanwhile in Madrid:

Detective Baldomero placed little relevance on the chance encounter with Mr Blue Eyes, who continued into the club when the detective left. At the time it seemed to be a brief inconsequential meeting where neither party paid any attention, and they went about their business. The Detective looked up at the electric blue neon light swinging outside the main doors. Medianoche Exótica dance club was written in the light. Beneath this, another sign lit individual letters before flashing three times as it spelt out the word "Chicas." He accepted this was a modern-day brothel and the women inside turned tricks for the business, but it wasn't why he was here. Baldomero's bloodhound instinct told him something associated this place with the deceased girl, but the young girls inside when questioned became tighter than the corsets that their ample breasts spilled out from. Nor could he gain any information from the older woman when he quizzed her. She appeared evasive and kept a close, mistrusting eye on him. Her callous disregard to his queries made Baldomero suspicious. So, when he stepped out, Baldomero knew he'd be coming back. At this stage he hadn't any evidence to suggest a crime. With such lack of proof he couldn't pursue matters further and went back to the station.

Back in his office he sat and mulled things over, perhaps there's evidence of other dope related incidents, he deliberated. Baldomero logged into the database and extended his research. This time he cast his net further, wishing to identify similar drug-related deaths which had taken place over the previous six months. There were many overdoses, but nothing came up in Madrid that he didn't previously know about. Unperturbed, he carried out a comprehensive investigation for Spain and Europe. Again, many deaths had been registered, and many drug-related crimes, but only one produced the same factors. They identified a known junkie living near Salou. Something else to go through, he speculated. One other death had occurred which Baldomero found odd because this held identical chemical markers as the dead woman he was investigating. This tragic death happened in England. The incident report outlined a young adolescent who was thought to have run away . The report put her death down to an alcohol and heroin induced overdose, the testimony said death by misadventure.

Kerry Wells was the adolescent's name and the investigator who had headed this case was Inspector Collins.

"Might be worth my time to speak to Inspector Collins," Baldomero decided. The phone buzzed in his pocket. He answered in a sharp tone, "Baldomero."

"We may have a picture of the suspect." A voice revealed, relating to the hideous murder of Curly. "It isn't the finest picture. Taken off the train station's CCTV, it's grainy, but we may clean it up. I think it's the last person the victim met."

Appreciative, "Email it to me and I will look into it." Baldomero said.

Drunken Brawl

Celia was in a panic. The policia had found Stefania's corpse. The one saving factor was they hadn't associated Stefania with the club. Celia made certain all her girls were untraceable. It would never do if a husband, boyfriend, or family member came searching and tracked them back here. Celia did what she preferred to call washing away their old laundry. Any trace of a previous existence would be eliminated and once the Eagle talons of narcotics had them in its grip, the young woman soon forgot their past lives.

The detective's appearance couldn't have been timed worse. The indignant Celia watched the officer leave. But, within an instant she wished for his immediate return. When confronted with the narcissistic Mr Blue Eyes.

Those piercing, sapphire eyes with vicious intent just below their surface scoured out her soul.

She poured herself a drink to avert eye contact from his searing stare.

Jaded after his journey and irritated by the snooping Inspector Collins, Mr Blue Eyes glared at her. Bruising to Celia's face looked as if she'd been in a boxing match. Unable to stand upright, she hunched like an old crone and made the excuse of falling when drunk.

"What do you mean? The police are investigating Stefania?" an indignant Mr Blue Eyes asked. "Drulovic has cleaned this little shambles up. Are you telling me he hasn't?"

"I... I...don't know." A disheartened Celia said. "You'll need to ask him. But tonight I have fended off questions from an officer of the civil guard. He showed my girls an image of a dead woman. It was a ghastly picture, but I recognized Stefania."

He was outraged. "Get Drulovic here now." Blue Eyes demanded.

— □ —

In front of him sat a regretful Doctor Drulovic. Blue Eyes spoke in his gentle, charismatic way. "After the girl overdosed back home, you assured me all the bad heroin was gone?"

"It is, it was," protested Drulovic. "I destroyed it myself; my only assumption is Stefania must've hidden some."

"We're agreed then?" Blue Eyes held his cool demeanour. "It's the same shite that killed Kerry in England?"

Drulovic sighed. "Yes, it appears to be. Without a coroner's opinion we cannot be certain."

"Well, I'm pretty certain." Blue Eyes' calm facade slipped to show the molten anger which raged inside. "You were supposed to dispose of her clean? No, come back. No police." He was furious now. "So? What the hell happened, and why are Spanish authorities snooping around my club?"

"I didn't have the luxury of time with this one. It was getting fragrant and beyond credible explanation," Drulovic explained. "So I thought..."

"You thought... You thought?" Blue Eyes interjected without disguising his derisive tone. "There wasn't any thinking from what I can see. And who's stupid idea was it to dispose of her in the river?"

Drulovic flinched under this scathing attack. "We weighed the body down. I don't know what happened, but she must have broken loose."

"You think…?" His words were steeped in sarcasm.

As if flipping a switch, Blue Eyes became sedate, "This better not happen with the replacement."

"And when will she be here?" Drulovic asked, eager at the chance to discuss something else.

"Soon enough. You get her hooked as quick as you can." Blue Eyes instructed. "Leave the rest to me. This time Doc, be certain there aren't any screw-ups. I have too many questions in England, because of you."

— ☐ —

He watched the doctor go. Not giving it any consideration when he first entered, but the room stank. A variety of stale cigarettes, cheap perfume, and rubbish clung to his nostrils. Celia was an odd woman who nagged at the girls to keep the club clean, even though this was her workspace. Blue Eyes tutted, "And, there is this matter of Stefania stashing her dope. Celia would've known all about it. Maybe I should grant Marco his wish." With him in his thoughts, Mr Blue Eyes pulled his phone from his jacket pocket and called Marco.

The indigo hue bled shadows into the night as sunlight vanished from the world. Marco drove into the murky depths of a restaurant's car-park. It had been a busy day and his belly growled like a pit-bull. The shrill ring of his phone chirped into the quietness of the Range Rover. He parked in the farthest corner and answered, "Yes."

Mr Blue Eyes spoke, unperturbed. "I'm at the club. How's it going at your end?"

"Brodie's on board," Marco replied.

"So, what's the plan now?"

"We wait." He listened to a hiss of concern from Blue Eyes, "I will collect the package from the bar."

Disapproving, "I'm not happy with it. Too many people involved. Too much at risk," replied Blue Eyes.

"Nothing I can't sort out. After."

"I will be the one to sort it out." Said a frank Blue Eyes. "You concentrate on securing our package."

— ☐ —

Mr Blue Eyes stood and stretched his arms above his head. That's enough business for one day, he decided. Time to unwind. He wandered through the club towards the lap dancing stage. Music pummelled his chest the further he went. He stopped to watch the girls dance. Twisting their lithe oil glistened bodies around the smooth poles. Between the girls on the dance podium stood an intoxicated man who slurred obscenities as he flung money towards them. Blue Eyes ignored the loudmouth and pointed at the girl dancing in front of the sweat-drizzled Spaniard.

Her long black hair and Latino looks stirred his primal hunger.

She mesmerized Blue Eyes, and he held out his hand to aid her down from the podium. She tottered in strappy six-inch stiletto sandals toward him with a provocative swagger. That's when the drunk grasped and unbalanced her. He pulled the Latino girl away from Blue Eyes. "Dónde crees que vas, Perra?" (Where do you think you are going?) the demeaning drunk snarled.

She lurched backward and slapped away his clammy palm.

Jonas, whose duty it was to look after the girls, started toward the aggressor but Mr Blue Eyes gave a signal to hold back and approached the obnoxious drunkard. His approach was ice cool, "Would you be kind enough to let go, please?"

A raging bull after the matador's cape became the man who turned on Mr Blue Eyes. The enraged drunk snarled. "Mind your goddamn business. English pig." His rage surged, and he swung a boulder-like fist at Blue Eyes.

Moving with the nimble mastery of a ballroom dancer's cha-cha, Blue Eyes stepped to his left to outmanoeuvre this drunken lout. With the speed of a rattlesnake, he landed a knife-hand blow into the larynx of the advancing assailant.

The drunk held his throat as he gagged. He flew past Blue Eyes, who booted the back of the man's knees and made his legs collapse beneath him. He buckled to the floor, slamming his face against an adjacent counter. The ebbing tidal swell of unconsciousness brought darkness to his world, and he face planted the floor, still and incapacitated.

Holding out his hand to the girl, Mr Blue Eyes kept composed and had a reverent tone when he said, in perfect Spanish, "I'm sorry about him," and smiled. "Shall we go somewhere a little less crowded?"

A Night of Trickery

Joe and Hanna were vultures circling carrion as they watched tourists for their next intended victim. They were scammers awaiting the innocent and preyed on the gullible. They roamed the music filled street, relishing the laughter which fluttered into the evening.

Joe had started to get on Hanna's nerves. Frustrated, "Can we stop for a drink at least?" he implored, "I don't reckon we're gonna av any luck tonight."

Hanna turned to him. "I suppose, wiv been walking a while. So we hav. Perhaps you're right."

Bordering the concrete causeway at the rear of the waterfront was a modest bar. Perfect to observe the bobbing heads of tourists. It was when they sat that Hanna glimpsed Kirsty and Steve stepping out from their limousine. Holy mother, you've answered our prayers tonight, and this energized Hanna. It's time to put on a show, and she gave Joe a wicked smirk.

"What's wrong, babe?" Joe asked just as Kirsty and Steve walked past. He watched them head into Brodie's bar.

— ☐ —

Brodie's bar resembled an old-style British country pub. The imitation oak beams would have been ideal if in the honeycomb cobbled lanes of the British Cotswolds. However, on the central strip of Salou and between all the other bars and clubs; the building looked fake.

Joe couldn't believe their luck. "Feckin typical," he declared with an aggrieved sigh. "We've lost the last few hurs searchin fo the next payday, only fo it to walk by." Turning to stare at Hanna, he struggled to hide his irritated mood. "Jesus, Mary and Joseph, we've been wandering about for nothin," he continued, "All we needed to do was stay here and let them come to us."

Excited and quick on her feet, Hanna said, "Yer comin? Or yer just gonna gawp at em?"

Joe gulped down his beer. "Yer, yer for feck's sake." His frustration showed by his impatience. "I'm coming; I'm coming. Jeez."

"Hang up gurl, be-jeez," he gasped, "Jay-sus, Mary…let's get us a couple of drinks and check em out first."

— □ —

Joe and Hanna slithered further into the pub and pushed between the sweat-slicked bodies that packed the dance floor. Hanna shouted, but the thumping dance music drowned out her words, so she pointed toward a door which led to the terrace and headed for it. Sat alone was Kirsty, both Joe and Hanna stared at each other and grinned. Joe let Hanna lead the way as they ambled toward the lone girl.

This is our best chance, Hanna decided, and with a jubilant bounce she strode towards Kirsty. "Jeez, it's hot in there," she declared, her actions animated as she wafted her hands in front of her face. "Do you mind if we join yer, sweetie?" and before Kirsty could attempt an answer, Hanna plopped herself into the opposite chair. "There ain't any other tables." Hanna's Irish twang gave her a charming appeal, which put Kirsty at ease. "And you sweetie," she flipped a lock of fire red hair aside and pointed at Kirsty with playful exuberance, "You're looking a little lost, sat here all alone?"

Kirsty's cheeks felt warm, and she couldn't suppress the grin as she blushed. She was reminded of the bubbling confidence Abigail, Kirsty's best friend, demonstrated. Of course the girl in front of her whose lobster complexion, pixie nose which was a spatter of freckles and jade eyes, was nothing like Abigail. But her persona was a near match, and Kirsty felt an instant kinship to this likeable girl. "Of course, I don't mind," Kirsty said, "but, I'm not alone." She was all in a quandary as she searched for Steve. "I'm here with my boyfriend," Kirsty said, as an explanation. "He's gone off to the bar."

"Well, we can keep yer company," beamed Hanna. "Just while yer wait."

Joe perched himself on the side of Hanna's seat. "I can't leave yer fo five minutes before yer off disturbing good folk," He spoke in a light-hearted, jovial way.

"Well, what do you expect," Hanna giggled. Looking at Kirsty, "This is me fella, Joe." She glanced toward Joe with, this is our next payday look, and replied, "You left me standing on my own while you made a prat of yerself," she said, mocking him. "I got bored and needed some fresh air. It's too hot in there." looking at Kirsty as she pointed back inside, "I'm but a sweet simple fae from the emerald Isle, I weren't built for this heat."

Enjoying her satirical explanation, "Aww jeez go on wit yer," Joe thought her hilarious, and sported a crescent moon grin. "A sweet fae, av you eva hurd such a ting," grinning at Kirsty he shook his head, "That's moi Hanna for yer, head full o silly feckin nonsense. So she has."

Enjoying their whimsical display, "My names Kirsty," she said, "and my boyfriend." She looked at her engagement ring and grinned. Her heart skipped when she heard herself say. "Sorry; My fiancé, wherever he's gone, is Steve." Kirsty had fallen for their trickery and couldn't wait to introduce her new friends when Steve returned. He raised an eyebrow at Kirsty as he dodged between the bustle on the terrace. "So? Who's this then?" Steve inquired as he placed drinks on the table.

Kirsty stood and wrapped her arm around his waist. She nuzzled his cheek with a kiss. "This is Steve," Kirsty said.

Kirsty and Steve found their new friends fun, but had escaped them for the moment so they could dance. They weren't aware of the bitter conversation Hanna and Joe were having with Brodie.

"Save yer breath and quit the bullshit." Brodie's scathing tone silenced the pair before they started. "I bailed yer out months ago, and yer aven't offered me a single euro," Brodie said as he continued.

"We will. We're working on it," insisted Joe.

Joe and Hanna had worked at Brodie's bar until they caught Joe for drug possession. Joe hadn't anybody else to call and had borrowed money from Brodie to pay his bail.

The Irish couple showed their evasiveness as they slunk into the chairs. Their eyes looked anywhere but into Brodie's. Hanna chewed her bottom lip as she squirmed with her hands, scrunching the pink material of her sarong skirt.

"You're both something, yer know that?" Brodie said with a snarl. Staying their protests again by holding up his palm. "I didn't say yer could speak." Anger trembled at his words. "Yer pair of idiots have cost me and ya canny be bothered to offer to pay me back."

"We're sorry." Hanna began, but her apologetic tone failed to satisfy. "We didn't mean to take the piss..."

Brodie's cheeks flushed. "I'm nea-bothard, so keep yer trap shut." He was becoming aggressive, and others now glanced over. He paused. Took long slow breaths and settled himself, "I haven't told yer can speak, so just clam it shut 'n' listen."

Brodie explained what he needed of them.

"Let me get this straight," Joe replied, and smirked at their old boss. "You want Hanna and me to roofie Kirsty an Steve an you will let us off what we owe?"

"Yes. That's all. Nice and simple." Brodie's smile was empty and humourless. "Plus, yer get ta keep any cash or jewellery yer choose."

Joe showed he was always the scammer. "Do we get paid anything? For our troubles?" he asked in an egotistical fashion.

Brodie's face burned crimson. "Yer — cheeky lil shite." Furious words hissed between clenched teeth. His tone sank to a growl, "Not only did I av to bails yer out, but I catch yer selling crap in me boozer." Again he glowered hard at Hanna, who withered before him. "But I also catch yer bird fleecin me guests." He towered above them.

Brodie trembled, and his erratic breathing gushed from flared nostrils. "But that isn't enough for a greedy little shite like yer…" His chest clanged, a sharp stabbing behind the breastbone, "… Now you're expecting to be paid. You're lucky you can still walk! Yer — arrogant strip o piss."

Joe burnt imaginary holes in the floor with his stare, wanting it to swallow him whole. "I… I… I'm s… s sorry, I didn't mean to… I… I… I only meant…"

It was Hanna who turned on him. She scowled stiletto knife eyes and said. "Will yer, for once, shut yer flapping gob?" her anger rivalled Brodie's. "You're going to make things worse… as feckin usual." She was furious and had to look away. "We'll help," she resigned with a sigh, "All's we ask is yer forgive us over the trouble we've caused."

Betrayal

The carnival atmosphere of Brodie's Bar was buzzing. A kaleidoscope of coloured strobe-lights pulsed to the thump of vibrant dance music. An energetic Kirsty danced, cheerful and exuberant even if a little intoxicated. She felt on top of the world and nobody could change that. Looking at her new engagement ring, she had her Steve, Kirsty grinned and flung her arms above her head whilst she twirled to the rhythm which moved her limbs. Mrs Douglas, she sighed to herself, I'm going to be Mrs Douglas. She was so thrilled and couldn't wait to tell Abigail. Laughing, Kirsty smiled at Steve; this was the perfect way to celebrate. Nothing could go wrong, or so she thought.

Joe's malicious stare watched as the impressionable pair danced. He kept lookout whilst Hanna rifled through Kirsty's purse. Taking bank cards and Kirsty's driving licence. The licence they could move quick enough, there's always someone who'd buy it, grinned Hanna. The debit cards would work contactless until reported missing. Hanna doubted Kirsty would be calling the bank.

Holding up the cards, "Cher-Ching," she declared, her mannerism derisive as she smirked. "Jackpot."

Joe's eyes were alight as his excitement grew, he said, "Stay close to this pair," pointing at Kirsty and Steve, "I'm going to see Brodie for the drinks," and he headed to the bar. Taking a diversion toward the restroom for a livener of cocaine.

— □ —

Brodie pretended to polish glasses at the edge of the bar, a farcical act of bar maintenance. An excuse to maintain a visual on his destined victims. He rang and told Marco, "They're here."

"Fine." came Marco's caustic response.

"They'll be ready in the early hours." The bar owner informed.

"I'm on my way..." was Marco's curt reply.

Click... the line went dead.

Brodie waited for Joe, who wormed toward him. The lad was high, that was plain to see. "We're ready whenever you are?" The Irishman said.

"Okay great. I will bring drinks over. Four beers, OK?"

"Yeah, that's a start," Joe responded with a flippant snicker. Then continued, "They're celebrating their engagement."

"Even better," Brodie grinned. His manner became hard and one of caution. "Oh yeah, just one last thing, bonnie-lad. If yea know what's safe for ye, yer'll lay off the shite yer've been snortin."

— □ —

Brodie opened a bottle of Moet Chandon and filled two glasses half full. Then, as per Marco's instruction; he slipped two pills of Rohypnol into each. Waiting as they dissolved before topping up and taking them to the couple.

Brodie shouted over the music, "Someone tells me you two are celebrating." He presented the drinks. "This is for you two." passing first to Kirsty and then Steve a glass of bubbly. "Congratulations on your engagement." He claimed, "This is my finest champagne, so enjoy."

Kirsty drank a little. It tasted sweet and tickled her tongue. She gave a joyous sideways glance at Steve and giggled. "Cheers. My husband to be," and clinked his glass in a playful salute before gulping down the entire drug-laced drink.

Steve followed suit and grabbed Kirsty by the hand, "Now it's party time." he said and tugged her toward the dance floor, "Come on. I want to dance."

— □ —

They moved further between the mass of gyrating bodies and, to begin with, all looked fine. But, after ten minutes Steve felt penned in and was overwhelmed by a sense of foreboding. Perhaps it's the booze, he wondered as the proximity of individuals became claustrophobic. Steve wasn't dancing any more. He blinked, but images became a fairground's hall of mirrors. Strobe-lighting compounded the issue, and he seemed to have one leg shorter than the other as he lurched across a dance floor which slipped from him. A sluggishness now ebbed at him, making it seem as if his limbs were sinking into quicksand.

Kirsty was struggling, too. Her eyes rolled, revealing their whites. She slunk forwards in a zombie fashion and faltered, almost tumbled, toward Steve. Anybody nearby would presume she was drunk. But this was different, more like being stuck on a merry-go-round, powerless to get off. Kirsty panicked.

— □ —

Joe was the first to notice Kirsty and Steve. Cupping his hand to Hanna's ear, he shouted, "Are you coming — We have their cards. I can't watch this." Pointing to Kirsty and Steve, "It's time to ditch this pair."

"Shame, I like em." sighed a dispassionate Hanna, "and I wanted her ring."

"Yeh," a belligerent Joe admitted, "That's why I wanna ditch em. Next you'll be wantin me to propose. Besides, look at them," he pointed at Kirsty, "They're stumbling about like a couple of crack whore zombies."

Hanna noticed how flushed Kirsty's face was, Steve's too. Both seemed wasted "Yeh, I agree. Let's get going."

They headed toward the exit but were intercepted by Brodie. "An where are ye gunnin?"

"We're done," resigned Joe. "Time to get out of here."

Wrapping his arms around their shoulders and spinning them back towards the bar. "Yer pair need to stay — where I can see yer. I will tell yer when it's time to leave."

— ☐ —

Kirsty's washing machine vision was on spin. She thrust out her arms to steady herself. "Woe, I don't feel… Right."

"Me either," Steve slurred, and shook his head. "It's weird."

Closing her eyes, Kirsty blinked several times. It didn't work. A stool stood next to a table, and she perched between them. "I'm burning up." She slumped upon the stool. Sweat dripped dew drops from her brow as her pulse thrummed a racehorse against her temple.

Steve stared at Kirsty, but couldn't determine which of her spinning images was the true one. His hands flailed in the air as if doing a poor impersonation of a pianist. He tottered toward her and fell, smashing his face upon the table's edge. Warmth poured from a deep gash in his forehead. The jolt sent concussion throughout his skull and he dropped hard. This time his chin collided, and everything went black.

Unable to do a thing for Steve, Kirsty fluttered in and out of consciousness. *It's okay, it's only a silly dream.* She smiled a wistful, dreamlike smile. A voice from some place deep inside spoke. *That's it, just relax.* Said the enticing voice. *Hush now, go to sleep, it cajoled,* and Kirsty floated upon an ever-darkening void.

— ☐ —

Brodie had remained close. Waiting as the drugs took hold. Then, with help from Hanna and a reluctant Joe, he gathered Kirsty and Steve up to carry them through to the back.

"So, what now?" Asked Joe.

"Yer pair," Brodie looked at them. "Yer canny bugger off. I will call yer soon enough. When the time is right."

"What about the gear? When will we have that?"

"Joe?" Hanna groaned. "Drop it, will yer."

"I'd listen to her — if I were you." Brodie patronized and patted Joe's cheek.

Joe shoved the Scotsman away. "Okay, we'll speak soon?"

"That's what he said, wasn't it." Hanna snapped. "Jesus Joe, you're dumb. Now come on, will yer? It's time we weren't here."

— ☐ —

It was just past midnight when Mr Blue Eyes climbed on board the company jet. The smell of body odour, sex and cheap perfume clung to his nostrils, a reminder of the wanton lust he had gratified. She had been a brief distraction, but he hadn't wished to linger at the club, not with the detective snooping around. He had rung Andy, his pilot, and instructed him to charter a course to Reus airport. Marco had been in touch to update him on the progress of their package. They had captured them thanks to another couple. The involvement of another couple wasn't what Blue Eyes wanted. More people meant more mouths to keep silent. The feeling of being caught in an avalanche wouldn't disperse. The first snowdrifts had shifted and soon would tumble out of control. It was time he put a stop to the slide and brought stability back to the situation.

He called Brodie. "Fergus, my friend." He kept his tone frank. "I understand my associate — Marco — visited earlier this evening?"

There was a brief pause, "Aye he did," a docile Brodie replied, "I did what he required, nea-botha."

Blue Eyes became derisive. "You had a little help?"

"Aye. I did ave a'lil hand," said Brodie.

"I require their address?" Blue eyes demanded.

"How come?"

More assertive, "I want their address," Blue Eyes insisted.

Brodie had supplied what he sought so; Blue Eyes sat back to sleep. They would land in just over two hours. He needed to rest no matter how brief that might be, he would welcome it with enthusiasm. He had lots to take care of in the impending hours, individuals to interrogate, others to silence. His thoughts went to Steve, and the fury of his betrayal ignited the embers of rage. He had a thirst for vengeance only he could satiate. But to create a little order to the crushing avalanche, Blue Eyes needed to slip deep and blend into the shadows.

The Man of Shadows

A black ski mask concealed his face. Only the glimmer of his blue eyes was visible. The sultry night offered brief respite as his breath warmed his head beneath the fabric mask. Dressed in black to meld into the depths of the nocturnal shadow. A need to be nimble, so he travelled light. The tar-pit of night was his protector and stealth, his ally. Unseen and unheard, he neared their building.

A silhouette of seaside apartment blocks loomed from out of the blackness. This unappealing structure was where they lived in a ground-floor flat and the man of shadows crept, up to the front door. In his hand was a wallet of metal picks, biting on a small penlight as he shone it at the keyhole. With expert insertion of the slim tension wrench, he applied minor pressure. Pushing another pick into the top above the first, he provided a little more leverage upon the wrench. A metallic click rewarded his skilful handling and freed the door and, in silence he entered.

His next task. Locate the electricity fuses. Again, wielding his penlight, he examined the foyer before heading further inside. It was a modest flat; the bedroom faced the entrance, and the hall turned toward his right. Instinct told him to discount the bedroom and follow the slim corridor into a lounge. An open-plan kitchenette to his right, and a wide opening of plate glass doors to his left, which led onto a small veranda. Opposite him, the framework of a cupboard door fitted into the adjacent wall. It was low down to the floor and housed the fuse board plus the master power switch. He snapped this into its off position, extinguished his penlight and dissolved into a shroud of shadow.

3:30 am:

Joe and Hanna headed home. Joe had smoked too much. His chest felt tight and his bagpipe breath wheezed. His thoughts were full of regret as they strolled in silence.

Hanna thought about it too, and replayed the evening over and over in her mind. "What've we done, Joe?"

"Don't think about it, babe."

They walked a little further, and she wept. He sought to reassure her, but she shrugged him aside.

"Great." Joe said with a disinterested grunt, and rolled his eyes to the heavens, releasing a dispirited sigh. She always got this way after a large payday. He realized it would change tomorrow once they started spending on the bank cards.

"We're lousy, horrid people, Joe," the drink made her emotional, and she snivelled, "I'm going to mass tomorrow, I need confession."

"For fek sake, that's just the booze talking," he shouted, infuriated by her shame. "And yer not going anywhere. Yer not fessin anytin — you, hear me?"

A chasm opened between them as Hanna dawdled behind a sulking Joe who stomped ahead. "Come on, woman?" His words caustic as he yelled, "Hurry ye arse, will yer."

Angered by him, "Will yer stop feckin shouting," Hanna screamed.

They reached their flat in silence.

"I don't care what yer say." she said in frustration and stepped inside. "I'm gonna tell someone. Like the cops or summat."

"Don't talk daft, yer've ad too much drink." Joe struggled to remain calm. He wanted sex, but knew his chances were diminishing. "Wait until morning, and we'll decide." He clicked the entrance light switch. Nothing happened. He moved over to the bedroom and tried the light in there. The darkness reigned. "Feckin great."

Using the torch of his mobile phone, "Power's out," he explained.

"Is it a power cut?"

"Dunno? Maybe? I'll check the breaker."

"I'm gonna stay in the bedroom," She strode toward the blackened room. "Shout me if it's a power cut."

— ☐ —

The man in the shadow listened to the approaching target. More satisfied than ever, this was the correct course of action after hearing their conversation about confessing. Excitement sailed his adrenalin sea, a tidal rush received from the unknown influences of what might be. It was this part he enjoyed most. He was ready and waiting.

A sword beam of light sliced through the blackness. Not bright enough to saturate the room, but ample to disperse many a hiding place and the shadows which offered refuge. He unsheathed the curved 7-inch honed blade of blackened scalpel sharp steel and smirked. A person's silhouette appeared from behind the light as it entered the lounge, oblivious of death, who lurked among the shadows and crept with stealth toward him. The full moon betrayed the shadow as it cast against the adjacent wall, giving it a cinema screen of silver light where silhouetted shapes danced. The darkened form of Joe grew large in the moonlight, but a second person morphed from the darkness.

Joe stopped walking and was a little confused, but guessed Hanna had followed him after all. "I thought…" He began but didn't get to finish his sentence.

His head jerked backwards from an unknown force. The impact was unexpected and tore into the critical tissue within his throat. Joe didn't see the blade as it sliced into his carotid arteries and jugular vein in one fluid strike. The kiss of sharpened steel glided past his trachea with slight resistance until it struck Joe's C3 vertebrae. The mobile phone clattered from his grasp. Torch facing up to dance a halo of light around him. Joe brought his hands to his throat, but couldn't fathom why a warm coppery slickness filled his mouth. Its oiliness clogged his oesophagus and gushed from his lips. He stumbled, then slipped. Going down on one knee as the light waned and shadows became darker. A rasping wet cough was his final sound, and he slouched towards death's abyss.

— ☐ —

In the bedroom, sat on the bed, Hanna listened to the hush of the room. She could hear Joe fumble around in the darkness, and heard him talk.

"Who're ya talking to?" She hollered, a little concerned. A curious noise distilled the quietness, a spatter like raindrops accompanied a bubbling gurgle noise. Then a thud as something dropped. *What's he doing?* She wondered, becoming unsettled. A chill ran up her spine as imaginary spiders danced hair covered legs across the nap of her neck. She trembled and stood up. Walking over to the door she hesitated. Something didn't seem normal. The darkness felt cruel. "You're freaking yourself out, Hann," she whispered to nobody and let out a nervous chuckle. "It's Joe, he's trying to spook you." *It's working*, admitted Hanna. "The feckin prat has fallen over or sommat." She opened the door and entered the corridor.

Joe's assailant didn't stick around to admire his handy work. Experience told him, he had dealt a fatal blow, and left the man to die. Now his attention shifted toward the young woman. He became ink on dark blotting paper within the darkness, which absorbed him once more. He slithered into the hallway. Facing him was a small windowless room, and he dived into it the moment Hanna stepped into the corridor. Shapes in the blackness, a toilet and washbasin visible enough to recognize. He was in the bathroom.

He watched for her to pass.

A noise like wet flatulence gurgled the air, then all became silent.

"Joe?" her wretched voice called out but there was no answer. Concerned, she called again, "You okay? Babe? You're scaring me now."

She took reluctant steps along the corridor, past the open bathroom door, guided by the poor light coming from the lounge. It was the pungent metallic stench which clung to her nose and made her gag, which informed her Joe wasn't OK. Each step sent her heart thundering into overdrive.

Hanna knew the crumpled heap was Joe. He was a puppet whose strings had been cut, seated in the feeble lighting of his mobile torch. Hanna could see his limbs jutting out at abnormal angles, his head sagged onto his chest. She knew he was dead. Panic gripped her, and she became an ice statue of fright. She wanted to run and never look back. But fear held her locked rigid. Her scream when it started, came up from her bowels, but only silence left her mouth.

— □ —

He watched the slim silhouette of Hanna pass the bathroom and pursued. His assault was as agile as a praying mantis and was behind her with lightning speed to lift her up and backward, slipping the dagger up under her ribcage toward her vital organs. Penetrating deep. Within an instant Hanna's body went limp, and he eased her to the floor. Stroking her delicate cheek, and waited for her last gasp to slither from between her lips.

Mr Blue Eyes walked into each room and ransacked the flat as if a burglary had gone bad. Satisfied, he closed the apartment's door and once again he delved amongst the shadows.

— ☐ —

Dawn:

Alejandro Gonzalo looked out across the bay, enjoying a sunrise which bled upon the lilac sky. These early mornings were the most temperate when the world was not yet awake. It had been six months since retiring, but he was struggling to adapt. His morning walk never failed to clear his mind, there was something about the jasmine infused sea-air he found awe-inspiring. More adapted to the commotion and fume polluted city of Madrid as one of the capital's finest most revered prosecutors, life by the ocean was a little slow. Gonzalo faced a fresh challenge in helping his beloved Mariana run her late father's restaurant. The ambience of Capellans beach, together with the slower tempo of retirement, was sending him crazy. This morning he'd stayed to appreciate the coral brushed dawn swelled with terracotta hues. He'd sat to view the sunrise while he smoked his favourite Montecristo cigar away from Mariana's disapproving stare. The buttons of his shirt strained against his stout belly as he inhaled. This was his routine, granting himself one cigar a day, and he wished to savour its smoothness. Date palms ruffled in the breeze, as did his sparse silver hair. The electronic tune of Mozart played, and he lost the moment. Gonzalo reached for his mobile. He glanced at the caller display and smirked.

"Nicolas," said a jovial Gonzalo, using Baldomero's first name. "Nice and early. You can't be calling to organize a visit?" he continued, voice bubbling with humour. Gonzalo sported a crescent moon smile while he fiddled with his puro. "It's great to hear from you, my friend. What's your trouble?"

Baldomero never ceased to be entertained by his old friend, but with reverence, replied, "How's retirement, Al?" enjoying his old friend's jubilant personality, even if they were hundreds of miles apart. "I would have thought Mariana would be fed up with you — by now?" he added in jocular fashion. "Speaking of her, how is Mariana? And the kids? Hope they're well."

"She keeps me busy, too busy." Gonzalo laughed. "And she couldn't ever become fed up with me," he chuckled. "Who else would she order about, eh?" Gonzalo roared. "We're as chaotic as usual, but, she's happiest when we're busy."

Getting straight to business, "A case I'm working on may bring me over your way. Tell Mariana I will visit soon." Baldomero said.

Keeping light- hearted, "So, what's this case? The one which may drag you kicking and screaming in my direction." Asked Gonzalo, but he could sense the time for comical remarks had passed, and became sincere. "How can I help?"

Powerless and Alone

Kirsty moved as she woke. *Why do I ache so much?* Her confused inner voice groaned. *What happened last night?* She slithered back into the realms of oblivion and sailed between delirium and reality. Seconds turned into minutes, then minutes into hours. Shifting position, struggling to loosen the bite of cramp which chomped her muscles. It took an age for Kirsty's sluggish brain to understand both arms and legs were bound. Her clamshell eyes opened as if thick with silt, but something covered her head, making it near impossible to see beyond its blackness.

She sighed and plunged into a quagmire of nightmarish sleep. Dreaming; she was a young child, badgering her parents to take her to the fairground. Insisting on riding the spinning teacups, which whirled and twirled over and over until perpetual motion made her nauseous. Now, the same sensations of spinning hit her. Each time she raised her head, the sharpness of a thousand needles pricked her throat when bile seared up from her gut.

— ▢ —

Steve dangled. Hands tied above him, a Vulture's beak of cramp tore into his biceps whilst its talons shredded into his triceps. His jellied shoulders trembled under the strain to make his tip-toed feet skitter beneath him. He tried but failed to hold his weight, as the struggle forced him to pitch a metronomic arc. Steve's head, like Kirsty's, was covered with a hood and all he could do was listen to the muffled mewling noises, like that of a tormented beast. He sought to get a fix on these sounds until he realized they derived from himself. Macabre panic drove him to fear.

What's going on? Steve's tiptoes became more sure-footed, and he could hold himself. Easing the spin further with the extreme tips of his toes. His brain strove to recover his equilibrium. *What is happening? Where am I?* A maelstrom of thought surged his terror. *What's happened to Kirsty?* Twisting left, then right, searching up, then down, wishing to shake loose from the hooded deprivation. But this slight movement caused his stability to shift, and the oscillations began once more. Steve's tortured limbs screeched a banshee's wail, but he bit into an obstruction that stifled his mouth.

— □ —

Marco watched the couple rouse. Steve, with his arms tied above his head, trussed to the ceiling. His pensive mood made him contemplate, *what trophy will I gain from you?* He wondered on approach. He discarded the hood covering Steve's head and stared hard into his hostage's horrified eyes. In absolute control, Marco moved across to Kirsty. Savouring the heat of her skin as it trembled away from his touch. Remaining silent, he got rid of her hood before returning to Steve to remove the gag. Steve gave a blocked vacuum cleaner whoop as he inhaled. His captor grinned, then gave Steve's limp body a hefty shove. Swinging him as if he were nothing more than a pig carcass at an abattoir. His agonized screams were swallowed by the leather clad walls of their makeshift dungeon. Blinded by tears, "Who are you?" Steve said, his question came out as a bleak hiss. "What do you want with us?"

Marco ignored him and strode through to a separate room.

"Please?" Steve implored. "Please let us go."

Hushed twittering of a discussion, a mix of English and Spanish, emanated from the other room.

"Please, I have money," He pleaded, "I can give you cash." He lifted his head and whispered to Kirsty, "I'm sorry, darling."

Kirsty watched a second man, who walked in front of her and blocked her view. He faced Steve.

The original captor had reappeared. Gripped in each of his hands were two objects. Kirsty recognized a syringe, but what it held she couldn't hasten to guess. The other item resembled a long leather shoelace and was looped over a small wooden block. The ogre of a man pinned her down to the floor as he grasped her by the left arm. She felt the scrape of a needle, and the room swam. Coloured rainbows spiralled her vision, and voices became distorted echoes as if shouting into a cavernous room.

— ☐ —

"Steve, Steve, Steve?" Mr Blue Eyes said.

"What... do you want... with us?" snorted a defiant Steve. "You bastard."

"Why... oh... why have you let it get to this?" continued an arrogant Mr Blue Eyes. "All you had to do…" He settled his solid hand on Steve's head. "The only thing you needed to do was keep your mouth shut." Increasing pressure, he pushed downward.

The shriek which exploded from Steve was high-pitched, a screech of eternal damnation. The pressure was continuous, and the excessive weight tore through Steve's overburdened shoulders. Something gave a sickening pop. Then, as sudden as it had begun, the hefty hand on Steve's head was released.

"Why did you talk to that interfering policewoman — eh?" Blue Eyes asked. "You know the one I mean- Collins?"

Steve panted and dribbled, "You... told... me... the girl... was... okay." each word juddered between spasms of suffering.

Mr Blue Eyes turned to Marco. "Do it," he commanded. Without further provocation, Marco drove his fist hard into Steve's gut. Air compressed out from his lungs but failed to return. Something substantial inside Steve's shoulders gave a loud cracking snap and sent fresh agony into his tormented tendons. Steve danced close to the precipice of unconsciousness.

"I thought we understood one another, Steve?" Blue Eyes was frank in his words. "You stay out of my life, and I stay out of yours. That was the deal."

"But ... that ... poor ... girl." Steve squealed with wretched gasps. "I ... she ... was ...with ... you ...and ...now," he swung, "She's ...dead." Another blow smashed his gut, ribs snapped like twigs and his mouth overflowed with copper tasting bile.

With a fierceness only matched by Marco's blows, Blue Eyes snarled, "Enough is enough." Gripping Steve's sweat-soaked hair, "I'm not interested in what you have or haven't reported to the police." Pulling him back to stare into Steve's blood crazed eyes. "I told you what would happen?" releasing him, Steve's head sagged to his chest. "I warned you, never cross me." Blue Eyes nodded at Marco, "It's time."

Marco went in behind Steve and slid the small leather shoelace object around Steve's throat and drew the garrotte backward.

Blue Eyes turned to Kirsty. "As for your pretty little girlfriend — She is mine now." He gave Marco a nod of authority, observing how the muscles of Marco's forearms trembled when he tugged the ligature tight and sent Steve into the perpetual darkness of death.

— ▢ —

Mr Blue Eyes reached for Kirsty and ripped the gag from out of her mouth. "Look at me, slut." forceful in his demand. Apathetic as he watched the lucidness of her eyes set on his, albeit brief; then she slid away. He shook the delirium from her and repeated with a growl, "I said look at me."

The aberration laughed out loud. A maniacal cackle of malice staring up at the demon which had morphed into its human form. "W...w...what ...do ...you w...w...want f...from ...us," she sputtered. A thousand wasps swarmed across her face as the palm of his hand slapped her. A crimson stream dripped from her lips. "I didn't tell you to speak. Did I?" He snagged a fistful of hair. "You are mine now." He flung back his head and laughed a thunderous roar. "You're mine; I own you,"

Then, the sharp jab of a needle welcomed Kirsty onto the cruise ship of fantasy, where she would float off into an abyss. Steering her through the cancerous blackness. Kirsty was trapped by two cerulean orbs which swirled as belligerent fireflies. Abhorrent, cold, and menacing, her jailer who kept her powerless and alone.

PART 2

Missed Flight

Doctor Drulovic checked over the young woman who had been with him over the previous two weeks. Her dependence was almost accomplished, which meant her compliance would soon follow. He smirked, a contemptuous smirk which crinkled the crows' feet around his graphite eyes. He detested women, shrugging callously. More so, the pretty ones like Kirsty, and he plucked, with thumb and forefinger, the delicate skin at the rear of her arms. He gripped her flesh in much the same manner as he'd have grasped a rusted doorknob. Using all his force to twist. Nothing, not a single murmur. Yet, he realized the pain would be excruciating. She'd react if conscious. Only her wind rattled, bulrush reed breath suggested life. Then her head jerked towards him. Crimson moth eyelids flickered but declined to open. Disappointed to be denied his fun, Drulovic walked to the bedside cabinet and gathered the syringe with its amber narcotic and rubber tubing.

The tube he strapped tourniquet style above Kirsty's left elbow and patted the skin. Tap—pat—tap. Purple tree root veins ran along her emaciated arm, and Drulovic used one of these to inject her medication. She murmured a flute concerto sigh. This time her eyelids fluttered open. The black penny eyes of Kirsty's China doll face looked out at the room without clarity.

— ▢ —

Freshly baked pastries and ground coffee made Abigail's stomach growl almost as loud as the aeroplanes rumbling overhead. The coffee shop inside the arrivals lounge of Birmingham airport was tempting. She squinted through the window with her chocolate drop eyes and examined the baked goods. Abigail's mouth salivated. She had skipped breakfast to collect her friends, and they were late. Abigail turned her attention to the most recent group of returning passengers. Neither Kirsty nor Steve were amongst them. She sighed her disappointment and went back to the temptations of the coffee shop.

Kirsty's usual updates over Facebook or Instagram, even Snapchat had all been quiet. *It wasn't like her.* Steve was good for Kirsty, Abigail agreed, *albeit a little egotistical,* she beamed a light-hearted smile. She wasn't being nasty and meant no harm, but losing communication failed to surprise Abigail. *It will be one of Steve's holiday rules for certain,* she concluded. *Done to make him the complete centre of Kirsty's attention. Now,* Abs, she scolded, *do I detect a little jealousy?* Laughing at her pessimism. *Now who's being self-centred and egotistical?*

— ☐ —

Drulovic squeezed his gnarled fingers over the mound of Kirsty's bee-sting sized breasts. Her skin was ashen grey and a severe contrast against his sun leathered hands. She lay down upon a stained mattress with her once lustrous hair splayed beneath her; it was now lank and dull, slick with perspiration. Towering over her, Drulovic drooled, and he licked his lips, reptilian style. His breathing increased along with arousal. White spittle appeared at the corners of his mouth, and a tingle of pleasure tormented his impotent loins. *She'd laugh at me,* he thought with resentful anger. "Like all the others," he said with an accusatory whisper. *She'd humiliate his pathetic manhood and make fun of his crippled frame. Just like his two bitch sisters.* He nodded, incensed by the recollection of his older sisters.

"It's not my fault," Drulovic hissed, furious at Kirsty, and rubbed her breasts as if he were kneading bread dough. Frustration flared. "I can't help my weakened legs — it was polio — that's why I'm like this."

She didn't answer.

Unperturbed, he glided his hands down over her navel. Taking her lack of response as a challenge to gain reaction; he advanced further towards her pubic area.

"Poppa — the drunken bastard — used to whip me."

He clawed at the flesh of her inner thigh, drawing crimson tracks over her chalk skin.

"The point is," he panted, aggressive breaths, "The ironic part is... I enjoyed the beatings." He laughed a farcical laugh and delved his reptilian hands deeper, snaking down between her thighs.

"My sisters..." Kirsty's delicate down of pubic hair brushed against his palm. "...Well — they'd join in with Poppa."

He relished her warmth, which now enveloped his fingers with her slickness and he renewed the invasion with vigour.

"You're going to beg me to hurt you," Drulovic said with bitterness.

"The simple beauty of pain," He chuckled. "Its rawness is complex and exquisite. Something real, something divine."

— ☐ —

The cogs of time were well oiled, and seconds slipped into minutes and minutes into hours. Abigail was bored but amused herself with a lone game of eye spy. This became tedious. Even people watching, which she often enjoyed, failed to satisfy her. She gave a deflated sigh and leant upon the coffee shop's chrome railing. Chin cradled in her palms, she glanced at the monitor screen for incoming flights. The aeroplane travelling from Reus airport had landed two hours ago.

"Come on, Kirst — What's the hold-up?" She spoke with a dispirited whisper. "Give it a little longer." Abigail huffed. "Patience is a virtue...?" This amused her, and she responded with a pig snort of laughter, shrugged, and said. "Virtue isn't an attribute of mine."

Peering into the somewhat dwindled crowd of returning passengers. At the far end of the foyer was an information booth.

"I assume that's where I should inquire?" She resigned and headed towards the counter.

Abigail smiled at the pleasant Indian girl, who sat at the counter. A name badge fastened to the information clerk's tunic lapel introduced her as Janisha, she chewed on the ends of dense, single braid of black hair. Absorbed by what she was studying on her computer monitor screen, her perfectly manicured nails, machine-gunned, across the keys of her keyboard. Her braid slipped from her mouth as she looked up and. said, "Hello. How may I help you?"

Abigail explained, while Janisha clicked away at the keyboard.

"I'm sorry, could you repeat their names?" She asked, without glancing up from the monitor, "Who is it you're checking for?" she returned to chewing her hair and this muffled her words. "What flight were they on? Do you have a flight number?"

Abigail struggled to conceal the frustration in her tone. "I'm trying to find a Miss Kirsty Edwards and Mr Steve Douglas. They're scheduled to be on the 10:45 am flight."

It was now 1.30pm.

"Flying in from Reus airport — Spain. Flight: FR2296?"

Janisha scrolled down a register from the manifest. "Yes — okay, I have it." she smiled. "Miss Kirsty Edwards and Mr Steven Douglas?" She glanced up at Abigail. "They were expected to be on the arrival from Reus — but neither of them boarded."

Confused, Abigail replied, "Well. That's ridiculous." She snorted a satiric laugh. "Of course, they boarded — Why wouldn't they?"

More rhythmic clicking of the keyboard. Janisha shook her head and feigned an apology toward Abigail.

"Sorry. But it suggests they didn't get on the flight from Reus."

Rummaging into the depths of her handbag. Abigail searched for the small handwritten note presented to her by Kirsty. The times, dates and flight numbers were written upon it, which she showed Janisha.

"Look, I have the right details. Kirsty wrote them down. They're correct." Abigail slapped it onto the desk. "Please recheck this arrival?"

Dismissing the note, Janisha squinted at the monitor screen and sighed.

A couple of seconds passed, and she glanced up.

"You have the correct information. But your friends couldn't have got on. It would say so — here." She tapped the screen with her nail, "If they had been on board, it would show up, but it doesn't." Janisha felt the intensity of dissatisfaction from Abigail's glare. "It indicates two individuals have missed this departure. Giving the names you are conducting inquiries about." She tried to appear sympathetic. "There is another arrival from Reus." She glimpsed at her wristwatch. "It's expected to touch down at 3 pm."

— □ —

A knock at the door interrupted Drulovic.

"Who is it? I'm busy," He answered with a furious growl.

"I've got to check in on Stef..." Celia shouted before she corrected. "... The new girl. I want to check on her." A cannon volley of thumps rattled the door, "Let me in."

Looking down at Kirsty, "What an interfering old whore," said Drulovic with a mean-spirited hiss. Crimson anger burned his liver-spotted cheeks. Calling over his shoulder at the locked door, he shouted, "She's fine."

Drulovic squeezed Kirsty's slender hand within his vice clutching grip.

A mouse-like whimper broke from Kirsty. Her eyes opened, black marbles in deep dish sockets. They rolled separate from one another and failed to find him or the cause of discomfort before she slipped on the glacial precipice that was unconsciousness.

Celia, refusing to let up, thundered her fist against the door.

Incensed by her persistence, "I told you... I'm busy," he boomed. "Come back later."

"I don't care," answered a defiant Celia and yelled, "I know all about you, Doctor."

Her fists became an elephant stampede which hammered the door in its frame.

"You're a sick masochistic bastard, now let me in." Her hand throbbed. "Open this God-damn door."

Infuriated, Drulovic snarled at the air. "Why can't they allow me to tend to my patient."

Gripping two of Kirsty's fingers, he twisted them back until the white of knuckle-bone bleached her skin. Any further pressure and the sprigs of her fingers would snap. The drug-induced darkness which claimed Kirsty kept her hidden.

"I am not going anywhere," Celia insisted. "Let me in. Now." She cupped her palms around her mouth and pushed them against the frigid wooden door, and threatened, "If I have to call Marco?"

Disappointed, "Fine — give me a minute." Drulovic answered.

Celia stood, fists on hips, as the dragging scrape of the latch clicked and the door opened. Drulovic shuffled to one side to allow her entry.

"I reckon a little more of this." he held up the empty syringe. "She'll be ready to earn her keep."

Celia ignored the doctor and went straight to Kirsty. Words steeped with cynicism as she responded, "That's if — you haven't killed her first."

— ▢ —

Abigail called Joyce, Kirsty's mother, for the third time in as many hours. She made an anxious sigh and said, "I haven't heard from either Kirsty or Steve." Hesitated before adding, "Have you? Has Kirsty called saying they're delayed?"

Abigail regretted asking the question. She closed her eyes and squeezed with thumb and forefinger across the bridge of her nose whilst Joyce panicked.

"I was asking…" snapped an impatient Abigail. She drew a deep breath then started over; this time she kept her tone restrained.

"… I'm trying to see if either has been in touch. In case they missed the flight." Abigail listened to the worried warbling of Joyce's voice. *Well, this was a mistake,* she decided. *Joyce sounds frantic.*

"It'll be okay," Abigail soothed, her tone persuasive. "They'll have missed their flight. That's all. Please, Joyce. Try not to panic." She finished the call and exhaled a massive sigh of relief. Frustrated, *you owe me big time, Kirst. You're such a spud brain.* It was 4:30 pm and the arrivals' display confirmed the 3 pm flight from Reus had landed on time. There were still no signs of her missing friends. *This is getting stupid,* Abigail decided, and returned to the information booth.

"Hello, is Janisha about? I spoke with her earlier." Abigail asked a plump, middle-aged woman. Her name badge read Liz. Cradled beneath a shock of peacock blue eyeshadow were her tired chestnut eyes, and lipstick lips daubed a shade of mulled wine. Her smile crinkled her cheeks and risked cracking their plum blushed fullness. Liz explained she was Janisha's colleague.

"Janisha has finished for the day."

Cloying dewberry perfume choked Abigail when she said, "I'm looking for my friends. They should have arrived earlier this afternoon."

She gave Liz the same note she had shown Janisha. "Would you be good enough to check for me?" Then, as an afterthought, she added. "I don't mean to waste your time. Can you look at both — this one…" she tapped the note, "… and the flight which landed at 3 pm? Just in case I have missed them?"

Liz's skills were more cumbersome than her colleagues and she jabbed her stubby digits on the keyboard. She said, "I have looked at both flights." Her tone sounded regretful as she shook her head. "Your friends haven't boarded either. Please try not to worry. I know how you must feel, but I'm certain there is a good explanation."

Her plump hands were milk on chocolate when she placed them upon Abigail's. "I will carry out a few calls and see if I can find out what may have happened. Can you give, say, twenty minutes?"

"I will be back in twenty."

Now, for the first time, Abigail felt nervous. Something wasn't right. She couldn't describe it. It was the same sense of apprehension she experienced when visiting the dentist. Seconds seemed to bind against one another, and minutes appeared to become hours. After twenty minutes, Liz came back to Abigail and explained.

"I have spoken with my colleagues at Reus airport."

"OK. Did my friends miss the flight?" Said Abigail.

"Well." Liz braced herself. "There isn't any record of either passenger checking in for today's flight."

"I know this already," failing to hide her aggrieved manner. Making the older woman docile and shrink away like a terrified mouse. "Otherwise — I wouldn't be wasting my time by having this pointless conversation." Abigail's face flushed a deep mocha. Conscious of other people watching her. She became tolerant.

"Sorry..."

Abigail looked down at the pale-faced clerk.

"Sorry," Abigail repeated. "I didn't mean to be rude. It's just," she searched for the right words. "This isn't like them." She stated, disheartened, "I haven't missed them. They didn't miss their flight."

Sshh — My Sweet Darling

Detective Baldomero beamed at Mariana Gonzalo when she neared. She brought upon an oval tray two plates of tapas and three glasses half filled with ice and a decanter of iced water. She had also produced three bottles of beer. Her hair gleamed a natural teal, which she had tied up away from her bronzed face. Her eyes, dark brown, almost as black as obsidian glass, sparkled with delight. "Nicky," Mariana said as her cheerful smile creased across her face. "Such a lovely surprise." She placed the tray on the dinner table. Leant forwards and brushed each of his cheeks with hers.

Knowing better than to offer his help, Baldomero watched her place the food and drinks before him. The beer hissed as she flipped their crimped caps, and amber froth bubbled from their neck. He picked up the nearest beer and took a generous swig. Baldomero had always detested being called Nicky, but smiled to himself as Mariana sat upon her husband's knee. He said, "Al has just been telling me about Carlo," and swigged another mouthful of beer, enjoying its coolness. "You must be real proud?"

"Yes. And worried," concern etched her tone as she nodded, "You appreciate how dangerous the world is." The shine left her eyes, and she became solemn, "I pray for his safety, each day." She crossed herself and kissed a small rosary beaded necklace dangling about her lissom neck.

"He will be okay." Baldomero said with ardent reproach, as he placed his beer down. "I was just saying how Carlo has been assigned to a friend of mine. She will keep an eye on him."

"She?" Mariana quizzed in a mischievous manner. "And is this she, a special friend?" Mariana pried, with a playful touch of Baldomero's knee.

The detective felt warmth on his cheeks. Mariana always did this, always wished to know when he was going to settle down and get married, have children. He became evasive. "Not at all. She is a respected colleague." He laughed.

A crashing noise of crockery made Mariana sigh and tap the thigh of Alejandro. "I had better see what they're up to. Before our other dear children, ruin us." She grinned as she stood. "Lovely to see you, Nicky. But when are you going to bring a girlfriend or a wife?"

"Ha ..." Baldomero rebuked. "I got married long ago. To the job. I don't have the time for anything else."

"Nonsense ..." she started, but another crash followed by angry raised voices caused her to glance towards the kitchen. "Don't think this conversation is over, Nicky," she whispered as she leant forward and brushed her cheek against his. "Are you here for long?"

"Not certain, a week, maybe longer." Baldomero shrugged.

"Visit again before you leave. Won't you?" She was gone before he could reply, walking toward the kitchen, glancing over her shoulder at both Gonzalo and Baldomero with a smile, "You're always welcome."

— ☐ —

Kirsty woke as if roused from a maelstrom of narcotic slumber. Shadows crept within the obsidian room. A dusting of amber light from the dwindling sun spliced through the curtains. Her ghostly skin appeared almost porcelain as a chill puckered her naked goose-bumped flesh. Kirsty's liquid vision swam when nausea wracked her body.

I must be sick, thought Kirsty. *That would explain the doctor's many visits. The doctor who brings my medicine.* "I don't like him," she proclaimed in a detached whisper. "He's a bad man." speaking louder. "Shh!"

Holding a hand over her mouth with a slap of worry, she'd be heard.

They'll hear you... you fool. Her inner voice screamed its caution.

The same routine, always when I wake. The doctor comes with my medication. Sometimes the other guy is with him. They both scare me. She shivered, as if seized by an icy draft. *They do things... nasty things.* Her wretched thoughts raced. *Things doctors shouldn't do.*

Lying silent and still. Hoping. Praying even to be spared for just one night.

Something dreadful has taken place. She knew this much, but each time her brain dipped within the sludge, the memories were as inaccessible as the depths of the deep, black ocean. Guarded by two bright-blue pearls, the enticing and predatory lanternfish of her mind. Kirsty retreated, for she feared what lay beyond the veil of hidden memory.

— ☐ —

Gonzalo fumbled inside his trouser pocket for a set of wire-framed specs. He perched them upon the bridge of his nose and read.

"I have the charge sheet here about Joseph O'Flanagan. This was the crime report for his possession charge. They found him, along with his girlfriend, murdered. It's a damn coincidence," He declared, with scepticism, and handed over the document to Baldomero. "The news reported it's drug-related." His grim expression appeared doubtful. "A drug deal turned sour?" He glanced up at Baldomero and said. "Reading the report? I see nothing here you can't handle. So, what's got you thinking your crimes in Madrid are connected?"

"Okay," Baldomero agreed. "First assumption, this looks pretty straightforward." He leant in close and took out a 10 x 11-inch tablet. He swiped the screen and dragged up several photographs of the murder scene. "Look at the method which killed them?"

Gonzalo pushed up his specs and studied the pictures. A male in his early to mid-twenties slumped into a crouch position. Taking an educated guess; Gonzalo came to the supposition the victim had died at the point of attack. Not showing awareness and displaying all the signs, he'd been surprised. The flesh surrounding the mortal wound was a clean, smooth cut, almost clinical in its precision. This told Gonzalo, the weapon had been a very sharp blade. The large blood splatter which arced a reddish-brown rainbow across the wall showed blood loss was tremendous and death would have been swift. Gonzalo swiped through the images and inspected each one. Something seemed odd.

The next sequence of pictures was the female victim. Again, this fatality was in her early to mid-twenties. Her attack had been different. Not as brutal as the male victim. But it displayed signs of surprise. She was on her right side. A puncture wound just below her left rib, toward the base of her sternum. Very little blood loss, which determined the heart had stopped within moments of the assault. Again, the precision of this attack set alarm bells clanging. Gonzalo had encountered this type of killing before when an American ex-marine had been in a bar fight. The marine had murdered the man he was fighting in much the same manner as this girl in the picture.

More pictures showed the flat was ransacked, as if someone had been searching for something. Gonzalo sat back and stared at Baldomero, "I can understand why you're suspicious." Tapping the screen, which displayed a bedroom in chaos. "This is a red herring."

Gonzalo declared with a disparaging shake of the head, "It has all the trademarks of an assassination. Not a burglary." He scrutinized the images. "This all looks…" he flattened his goatee as he swiped from one image to another, "… Staged."

Baldomero nodded in agreement. "Just look at how they were murdered. Especially the male victim, throat slit to the point of near decapitation. The blood splatter." Baldomero had picked up the tablet from Gonzalo. He returned to the first brutal picture. "This blood loss would have finished him in minutes, if not seconds. Yet, there's no evidence of his assailant. It's as if the assault happened by magic." Baldomero took a sip of beer, allowing Gonzalo time to process what he was being told. "It isn't as if the perp has tried to clean the crime scene. Whoever did this was damned quick and proficient at it. He knew where to stand without becoming covered in blood and how to avoid leaving evidence."

"Look here, at the girl." Baldomero swiped across to the female victim. "I'm certain you will agree. Someone with previous military training executed this. Special forces, maybe?" He leant back in his chair and arched his back. Gonzalo's face was creased with concentration, and he sat facing the detective in silence.

Time had galloped on and the restaurant was now full of tourists. The sun was hanging low in the sky and splayed its orange amber fingers across the cobbled square, and the shadows grew in front of the restaurant's gazebo. Clicking the touch screen again, Baldomero pulled up a CCTV picture of Kirsty and Steve. Turning the tablet to face Gonzalo, he said, "This couple were the last ones with the victims. I need to talk to them." A server moved in and cleared the dishes. Baldomero waited for him to leave before continuing.

"Do you think they have anything to do with the murders?" Gonzalo asked.

"No... Maybe... I don't know." It was Baldomero's time to be sceptical. "I will need to interview them."

He tapped the tablet screen, and a different series of images appeared. "Do you see this man in the background?" Baldomero was apologetic. "We took it from the metro station camera, the one facing Bravo Murillo Metro station. It's not the best,"

"I recognize the one," said Gonzalo.

He looked at the picture. The guy was familiar. "Yes, I see him. What about him?"

Baldomero swiped the screen until another picture of the man became visible. This image was an enlargement of the man's face. The look of puzzlement upon Gonzalo's face altered to one of fascinated recognition.

Before Gonzalo could react, Baldomero swiped onto another brutal crime scene. "This is a homicide which took place in Madrid. The casualty was a petty criminal. A junky and drug dealer. A bit of a sleaze bag, but harmless enough." Swiping through the images until he stopped at another CCTV picture. "This is another picture taken from a different camera at the Metro station. It reveals the fellow in the first picture meeting with the unfortunate fellow we found murdered. He is most probably the last person with the victim, and is a significant interest." Baldomero was on a roll, and he finished his beer while he gathered his thoughts.

"I agree he's a suspect, and I also know who this man is." Gonzalo said, becoming frank with Baldomero. "But you knew that. Didn't you? It is why you have brought this to me."

Baldomero nodded. "I tried the usual facial recognition searches. The quality of the pictures are gritty to be indisputable. Especially this one." He had swiped the screen until a blown-up picture of the individual in the CCTV image was displayed. "After a more advanced search, I turned up with a viable suspect."

"Marco Branco," Gonzalo announced. "That is the man who is in these images." he shook his head in disbelief. "But how does this link in with the murders here," He picked up the tablet and scrutinized the picture. "He was my one case. The one who I never got as far as the court steps."

Baldomero raised his eyebrows, "It would explain why you were so meticulous, whenever we investigated a crime."

"Correct." Gonzalo placed the tablet down on the table. "This person is a sociopath. I knew it when he was a boy. They should have locked him up back then. But they were too scared to convict a minor. Just in case they'd got it wrong." He tapped the picture and cautioned, "Be careful with this fellow. He is vicious. After we released him, he just vanished. I tried to keep tabs on him, but he disappeared. He must have had support. I could never find out who that could be, and the file has been cold ever since."

"Well, that fits." Baldomero shrugged, then swiped to another picture. This one of the high-street in Salou showed Marco about to enter Brodie's bar. "They took this on the day of the dual murder. I can't believe Marco Branco's appearance here is a coincidence."

"The Madrid case sounds very much like Marco," Gonzalo admitted. "But, the case of the double homicide?" he gave a negative shake of his head. "That's someone else. It is too surgical for Marco. My best guess is: He may be involved, somehow, but he didn't kill them."

"I hate asking," said Baldomero, "but could you help me with this?"

"I will look through my old files," Gonzalo said. He grinned and stood up from the table. "We're getting busy. I know the bar owner, Brodie. I will ask him a few questions."

— ☐ —

Only when Kirsty felt the roughness of hands upon her nakedness did she understand her vulnerabilities. Unsure of who forced her over flat onto her abdomen. She was rigid, paralytic with fear, and realized their intentions were much more perverse. Her heart thundered a freight train in her chest, and panic clenched her stomach tight. She sought to move, but couldn't. Tried to resist, but someone punched her at the nap of her neck and fireflies filled her vision.

The creature didn't speak. Only grunted as he pinned her down. Her fear-induced paralysis fell away. Able to writhe and squirm, she attempted to fight off this monster. He was strong, too aggressive. Kirsty was weak, and strength sapped as she tore at the mattress. *Oh, God... no... please God... no... not this.* Her scream ripped into the bed, but was ineffective. He forced her legs apart and thrust himself inside. Sheer helplessness made Kirsty scream again and again until his pounding muted her. They stuffed the sheet from the bed into her mouth, gagging her. She gave up. A surreal calmness descended while she resigned to this violation.

Turning her face from the bedsheet,

"Please stop." She pleaded, "You don't have to do this."

The blue-eyed beast answered through clenched teeth. Words were a vortex of abhorrent growls.

"Girls like you." He grunted with each thrust. "Deserve," forcing himself into her. "To be treated — like this."

Her passive approach was of no use. Kirsty bucked like an unbroken horse; wild with fear, she squirmed beneath him. Nothing helped. She felt the warm clamminess and blazing fire of his mouth biting into her naked shoulders. His teeth slashing at her skin. Hot crimson fluid oozed into the crook of her neck. It empowered him. Invigorated him. Her anguished screams delighted its audience, spurring him on. He hissed.

"That's it, scream." He said, "Screech loud and hard — no one will help."

Then he bashed her head against the mattress, squeezing his fingers around her throat.

Kirsty could resist no longer and allowed him to use her limp, defeated body. Her mind drifted, seeking its tranquil place. Its sanctuary.

Cutting off her breathing. "I could kill you and…" He grunted, "No-one would ever find you."

His hands remained around Kirsty's neck for the duration. She couldn't breathe. Numbed to the physical pain, she floated above herself and watched him shudder toward climax. He released his grip before death could take her from him. His panting breaths slowed, and he held on to her. Caressing her trembling body as if they were lovers, he spoke with soft, consoling tones, "Shhh," he panted, "Shhh — My Sweet Darling, it's all okay — it's over now."

The Station

Baked scones wafted a delightful scent of devilish temptation into the room. However, it did little to raise the oppressive atmosphere which weighed upon its occupants. Ruth reached over to a nest of tables placed within the forgotten space between the chimney breast and the bay window. A retro styled telephone together with directory notepad were among her selection of small Wade ornaments.

"I have Peter's number." She informed, giving an inquisitive look toward Abigail and Joyce. "You know who Peter is? Don't you?"

They made a negative shake of their heads.

"Peter is Steve's older brother." Ruth answered with a disapproved sigh. "They may be staying with Peter..." She became excited that her theory could carry some weight. "Or — perhaps — Peter has picked them up?"

"Don't talk daft..." said a flippant Mark.

"Well, it was just a suggestion," Ruth retorted with a scowl as she tried to remain optimistic.

"They never speak as it is — I doubt Steven would go anywhere near Peter," he argued, trying to remain realistic.

She looked over at Abigail and Joyce. "Peter owns property in Spain. It's a start at least. I will call him."

Abigail interrupted.

"I realized Steve had an older brother. But I didn't know his name." She glanced over to Joyce, who peered out through the bay window of lead-lined glass.

"How about you, Joyce?" Abigail asked. "Has Steve ever spoken to you about Peter?"

Rain misted the window into silver snakes of water rivulets, and Joyce watched these trickle over the bevelled edges.

"Joyce," Abigail said in an acerbic tone. "Has he mentioned Peter to you?"

"Err — sorry." Joyce replied, dispirited. "My head is a million miles away. Peter, no — I don't believe Steven has ever spoken to me about his brother."

Ruth's face was one of disappointment as she placed the phone onto its cradle.

"No answer," she said, discouraged. "I will give you his number." Handing Abigail a scribbled note. "Peter is a busy man. But if you keep trying, then I am certain you will get through. I've left a message and hopefully he'll ring me back."

"Huh," snorted a cynical Mark, and under his breath he mumbled, "When Hell freezes over."

— ▢ —

Kirsty's skin stank. A stench of rotting cabbage and stale vomit. With Celia's direction, Kirsty, who was in limbo between the dead and the living, shuffled toward the steaming waters of a rose-scented bathtub. She glided into its warmth and pulled her knees to her chest and clutched her arms around them. Burrowing her forehead into her drawn-up legs, she rocked forward, then backward. Bath water slapped against the tub in mini tsunamis of ripples as Kirsty stared; vacant and expressionless.

Celia used a sponge to wash Kirsty and ran it along her left shoulder lingering over the crimson bite marks of angered skin. The tenderness of her touch made Kirsty flinch.

"Hush. Pretty thing." Celia soothed, taking her time to bathe her. Once satisfied, she guided Kirsty from the tub and brought her, towel wrapped, into the bedroom where she twisted Kirsty's hair up, turban style, and sat her down on the bed.

Bluish smoke poured from Celia's nostrils from the cigarette she had just lit. She re-filled her lungs and removed the towel from Kirsty's hair. What shall I do with this; Celia wondered, picking up the damp strands?

Kirsty shivered as the onset of her drug withdrawal squeezed its vicious grip.

Peering from behind her polluted haze, "You are my English, Rosa." Celia announced. Kirsty's marbleized eyes fluttered, but she remained subdued.

"Yes–that's what I will call you." Shrouded with smog, Celia declared, "You will be my Rosa — that's your new working name."

Lucky Strike jammed between mulberry lips. Celia tugged a hairbrush at the damp straw hair. Ash dusted Kirsty's left leg when it settled on her thigh. "Well Rosa? How do you prefer your hairstyle?" she inquired, "I think — braided — Hmm?" water dripped icy rivers between Kirsty's shoulders. "Yes — braided will appeal to the customers."

Next, Celia applied makeup to Kirsty's corpse skin. This brought life into her cheeks. Smiling as she held up a small mirror.

Kirsty looked at the reflected image without reaction. A circus clown stared back, but there wasn't any humour in the eyes, just a despondent stare.

Celia's annoyance increased. "Please Rosa, — You must try to pull yourself together." she pleaded, "This isn't any good — You cannot be like this. They will hurt you — let me help?"

The bedroom door burst open as Marco stomped into the room, followed by a shuffling Doctor Drulovic. The briefest glimmer of unexpected excitement gave a twinkle in Kirsty's eyes. Celia's fears were confirmed, and she knew they'd caught Kirsty within their addictive web.

— ☐ —

Joyce had urged to go to the police earlier to report Kirsty missing. It was Abigail's suggestion to visit Ruth and Mark. It was a decision Abigail regretted and upon leaving, she had driven to the station.

A police officer entered to the right of the reception and strode toward them. His trimmed wisps of thinning ginger hair bounced with each stride.

"Hello, I'm Sergeant Phillips." he was courteous but formal. He glanced over his shoulder at the reception clerk and said. "I will use interview room one." His attention came back to Abigail and Joyce. "Care to accompany me, Ladies?"

"Now, I understand you wish to report a missing person?" Phillips said with earnest.

Answering for the pair of them, Abigail spoke. "Yes officer, well…"

Her arid throat seemed as if she was attempting to ingest a thistle. She gulped and coughed before starting over.

"It's actually two people." She cleared her throat again. "My friend Kirsty and her boyfriend, Steve."

"Kirsty is my daughter," interjected Joyce. "And this isn't like her. Not like her at all," she said, then continued. "Why?" she whimpered with a fervent appeal, "Why hasn't she called me?"

Joyce turned toward Abigail. Her tears glistened beneath the bright office lighting. Droplets ran over her cheeks, with smears of black mascara as tramlines. She rummaged for a tissue from inside her purse and avoided the officer's gaze.

Abigail squeezed her shoulder. Hints of worry had carved into Joyce's moon beam face.

"Excuse me for asking this." Interrupted Sergeant Phillips. "I understand how upsetting this all must be, but..."

He braced himself for the outrage to follow. Phillips continued his questions and kept direct but diplomatic. "Are you positive they're missing?"

"Well," Abigail was more astonished than angry at the query. "They expected me to pick them up."

She watched as the sergeant took note.

"Yesterday, from the airport. They expected me to collect them. But didn't show up."

He continued his questioning and remained neutral. "Did you inquire at the airport?" Phillips asked.

"Yes — Twice." replied Abigail. Heat rose within her coffee-coloured cheeks. She had been through this the previous day. *What is it going to take?* She became irritated, *Before someone thinks this is important?*

"They pointed out," she observed, dismayed, at the officer's blank expression. "The people at the airport explained; Kirsty and Steve may have missed their flight."

He started with a quiet nod of his head. "It seems likely..."

Abigail, exasperated, cut him off. "I stuck around for the later arrival to land." She said, her tone acerbic, "I'm not stupid." Her annoyance, caustic. "Neither of them were on that one, either?"

Opening her purse, she fished out the scrap of paper given to her at the airport and with a whack which rang within the small interview room, she shoved it in front of Phillips.

"I have the hotel phone number. You should check at least?"

Sergeant Philips was candid in his approach and said. "Nobody is referring to you as stupid — Miss Simmons."

He picked up the piece of paper she had given him. "I have a set procedure to follow. Please…" with compassion, he looked first at Abigail, then Joyce. "The quicker I can ask these questions, the sooner I can file the report and prepare my preliminary inquiries." He waited for his words to register. "Try to remain calm. Please proceed."

Abigail nodded. He is right, she realized, this isn't helping anyone, least of all Kirsty and Steve. Stay calm — Abs — persevere with him, and later you can start searching for them yourself.

"You don't seem to understand, officer." Her manner softened, but she remained a little fractious. "I called the number of the hotel — I even spoke to the receptionist." She paused. "She was most insistent — Kirsty and Steve checked in — but they never checked out."

Her scowl silenced him when he attempted to speak.

"Does that not seem odd to you, Officer?"

Abigail glanced at the time on her mobile phone. They'd been at the station for two-and-a-half hours. Two and a half hours of lost time answering the same pointless questions. This is becoming ludicrous, Abigail concluded.

Phillips didn't acknowledge the question but kept himself detached and said, "I only have a few more questions, if you would be patient with me a little longer?"

He ruffled through his written observations. "The two people who are missing… err, Kirsty and Steve?" Again, glancing at his notes to re-affirm the names. "They are together? As a courting couple?"

Sergeant Phillips wrote.

"Is that correct so far?" He looked up, his pen paused mid-sentence.

"Yes but…" Abigail replied.

"So?" Phillips interjected. "How can you be positive they are missing? Couldn't they just have extended their trip?" He moved on without giving a chance to argue. "I have to ask these questions because these are the questions my superiors will ask me."

"Well. Kirsty and Steve went on holiday a couple of weeks ago. But they haven't been seen since." Abigail explained, again, for the umpteenth time. She had resigned to the fact they were getting nowhere.

"Kirsty and Steve were both thrilled for this break," Joyce answered. "I haven't known my daughter this excited for years." She fidgeted in her seat like a small child. "Steve was going to propose." Her voice broke with a sob.

"It's alright, Joyce — they'll be okay," Abigail soothed, "I promise, we'll find them." she looked over at Phillips.

"Kirsty and Steve didn't check out of the hotel. Either the cleaners or the receptionist… I'm not sure who — found the room empty. No clothes. No suitcases. Not any sign at all. It was as if they had never arrived." She dabbed away her own frustrated tears. Disheartened, I'm sick of this, she thought. This is a complete waste of our time. "Now? Does that not seem a little peculiar — suspicious even?"

A quick glance at his notes.

"Could Miss Kirsty Edwards have turned down the marriage proposal from Mr Douglas?" He cringed, but needed to ask this question. "Perhaps they have gone someplace to sort matters out?"

Abigail was livid, her words jumbled when they spilled from her mouth.

"Now, you-you-you listen to me." She struggled to keep civil. "We're not just a couple of hysterical women, panicking for no reason. We have come to you for your help, and I don't appreciate your disinterested manner."

"I realize how upsetting this is." Phillips tried to be tactful and lightened the tone of his voice.

"I must investigate all the information presented to me. I cannot log a missing person's report until I have looked into all the factors." He paused once more. "The circumstances are; the couple have been missing since last night — it hasn't been 24 hours?"

Abigail's cauldron of anger boiled. She stood and knocked over the plastic chair; she'd been sitting on. "Well — this was a complete waste of our time."

Joyce, her voice wavering, added, "You don't appear to be listening — Officer- it is unusual and out of character for either of them to not call us."

Tears flowed hot rivers upon her cheeks.

"Please, find them?" Dabbing at her puffy, reddened eyes, she implored.

"Please help us find my daughter?"

— ▢ —

Turbulent clouds stirred intense violence about the heavens. The nor-easterly gale tore along the road and rain fell, throwing wet missiles down from a slate blackened sky. Abigail and Joyce ran along the high-street, towards a little coffee shop. The deluge pummelled the pavement in their wake as they tumbled into the coffee shop's entrance.

"So? What do you think?" Abigail asked.

Pebble-sized raindrops rattled against the windowed shopfront. Thick silvery lines traced criss-cross patterns across the glass. Water gurgled down gutters and spewed out of down-spouts. The deluge created a giant puddle outside the coffee shop's entrance. It reached almost into the road's centre and swallowed the curb as if the shop was sinking.

"I don't think he believed us. But we must proceed at their pace."

"I was considering travelling to Spain," Abigail declared, and shrugged. "Since the police here don't seem very interested. I may as well search for myself."

Nightmares and Pictures

Phantoms, dark and foreboding, morphed the shadows. Black and viscous, crude oil upon an ocean of nightmare. Fear imprisoned within Kirsty's mind. Glacial-blue eyes that shimmered as they rode upon the surf of this vast deep sea, malignant in their torment. She sat naked on the bed with her knees pulled tight in against her breasts. Revealing xylophone rib bones beneath goose-bumped flesh as she swayed back and forth. A babble of incoherent whisperings aimed at the blue-eyed spectre. Kirsty screeched her misery as her skin felt the tongues of flame lap over her flesh. It, too, was imagined, but in Kirsty's drug withdrawn state, it all looked real. Taking a few brief hours of withdrawal to grant the darkness safe passage and gain substance to the voices. These had emerged as whispers, but whipped to a crescendo of banshee shrieks. Kirsty held her head with both hands and wailed.

Steve haunted her on this first night. Devoid of life, cold and abhorrent as he lay next to her. Cadaverous hands fondled her skin. His touch produced an infernal fire, and Kirsty clawed herself to quench the flame. Steve's snake tongue slivered from a malignant mouth. Drawn back lips, which split to expose sulphurous yellow teeth. His breath gushed, a putrid stink of decay and death. She felt him burn deep as he invaded her. Steve slid into the turbulence of her mind and transformed into the blue orbs whose shrieks reverberated, "Shhh — My Sweet Darling — It's all okay, it's over now." They giggled, "Ha, ha ha hahaha…" Time lost all meaning, and she wasn't sure if it was morning or evening, day, or night.

She resurfaced from an unconscious slumber. The persistent itch of narcotic craving became cockroaches beneath her flesh. Trapped like a stricken swimmer as panic swelled her lungs. Her depleted chest burned in agony, and only her medicine would be her salvation.

— ☐ —

Baldomero was sitting in a broom-closet office at the Tarragona police station. They viewed him as an outsider. A suit from the capital, not to be trusted. He couldn't help but feel the resentment from the local officers. They mistrusted him, believed he was going to take charge of the case, but he was just an observer, nothing more. Invited by Chief Hernández as a favour because he had an interest in the victim. The detective hadn't any jurisdiction over the double homicide, but they feared him all the same. So, they shunned him into this miniscule office and left him to rot.

The quietness suited him and allowed him to work. Baldomero used his time to investigate further into the death of the woman for whom he was struggling to locate an identity. After days of wasted bureaucracy and hacking through red tape, he had gained access to documentation of the adolescent who had died in England. Now, as he stroked his moustache and studied the comparisons, he couldn't believe these were all coincidences. Both the woman in Madrid, and the girl in England, had the same 6- Acetyl morphine constituents in their blood-work. Both presented identical amounts of impurities and both held the same high levels: Papaverine and Thebaine. Other chemical trace markers were enough to give a definite chemical fingerprint. They matched the overdose death of Sebastián Garcia in Madrid and the heroin Joseph O'Flanagan had in his possession. All these individuals were now dead, either by overdose or murder, and their connections couldn't just be a fluke. The heroin must have emanated from the same source. This was conjecture on the detective's side, but he suspected the dealer known as Curly to be the origin. Again, he was guessing, but whoever killed Curly was involved in the rest of this mess. It was all linked, and then there was this appearance of Marco Branco. Someone who they recognized to be a murderous sociopath. But Baldomero wondered, how is he connected?

— □ —

Abigail had arrived in Spain two days earlier. She didn't waste any time and had first visited the Plaza Park hotel. She was told the same things as they had explained over the phone. However, the clerk Josephine had given the address of a restaurant where Steve had dined with Kirsty.

Abigail travelled by scooter, which she had hired earlier that morning. The taste of salt flavoured the air as it charged her face. The ever-evolving ocean sparkled turquoise and was nuzzled by a golden blanket of sandy coastline. Speckled upon its surface were many fishing boats, a scattering of jewels as each reflected beneath the high noon sun.

Abigail parked outside the restaurant and killed the engine. Standing, the scooter against a low wall of chalk white boulders bordering the arid scrubland. Patches of blazing colour of the many wild Gazanias bloomed in sporadic sunset orange clumps. Providing swathes of colour to an otherwise sparse and sun-bleached landscape. Hibiscus flowers grew along the restaurant's entrance. Blooms of coral-coloured trumpets danced upon the sea perfumed breeze.

Inside the restaurant, a bronze-faced waiter approached her with a smile. Showing him a photograph of Kirsty and Steve, Abigail asked.

"Have you seen this couple," she noticed recognition in his eyes. This made her even more curious. Getting excited, she continued. "Did you serve them?"

He took hold of the photo. "Ce — Ce — I... how you say?" He furrowed his brow as he searched for the words. "I memory them."

"You remember them?" She corrected.

"Ce — very..." he sounded embarrassed. "Erm — very — Hermosa." He circled his face, then pointed to Abigail's. He watched her blank expression. "Lo Siento — I am sorry — my English. Is no good." He turned to walk away. As an afterthought he stopped, glanced at Abigail and said. "You, wait." He went to the bar and spoke with a colleague.

This new waiter approached. "Hola, Buenos Dias," he greeted with an inquisitive smile.

"Jose," thumbing over his right shoulder at the original server, "Jose, was trying to tell you, your friend looked lovely. Just like you," he charmed. "My name is Felipe." he introduced and swatted at a fly buzzing about his face.

"You recognize my friends?" Abigail's excitement grew. This was the first verification that they had been seen, that they were OK.

"Ce -Yes; we never forget such a happy couple. So, in love, so content together." Felipe smiled; his pearl teeth gleamed in contrast against olive coloured skin. "It was his big secret," pointing at Steve, in the picture. "We hid flowers — made it — perfect for them." Felipe's grin filled up his face. "Ce, it was magnificent." He felt something was amiss, and his smile turned to one of concern. "Is everything okay?"

Abigail slumped into an adjacent chair. An impulse to talk to someone. "Well, I'm not sure." Her concern showed in the tears overflowing her eyes. "They should have arrived home, days ago." She wavered, striving to control her emotions. "They are missing." A frog in her voice caused her to croak. She gulped against the peach pit lump in her throat. "Nobody has seen them. Not since the night they were here."

"Well, I know they left in the same car that brought them here," replied Felipe, and ruffled his fingers through thick locks of black hair. "It was a limo. Very nice, I even take photos for them." He strolled toward the drinks bar.

"Remain here. I have a number for the limo company. If it helps?" At the bar, Felipe rifled through a small silver bucket, hunting for the business card he had kept. Felipe held it up and showed it to Abigail as he came back. "It isn't much," he added with a slight shrug. "I cannot help any further, I'm sorry, but it is the last I saw of them."

Abigail thanked Felipe as she left the restaurant. Outside, she leant against the wall next to the scooter and keyed the number from the card into her mobile phone.

— □ —

A curtain of silence settled upon the bedroom. Kirsty dared to look and cranked open her eyes. Her wide-eyed stare searched the shadows, but the ghoulish phantasm had gone. Instead, a woman now stood where the hellish creature had once. Ethereal was her presence. Awestruck, was she real? Kirsty wondered. Or is she just another dream? Kirsty couldn't be certain. The angel vanished into a vaporous mist, and the shadows moved once again. In her periphery, the blue orbs danced. Kirsty twisted her head from left to right, panic-stricken, she screeched. "Leave me alone…" she was defiant at first but then became meek. "I beg you. Pleeease - leave me — aloooone."

Spectral orbs sang within the darkness of her mind, "Shhh — My Sweet Darling — it's all okay, it's over now." Its cry thick with malice, which drifted on the echoes of infected memories.

Another voice, more earthbound, spoke, "Do you think — you will do as you're told?"

Kirsty peered into the lingering shadow. The angel had returned. Her shape emerged, melted away, and appeared again until a solid person stood before her. "I'm here to help you. I will look after you — Celia sent me."

Are you real? Kirsty questioned herself. *How do I know if you're real?*

"Please — help," Kirsty implored. "I'll do whatever you ask — please?" She implored, "I need my medicine."

— ☐ —

Abigail sped back along the coastline; its tranquil scenery slipped by unnoticed as she headed toward town. Where have they gone? She wondered. What's happened to them?

The limousine driver remembered Kirsty and Steve and recalled dropping them off outside Brodie's Bar. She parked up in front of Brodies and headed into the bar.

A sweat drizzled Scotsman greeted her, his manner jovial as he introduced himself as Brodie, the club's owner. His exuberance soon shifted to an incredulous mistrust the moment Abigail showed him a picture of Kirsty and Steve.

"I'm sorry, lass," he said with an aloof tone. "But we have so many comings and goings. I cannot recall these two ever being here." But he didn't glance at the photo and handed it back to Abigail.

It reminded her of her mother, who would lie and insist she hadn't been drinking. Her mom's bleary eyes, slurred speech and rum fragranced breath would tell a different story. Abigail had developed an inner instinct for lying. It was a skill which served her well. Now, as Abigail left the bar, she was positive that Brodie was lying. The mention of Kirsty and Steve and the sight of their picture made him evasive. *Guilty even. Guilt over what?* Abigail did not know. Glad to be back in the sun, she stopped to think, and it was there she saw Kirsty and Steve's picture. Outside a small supermarket, their picture in a newspaper propped in a turn-style stand.

She wouldn't have given any of them her attention, except for the picture on the front. She picked up the paper and unfolded it for a better look. She stared into a grainy black-and-white photo and into the two faces looking back at her. Although the picture was distorted, she easily recognized her Kirsty and Steve, printed on the cover of the El País newspaper.

— ☐ —

Chantelle, as per Celia's request, had checked on Kirsty several times. The first few occasions, the girl Celia referred to as Rosa was out of it. Over the course of the day, she had become more lucid, and this time Rosa had acknowledged Chantelle who said.

"Shh, Rosa. It's OK," Chantelle spoke with tender benevolence.

"Pleeease," Kirsty squealed, high-pitched and urgent. "I need my medicine." she pleaded, "please oh please... they crawl under my skin... I... I... can't stop them."

Chantelle listened to the ramblings. She appreciated what it was like to go through withdrawal. Had felt the same skin crawling sensations. Dealt with the same mania. It would pass once Rosa received her drugs, but she would never forget this sense of desolation. The first time was always the worst. The phantoms were so real, the madness overwhelming. Chantelle shuddered.

"I have what you need," said Chantelle, and held up the syringe. "But you'll have to show me you can use it."

After all, this was the whole reason the new girl was suffering complete withdrawal. It was to assess the depth of their grip over her. To force her to crave the needle more than life itself. For her to pursue an end to the torment.

"Pl... please," Kirsty said, with impatient anticipation. "Teach me how..."

"You know how," Chantelle said. "All you have to do is tie off and spike your vein." She showed by applying the rubber tube tourniquet to herself. Then removed it from her arm, and passed it over to Kirsty.

Her earthquake hands endeavoured to knot the tubing around her bicep, and it took three attempts for Kirsty to get it correct.

"That's it, Rosa," Chantelle coaxed in an instructional manner. "Not too tight now, you don't want the vein to collapse, just sufficient pressure. That's it, just like that."

"Li... li... like this," Kirsty quizzed as she examined her emerging veins.

"Just like that... now spike it." Chantelle passed over the syringe.

Kirsty snatched it with fierce impatience. But Chantelle had to hold her hands steady when she pricked her skin.

Kirsty looked up at Chantelle when she pushed down the syringe plunger and whispered, "Thank-you..."

Officer 572

The spattering of rain drummed the office windows to rattle a metronomic beat into the quietness. Broken by the ticking of the old clock fixed upon the wall. A wolf wind howled between the upper floors of the police station, as if the haunted souls of incarcerated phantoms contested for freedom. Sergeant Philips paid little attention, but added percussion as he tapped the keys on his computer keyboard. The bitter aroma of instant coffee, black and sugarless, wafted under his nose. His gritty eyes squinted at the bright computer screen as a heartbeat throbbed against his temple. *It's going to be a late one, again,* concluded Sergeant Phillips, but realized it was pointless to go home.

"Great night for the ducks — eh, Sarge," said Eddy with playful sarcasm. "You coming to the Nag's Head, for a pint?" Eddy was one of Sergeant Phillips' newest constables.

Phillips strained his eyes against the gloom. The computer's screen, the only light inside his office. Eddie's shape blocked out the illuminated corridor. "Not tonight, Ed You go on without me," He declined. "I have too much work I need to finish." He patted down on a stack of brown Manila envelopes.

"Turn the lights on for me?" Phillips asked. "That's a good lad?"

A clicking sound proceeded with the flicker of square fluorescent panels of bluish white light, and Phillips blinked beneath its glare. He pinched the bridge of his nose as he squinted.

"Don't work too hard — boss," came Eddie's shout as he hurried towards the exit further down the passageway.

Phillips was having computer issues. Each time he attempted a check on Steve Douglas, the police database froze. Standard bits of information. Such as the death of Steve's parents, and the names of the adoptive guardians, were easy enough to find out. The problems came when he tried to delve a little deeper; a message window would blink onto the screen saying unauthorized access attempt before his system returned to its start-up logo.

Phillips had talked to Mark and Ruth Douglas, Steve's adoptive parents, earlier that day, but that surmounted to nothing significant.

Clicking the computer mouse, first left-click, click, click — followed by the right. He gave up, frustrated, "Oh, for crying out loud — you stupid — cursed machine." A loud beep signalled a blank-blue screen as his computer crashed. "Aargh!" Incensed, he thumped his hand on the keyboard. "Stupid bloody thing."

The phone rang, a shrill warble. The caller I. D showed it was his boss calling.

"She's going to give me grief about working past my shift," Phillips assumed, and let it ring out. Seconds later, the ringing came again. He ignored it this second time, and then the third. The trill of a text notification buzzed his mobile. He knew, without reading, it would be from Inspector Sam Collins. He opened it up and confirmed his suspicion. The message displayed.

I know you're at your desk — answer the phone.

— ☐ —

Police Inspector Samaira Collins navigated beyond the five-day mountain of post and magazine landslides which swamped her doorway. She stepped beyond it and into the long entrance hallway of her two-bed flat before closing the front door behind her. Kicking off her heeled court-shoes, Collins leant against the cream walls. Rainwater dripped from her blazer to puddle upon the Buxton oak laminate floor beneath her stocking feet. Her soaked feet ached their fatigue as she massaged each and groaned out a yawn. "I need to stop sleeping at the station." A sceptical sigh slid from her lips as she stretched her arms. Collins knew this visit home would be a fleeting stay in unaccustomed comfort before the job kept her in the more familiar office.

Removing her wet coat as her phone vibrated, then beeped to signal an email notification. Patting away wet beads of rain, which glossed her honey toned face with the jacket sleeve as she reached inside the pocket for her phone. Collins had set up an alert to notify her when Steven Douglas' name was logged into the database. It was this warning which chattered and beeped as she headed further inside her modest flat. Entering the bathroom, she stripped out of her wet clothes and snuggled into a deep-pile peach bathrobe before turning the taps to fill the tub. She returned her attention to her messages on the phone screen.

Anything more than the basic police search would notify Collins. The people she was up against had friends everywhere. So, with Steve Douglas being a crucial component to her case. Collins wasn't certain who could be on the SFA corps payroll.

She interrupted her reading to add a large glug of chamomile and lavender liquid bath salts to the tub before proceeding. An alert showed earlier that afternoon: Sergeant Daniel Phillips, who was her subordinate, checked into Steven Douglas. She knew Phillips to be an exemplary officer who worked hard, but he lacked the requirements or motivation to progress further than sergeant.

Collins went through to her small lounge area and into the kitchen, opening the fridge. Why are you looking into Steven Douglas, she wondered with a disgruntled sigh, when inspecting the stalks of petrified celery, two shrivelled peppers and a box of eggs. Their best before date had expired two days ago. Closing the fridge. Take away it is, she determined, but called Phillips first. Collins became discouraged when he didn't acknowledge her third attempt, and sent Sergeant Phillips the message.

I know you're at your desk — answer the phone.

— ☐ —

Amber shades of sunlight glared into Collins' office, in which Sergeant Phillips sat. *At least the weather has improved,* he thought as he stared at the top of the inspector's head.

Inspector Collins read through his initial report of Joyce Edwards and Abigail Simmons' interview. She was conscious of Philips, but kept him waiting just a little longer. Without looking up, "Any luck with your missing persons' case — Sergeant?" she asked, rustling through the pages of documents.

"No leads; yet," He sighed. "I'm still to contact Miss Simmons. The friend who logged the report." He could feel his patience slip away. "Miss Simmons is in Spain." A further five minutes dragged by. Phillips said, "Boss? I want to avoid appearing rude," his brusque manner failed to hide his impertinence. "We're both busy people. Can you explain what this is about?"

Collins closed the file with a thump and raised her head. She held a stern, tight-lipped expression. One of no-nonsense authority as she stared across at him.

"Thank you for taking the time to see me." Her words were sincere. Flicking loose strands of charcoal hair away from her chestnut eyes. Hair slipped from the bun style she wore. "I realize how busy you are. I'm interested in your missing couple."

"I suspect they have, perhaps, had a squabble? And I'm confident they will turn up."

"So why all the interest?" She raised her eyebrows and made a questioning expression. "Why are you making such an effort?"

"I have been a police officer for a long time." Phillips began. "Sometimes a case — such as this, comes along ..." he hesitated.

In dogmatic fashion, Collins finished his sentence. "Sometimes. A case comes along, and, for whatever reason, it defies any logical explanation; the case grabs you by the short hairs and doesn't let go." She understood and did a thoughtful nod. "The more you investigate, the more it doesn't seem right."

"You hit the nail right on its head," Phillips agreed. "A huge part screams for me to pass the case over, let the Spanish authorities deal with it. But, my gut, call it police intuition if you prefer, is telling me there is something more to this." He paused and waited for an explanation to be offered. The pause turned into a long, uncomfortable silence. "So? How's my missing person's case tied into your investigation?"

"Like I explained over the phone last night, Sergeant." Said Collins, "Mr Douglas is willing to be a witness. It's my opinion there's an organized group trafficking in sex slavery."

"And now Douglas has gone missing?" Phillips said more a statement than a question. "That explains why you requested seeing me this morning."

"Sergeant. I appreciate all your efforts with this missing persons' case, but I fear you may stumble into my investigation." Opening her drawer, Collins got out and handed Phillips a folder. "Look over these."

— ☐ —

Phillips sipped at his second mug of coffee. It burnt his lips, but he savoured the bitterness and continued to read. A document from the Ministry of Defence showed a former military record and subsequent court-martial. The man these pages referred to was given as, "Officer 572." It gave his regiment of The Royal Marines 42 Commando unit, enlisted as a direct entry officer at eighteen, and Officer 572 had excelled. The first portion of his career was unblemished, and his ambitious progression guided Officer 572 towards the Special Air Service. However, it was while serving within the S.A.S that things went wrong.

Phillips referred to the de-classified details of S.A.S operations, within the troubled Balkan state of Bosnia, during the late nineties. The S.A.S Squadron, 'A,' assisted with intel gathering, and Officer 572 was part of the regiment sent on covert missions deep into Bosnia. Once deployed, they carried out several intelligence tasks, and became the eyes on the ground for the sector. The purpose of Squadron 'A' was to call in air-strikes upon strategic objectives and report intel on military activities. Officer 572 ordered ordinance in, to engage a suspected anti-aircraft unit. The provided coordinates were unconfirmed, but 572 gave the green light. The strike went ahead, and it decimated the neighbourhood. It became evident in the aftermath; it had wiped out a designated safe zone. A district which housed civilians. As officer 572 was the man in charge, they held him accountable.

Sergeant Phillips shuffled through the pages. Photos of demolished buildings and gruesome scenes of lifeless bodies. Strewn with blankets of powdered grey grit, torn limbs, mangled and twisted among the debris. Captured for eternity by photography. Phillips read the accompanying documents. A charge sheet against officer 572. The official classification provided a verdict of blue on blue, the military term for friendly fire. The British M.O.D upheld a separate charge of negligence and ended the career of officer 572 by dishonourable discharge. Looking up from the file, Phillips failed to hide his confusion. "I don't get it?" he frowned. "Why? — Why was he disgraced?"

"Well," she began with a cynical tone, "We," and tapped her fingers upon the military insignia of the court-martial documents. "The British Army — that is — didn't have any special forces on the ground during the Bosnian war." Her sardonic words put a sneer of distrust upon

Collins' face. "The unofficial statement," she pointed, with a pencil, toward the documents, "The record about this incident — is the S.A.S were conducting — black ops missions." She stared at Philips, "He — officer 572 — shouldn't have been there." Collins pointed to the images. "If you accept the official report, he handed out the wrong coordinates…"

"He gave out the incorrect position?" Phillips interrupted, shaking his head in disbelief. Staring at the pictures of destruction. "But how?" peering harder at the picture, as if it held the answers, "A man with this much training," looking back at Collins, "How could he make such a strategic error?"

"The government's official statement is officer 572 was declared not guilty. They put it down to diminished responsibilities after receiving the news of a tragic, family loss." Collins twisted the pencil between her teeth. "Of course, once you ask questions and poke around into military affairs; everything gets sealed up tighter than a nun's fairy."

— ☐ —

"After the armed forces, officer 572 started his own organization." Collins placed black and white surveillance photographs in front of the sergeant. "I know he has links to associate him with Russian and European crime syndicates." She pointed to several individuals in the black and white stills. None were people Phillips recognized. She held up a list of names. "This is a register of shareholders in a Spanish chemical company, called the SFA Corporation. Officer 572 is this company's majority shareholder. I'm positive this is a cover." She waited for Phillips to finish reading before continuing, "I believe that officer 572, runs a modern-day human trafficking and, prostitution ring; between here, Spain and the rest of Europe." She slammed her hand on the desk with a loud thwack. "Trouble is; this slimy bastard has an alibi — for everything." She felt the heat rise within her cheeks as her resentment became apparent. "I hadn't anything to allow a proper investigation." She handed over the findings of the Kerry Wells case, "This girl was identified to be with him before her body was discovered, but I couldn't get anyone to come forward." Collins leant back, a smug grin upon her face. "Not until Mr Steven Douglas contacted me."

Philips pushed back into his chair. It groaned beneath him, "OK, I admit I'm more than a little intrigued about how this is all connected." The eyelid over his left eye twitched, something which often occurred when he was tired and stressed. He pinched with thumb and forefinger the bridge of his nose to relieve the strain in his eyes. I should have brought my glasses, he thought. "And now it appears Steven Douglas is missing."

Standing up, a desire to stretch her legs. "Mr Douglas came to see me. He is the first and only reliable witness I have had."

Phillips read through the investigation report of Kerry Wells. His concerns for Miss Edwards and Mr Douglas were multiplying with each turn of the page. "There isn't sufficient evidence to support your theory," he said, frowning at the file. "I came here to talk about a missing person, a person whom you have contacted." He shoved the open documents across the desk. "I understand his significance ..." he picked up a few loose pages and allowed them to drop like single pieces of confetti. "... but is Mr Steven Douglas reliable? Reading through this; I can get his link to your suspect." he was becoming irritable, "But all your evidence is speculation and conjecture. You haven't any definite proof and this individual," he pointed to the man in an image standing in front of the SFA corporation logo, "His legal team will rip you apart." He drew a breath and became condemnatory as an inferno raged against his crimson cheeks. "Meanwhile, I'm wasting precious time that would be better spent trying to locate Miss Edwards and Mr Douglas."

"Mr Douglas is the sole witness who saw Kerry alive and with him." Collins jabbed her index finger at the same photograph. She was infuriated and raised her voice. This was getting heated, which annoyed her. *Time I pulled rank* she decided. Pointing toward the folder in front of Phillips. Collins' tone was biting, "Mr Douglas' statement puts Kerry in the back of a car owned and driven by that bastard." The inspector referenced the same figure Phillips had used. "This is the closest I have ever been to serve and conduct a section 18 search. It's imperative Steven Douglas is located — I need his help."

"This ..." he was censorious when he pointed to the file, "... this is maybe the reason why Mr Douglas, together with his girlfriend, have disappeared." Phillips accused, "This whole thing? — might have frightened them off."

"Yes — yes. The thought had crossed my mind." Collins gave a resigning nod before her demeanour changed and became stern once more. Time to close this down, she determined. "The Crown Prosecution has instructed me. You are not to take this missing persons' case any further."

"You're pulling my investigation." Phillips failed to disguise his derisive tone as he argued.

She held up her palm to stem his objection. "It's under Spanish jurisdiction. It should not tie up our police resources. I cannot allow you to waste any more time looking into this until approved by the C.P.S."

"Okay." He realized the dispute was lost, and he would need to be complicit. "So, for now, I must explain to Mrs Edwards and Abigail Simmons; I cannot look further into this? That the case is with the Spanish authorities?"

Collins gave a small but brief nod of her head and finished up. "That will be all, Sergeant."

Now or Never

Abigail stared for over five minutes at the photograph, a black and white CCTV image. It was without doubt a picture of Kirsty and Steve. The word 'Asasinado' headlined in bold font across the top of the tabloid. Abigail's knowledge of Spanish was poor, but she knew Asasinado, was Spanish for murder. Peering hard at the newspaper in a belief, some understanding would come back to her, but her long since forgotten school Spanish lessons didn't help to establish any sense of the written article. A phone number was at the bottom of the page. With nothing else to lose, she fished her mobile out and dialled. A female voice answered, again in Spanish, "¿Hola, como puedo ayudarte?"

Abigail chanced her luck and said, "Hello, do you speak English?"

"Yes, my name is Lucia. How may I help?" said the pleasant voice.

A waterfall of words came tumbling out of Abigail's mouth in one long sentence.

"I'm calling the number from the newspaper," she replied between nervous gasps, "It's my friends." Another snort, "I haven't seen them for weeks." Her capricious panic made her voice tremble. "They're missing. Can you help?" as an afterthought, Abigail added, "Please?"

"I am sorry," Lucia said. "Can you slow down?" She listened to Abigail's breathing ease. Lucia continued with a gentle tone, "I ran the column and printed the CCTV picture."

"What is the piece about?" Abigail's impassioned voice warbled, but she went on, "I understood Asasinado to mean murder?" Her words juddered, and she let out a small sob.

"All I can inform you, is the individuals in the picture were the last to be identified with a couple who were found, murdered." Lucia was considerate when she spoke. "I think you should call the police incident line," and, concluded by providing the police phone number. "Call this number." She instructed, "Once you have spoken to the police, I will meet you tomorrow."

— ▢ —

"Alejandro, what a pleasant surprise," stated the ebullient Brodie. "What kin ah git ye?"

Gonzalo skipped the pleasantries by being forthright. "I wished to inquire about the pair who were murdered?" he asked, and acknowledged how his question appeared to slap the bar owner's face crimson. That unsettled Brodie, he noticed.

Brodie was terse with his response. "Tis a dowie state o' affairs, that business." giving a disbelieving shake of his head. "Ah tellt th' polis a' ah ken. It wasn't much."

He was panicking. This was the second person in as many hours to be sitting at his bar asking questions. The friend of the couple he'd helped Marco abduct, and now Gonzalo. What next?

But Brodie was soon to regret this thought when Gonzalo asked, "What about Marco Branco?"

"Marco who?" stammered Brodie, but his evasive tone betrayed him.

"Marco Branco…" Gonzalo said as he recognized how the name had affected the now not so jovial Scotsman.

"Ah ne'er heard o' him," Brodie lied. "Ah sae mony comin' 'n' gaun it's hurd tae keep track." He stepped back from the granite top of the bar. "Ah wull be back in a moment, ah juist need tae check oan something."

Gonzalo saw through Brodie's lies, they were as transparent as glass, and his powers of perception honed from a career dealing with lawbreakers made him suspicious. If Brodie didn't know the man in question, then why had his persona changed from jubilant to evasive?

The bar owner went through to his office and posted a text to Mr Blue Eyes. It read; We have a problem...

— ▢ —

Chief Hernández informed Baldomero the preceding afternoon of the missing persons the detective was now looking into.

"It may amount to nothing," Hernández had said with a sceptical shrug. "The dual murders have held up all my personnel. Would you mind handling this?" And gave the detective the original report.

A young English woman had called the incident line. He had driven from the Tarragona office to meet her at the Salou police station. Baldomero had written the names taken from the murder victims' evidence log. These names were from the discovery of bank cards and driving licences which hadn't belonged to the victims. Now, these same names were at the top of the report. Mr Steven Douglas and Miss Kirsty Edwards who were declared missing by an anxious friend, Miss Abigail Simmons, who now sat waiting in the interview room.

Abigail listened to the buzz of hornets, which rumbled from the air conditioning. Regretting the high cut linen shorts she wore when the tops of her exposed legs became fused to the plastic chair she was sitting on.

The Policía Local of Salou was a modest building, which reminded Abigail of a beach hut. But inside housed sophisticated computer equipment and CCTV monitor screens. She peeled her legs away from the chair's plastic seat and stood up, to move beneath the air-con. She had stared at the blank, off-white walls and the windowed doorway wall for a little over forty minutes and the boredom became tedious.

If there was ever an example of a Spanish Matador, then it was the officer who entered. His intimidating six-foot plus height and oak beam shoulders, together with his sculpted biceps that strained against his shirt; was how Abigail imagined a bullfighter to be. He carried a stern expression, one of no nonsense, upon chiselled, handsome features. A persona of authority held deep within dark brown stiletto eyes set beneath the fringe of his bushy mono-eyebrow. His arched moustache formed a bridge over a pencil lined upper lip. This curved to a smile and although it was pleasant, it made Abigail's chest give an apprehensive stutter. He sat down at the small table and signalled for her to do the same.

His English was impeccable as he introduced himself, "I am Detective Baldomero," he said, matter-of-fact, "Of the Policía Nacional. I believe you wish to report someone missing?"

Brushing her hand up over her face, as if to remove hair from her eyes, then allowing it to wander up to check her cane row hair was intact. "Yes," she answered, but couldn't disguise her concern. "My two friends were on holiday, but they haven't come back to England. Have you apprehended them?"

"And why would they have been held?" came the detective's straightforward question as he scrutinized her reaction.

Abigail regretted her initial query, feeling as if she'd stumbled off the firm path and into marshland, she was now back tracking. "I'm sorry." She said, "That came out wrong."

She feigned an uncomfortable laugh, but Baldomero's granite cold eyes made her quick to continue. "I'm worried about my friends," She recovered. "No one has seen them — since their arrival. Almost a month ago."

Taking the initiative, his intention to keep her unbalanced, Baldomero asked, "Are your friends associated with drugs?"

"No, officer," Abigail, aghast over the suggestion, said, "Neither Kirsty nor Steve are into drugs."

Baldomero remained direct and to the point, he waited for Abigail to provide information, rather than interrogate her. He jotted notes in a small leather-bound notebook. "Can you give me their UK addresses and any contact details you have? Please."

Abigail complied, but was a little bewildered when he stood up from the table and left the room without saying another word. Peering between the slats of the blinds on the window, she could just make out him speaking with another officer. He passed over the information he'd collected before coming back. Baldomero eased himself into the chair and squeezed his hands prayer-like against his nose. He was blunt. "We haven't any leads on your friends." He observed her expectant look turn to disappointment, but he kept himself impartial. "We're keen to talk to your friends." He waited as if uncertain about what to disclose before sliding a small business card toward her. "If you hear from them? Could you please contact me?" he tapped an index finger by his number beneath his name. "I wish to establish their well-being."

"What's their connection to the murder? Why did you inquire about drugs?" Abigail asked, with an urgent plea.

He swallowed before speaking, "I have reported your friends as missing and our officers are looking into it." He hesitated before adding. "I'm not permitted to give out any more information of an ongoing case."

"But you haven't provided me with any clues?" Abigail said and failed to hide her disappointment.

His tone forthright. "You have my business card. Contact me day or night, whatever the hour." He meant to reassure her, when he smiled, but it didn't work. "We will do our best to find your friends." Holding out his hand to signal the meeting was over.

"I recognized Kirsty and Steve from the newspaper article. Are they OK?" She searched his face, looking for the slightest reaction, but he showed nothing.

"You gave the officers you spoke to on the phone yesterday all the relevant information, and they have begun a search. I needed to get an impression of your friends by speaking to you. I'm trying to figure out if they have any involvement with another case. Sorry if I appeared unconcerned, I cannot offer any further details." He became sincere. "I want to avoid building up your hopes or cause needless worry. We need to deal with facts, not emotions. Please be assured we're investigating their disappearance. I cannot provide anything further, but I will be in touch once I have something solid and factual to report."

— ☐ —

Kirsty's huddled heap lay on the bed. She wept. Not gut-wrenching sobs, but quiet shoulder jerking tears. Silent, wet pearls, which dripped off her cheeks to dampen her bare skin. She didn't weep over her predicament, or her forlorn despair. It wasn't Steve's gruesome demise, something Kirsty hadn't dwelled upon because of the forced narcotics. It was over the loss of her freedom, feeling her innocuous nature stolen and replaced with a deep-seated need of self-preservation. While the effects from her medicine subsided, she accepted the old Kirsty had died along with Steve. It resurrected her anew, more adaptive, more cunning and a willing participant. Gaining mental preparedness, knowing to gain freedom she would be required to fight; for she had nothing else to lose. In a few scant hours, the medicine's nagging itch would slither into her bowels and crawl beneath her chalky skin. *Escape must be now*, she concluded with conviction. *Now, or never*, and gathered herself for her attack as the female entered.

"Phew-wee, it stinks like you died already," Chantelle said with a nonchalant chuckle.

"Leave me alone," Kirsty said with a vitriolic growl.

The girl is dreaming, or hallucinating, Chantelle presumed, and kneeled at Kirsty's side. "Sshh. Rosa…" She reached to stroke Kirsty's hair.

Kirsty pulled back; her teeth bared in a rabid dog snarl as hatred filled her eyes.

"Hush now — you're safe." Chantelle said in a smooth tone.

A torrent of venomous profanities erupted as the screeching creature, which was Kirsty, pounced at Chantelle.

Knocking her backward beneath a melee of flailing limbs driven by a freight train rush which surprised Chantelle.

"Get away — get away — get away," Kirsty hissed with a fury never felt before. She lashed razor clawed fingernails, wracking across Chantelle's face.

"Leave me — leave — me, alone." She howled, her posture threatening like an angered cat.

Blood, a deep, full-bodied burgundy wine, flowed over Chantelle's cheek. This filled Kirsty with a newfound strength which buzzed on a power-grid of fury. She slapped out again. Rewarded by an anguished yelp. She was winning. Sensed the upper hand was hers. Kirsty pressed on with her assault.

— ☐ —

Abigail enjoyed the freshness of the breeze. The day itself was hot, but the breath of the wind carried the hints of an impending storm. The languid sea chased waves upon the coastline and clapped against the moored fishing boats. The distant horizon angered by charcoal grey, cumulus clouds that swarmed a clear blue sky, and Thor rattled upon his anvil as thunder grumbled faraway.

Abigail sat opposite the journalist. Lucia click-clacked her manicured nails upon the keys on her laptop before she glanced up and said, "You say your friends didn't come back to England?"

Abigail nodded and replied. "We don't have a clue where they've gone."

Lucia pressed a glass of mineral water to her soft peach lips, having a sip as she listened.

"Something isn't right. I just know it," continued Abigail. "Kirsty?" She had a look of bewilderment and shrugged. "Well, she would have called me by now." She paused. "The police weren't much help," she retorted. "Almost two hours of my life wasted this morning."

Abigail's face flushed dark mahogany, "I'm certain they're in trouble — but I'm the only one here who thinks it."

Lucia waited for Abigail to vent. "I'm confident the police don't suspect your friends are in any danger."

Abigail gave a questioning glance and asked, "Perhaps with your resources? I mean, at the newspaper. Could you help me?"

Lucia's sigh of reluctance provided Abigail with the answer. "Please, I wish to avoid upsetting you." She said and placed her hand on Abigail's wrist. "I will provide a missing person' advert in the paper, at no charge. I want to help you out." She gave Abigail's wrist a gentle squeeze of reassurance.

Seizing her opportunity, Abigail pleaded, "Could you post two adverts, one in English and one in Spanish?" She asked, "Just in case my friends look at the adverts. They won't understand it in Spanish?"

"I can run one advert for four weeks," Lucia said, "or two adverts for two weeks?"

"Two adverts — that's acceptable." Abigail nodded. "I'm positive I'll have found them by then"

— ☐ —

Chantelle's yelp was born more from surprise than pain. The attack was unexpected, but instinct took control. It was a more defensive block than a whack. The brittle smack resonated into the air. Chantelle grabbed Kirsty's hair and yanked back, hard. Survival instinct overriding all others gave her strength. She stared into the eyes of Kirsty and peered deep into a crazed void.

Surprise had caught Chantelle off guard, but she was ready when Kirsty didn't pull backward. From living rough upon the streets of Paris, Chantelle had learnt the skills to survive. She went with Kirsty and tumbled backward in an upturned beetle position, pulling Kirsty with her. Assisted by momentum and their combined weight, they went down to the floor. Chantelle kicked out, landing her foot between Kirsty's crotch. The blow landed true, and she used the drop's pendulum effect to catapult her assailant over her and through the air.

It was an unceremonious flight across the bedroom, which Kirsty travelled before crashing in a tangle of arms and legs. Chantelle was now the one with the upper hand, and didn't cease, aware Kirsty would soon recover her wits. Roles reversed and Chantelle became the aggressor. She scurried on hands and knees, chimp-style, and clawed on top with catlike quickness then punched her fist into the orbital socket of Kirsty's left eye. Slapping with her other palm, a lip splitting smack. Chantelle hit again, then again, and a third time before Kirsty fell limp, she held her arms over her head as she surrendered. But Chantelle added four pummelling punches. Each one drained energy, and sapped her strength until she slumped, exhausted, upon Kirsty.

They remained on top of each other for what seemed like an age, panting for breath. Chantelle spat, "If you try anything like this again, I will kill you."

Pete's Opinion

Gonzalo went for his regular morning stroll along the beach near Mariana's restaurant. He had paused outside the lifeguard station, and was now sitting in its vacant chair. Reaching for his mobile, he realized it was early, but he also appreciated his former friend, like himself, would be up at this hour. He called Baldomero.

"This is becoming like old times," answered a jocular Baldomero.

Gonzalo chuckled but remained on point, "I went to visit the club owner, Brodie." He said, "Brodie knows more than he's letting on. I could tell he was withholding something."

Baldomero knew he could count on his friend's instincts, but required something conclusive, better than an ex- prosecutors hunch. "What makes you so confident?"

"Come on, Nick, you know me." He became defiant, "I wouldn't suggest anything to you — if I didn't believe Brodie is covering for something." He understood the procedure and made a resigned groan, it was pointless to argue. "Okay, look, Nick," Gonzalo said, "I get how it works. If you'd been with me, you would agree. All I'm suggesting is… Brodie's worth another glance."

"I don't doubt you. Al," Baldomero countered. "But you know how I have to do this."

"I do," he conceded with a defeated grunt. "Try to gain a little distance. Come at this from a different angle, that's my recommendation," Gonzalo said, without disguising his irritation. "I couldn't detect any evidence to link Brodie and the murders or associate him to Marco Branco." Gonzalo kicked the sand at his feet. "Brodie became agitated when I mentioned Marco Branco. But that's all."

"But we don't have evidence of Marco having anything to do with them," Baldomero argued.

"We know that. But Brodie doesn't. It will cause him to sweat a little. Just watch him and see what kind of reaction you have." Gonzalo stood and started a slow trek back towards the restaurant. He laughed as he stared out at the horizon. "Shame we can't tap his phone." He became serious. "I'm telling you, Nick. Brodie is more involved. Worth a revisit. Put the squeeze on him. You have nothing to lose."

"Okay. I'll consider it. But as you said before, these murders are not Marco's style. They're too clean and too clinical for him. I prefer to avoid wasting more time and resources just because Brodie is acting a little suspicious." He hesitated before closing. "Thanks for going to see him, Al. I appreciate it."

— ☐ —

Abigail had returned home but could not get comfy lying-in bed. She sat up to stretch her arms high above her head and yawned. The bed creaked. She grumbled and wiped the sleep from her eyes. Two hours, they had delayed her departure, which meant she hadn't arrived home until pre-dawn, a little after 3 am. Her grit filled eyes stung when she squinted at the digital display on her phone. It was twenty-five minutes past nine. "Great," she moaned. Abigail flopped back upon the bed and sighed. "It's much too early."

Abigail's two-bed terraced house was at the end of a three-house block. There were nine blocks with three dwellings to each. Storm bellows blew in gusts through this quaint cul-de-sac and created a funnel effect. Today was one of those occasions, and a flute concerto whined. It had woken Abigail, who now pressed her pillow over her head to wipe out the complaining gale. But sleep didn't return. Something heavy pounced on her and attacked her feet. Sharp claws pierced the quilt as they gripped. Not enough to be painful, but sufficient to register their pin-like sharpness. A playful meow purred from the clawed owner.

"Morning Sammy," she greeted with tenderness, a ginger tom cat who stalked upon the duvet then nuzzled up into Abigail's chin before she got up and went for a shower.

Refreshed somewhat after showering, Abigail's afro hair dripped loose curls over her exposed shoulders. Seated in her kitchen with a towel wrapped about her midriff. Pastel lemon walls and beech effect worktops surrounded her with home comforts. The steaming cup of green tea sat before her made Abigail feel human again.

A feather touch of warm fur brushed against her naked legs, and she glanced down to find Sammy. The old ginger tom cat who had turned up one day, concluded he liked Abigail and remained ever since. Adopting her as much as she had him.

She grinned an endearing smile and said, "I expect you want me to feed you? Eh?" and stroked behind his ear.

Sammy nudged her hand aside and padded over to his empty dish. A loud meow was his response. Ignoring the cat, Abigail picked up her phone. It showed she had voicemail messages, and she pressed on the loudspeaker to listen while she fed Sammy. The first four messages were blank, instant hang-ups, with the click sound of a disconnected call. The next two were Sergeant Phillips, wishing to give her an update and enquire about her progress. He finished by stressing his eagerness to meet when she came back. The last message was Ruth, who'd called to explain about Steve's brother, Pete, had requested to see Abigail and would be at Ruth's home later?

Abigail rang Joyce to describe the result of the trip, speaking while she mounted the stairs two at once to head back up to her bedroom. Joyce failed to disguise her despondent tone in her voice when she asked.

"Do you expect your advert will do any good? Do they ever work? I don't think people give them any consideration?"

"Well, something's better than nothing," responded an acerbic Abigail, discouraged by Joyce's response. "Besides, I'm certain you feel as powerless as me. I needed to do something." A lull at the other end of the phone made her believe the line was dead. "Joyce? — You still there?"

A snuffling sound accompanied the subdued noises of a gentle sob, "Yes... I'm here," a melancholic Joyce responded. "Everything seems so... hopeless," she despaired. "Where on earth have they got to?"

"We'll find them, Joyce," Abigail, although being comforting, felt herself well-up. The warmth of a tear kissed her cheek. She was pensive and changed topic. Abigail asked about Pete.

"I've met him," Joyce said. "Such a charming man. Just like Steve." The tone of her voice was solemn, but Joyce's sobs eased. "I hope you don't mind, but I've arranged for you to meet him at Ruth's, this afternoon," she explained. "Ruth is expecting us. Is it okay with you? Do you wish to come to mine first? — for lunch?"

"That would be lovely," Abigail agreed. "I will be over at about 12.30."

"Okay, see you at 12.30," Joyce confirmed, and cut the call.

— ☐ —

"You stupid bitches," yelled a furious Celia. She glared first at Kirsty and then at Chantelle. "Don't you realize what you've done?" She glanced back at Kirsty, who was now drugged and catatonic. "Marco will kill me — hell; he'll slaughter us all." Turning her attention to Chantelle and clutching an enormous clump of hair, she yanked back her head.

Chantelle whimpered under the pain, but daren't retaliate.

A trenchant Celia continued. "The last thing I said," she spat, "The only direction I made, was to take care of her- not knock the hell out of her."

Chantelle squealed, "I... I'm sorry." She tugged at Celia's hand. "But, Rosa came at me." She implored, but Celia pulled harder on her hair. "Plea- aargh — please stop." She appealed, "I was defending myself." Celia released her grip, only to slap Chantelle hard enough to make teeth rattle. A thousand wasps stung her already inflamed, scratched face. Her legs crumpled, and Chantelle went down to her knees, more obedient than defiant, grovelling at Celia's feet.

Aggrieved, "Look at her," Celia snarled as she snatched Chantelle's head backward by her hair. Forcing her to glance at the circles of indigo-purple welts which swelled Kirsty's eyes. The right eye closed, cheeks puffed, a trout pout of swollen crimson, split lips, and weeping scabs. Beneath the lobe of Kirsty's left ear, blood had crusted into a rusted pool at her nape.

"You tell me?" Celia growled. "Explain how? How is she to earn her keep? Eh?" She belted her fist across Chantelle's skull.

The girl needs to understand, Celia told herself, regarding Chantelle. *She must realize who's in charge.* She spoke with a contemptuous tone, "You're going to have her clients." then pointed to Kirsty's hunched form, "But she gets the income."

"But — that's not fair — she was the one who attacked me." Chantelle argued, not caring about her belligerence.

"I don't care," Celia answered. "I have to assure them." She meant Marco. "I have to prove this girl is making money. I can't..." she jabbed a finger at Kirsty, "... in that state." She waited for the objection, but it didn't come. "If she doesn't show her worth — they'll kill her for certain."

"This is Peter, Steve's older brother," Ruth introduced when Abigail entered the room. The introduction was redundant because he bore a striking resemblance to Steve.

Pete's presentation was smart, in a blue-grey chequered Ralph Lauren polo jersey, black Emporio Armani jeans and a pair of Gucci leather Oxford shoes. It was clear he was doing well for himself. He held both Abigail and Joyce's hand in turn, leaning forward to place the gentlest kiss, as delicate as a butterfly's wing, upon Abigail's cheek. His expensive cologne engulfed her as it cascaded off him. It seemed the most natural of greetings, but it caused her heart to race and face to flush.

First to her, he spoke, "Hello, I'm Pete." Looking past Abigail, toward Joyce, who was standing behind her. Pete spoke with tenderness. "Hello again, Mrs Edwards. How are you bearing up?"

Joyce shrugged, "I'm beside myself with worry."

Abigail nodded, but became accusatory when she responded, "I didn't think you were interested?" For reasons Abigail couldn't fathom, she knew she wished to avoid liking him. But the harder she tried not to; the more enchanted she found herself. This confused and frustrated her, which showed in how acrimonious her voice was when she spoke.

Pete turned to her, "Yes." He made an apologetic sigh. "I'm sorry if I have given you that impression." with a conciliatory chuckle, he added, "Me and Steve have a strained relationship. We haven't ever been close."

Mark was brisk when he quipped, "Huh, that's an understatement."

"Oh shush," Ruth glared at her husband. "He's here now. Isn't he?"

Peter gave an embarrassed grin. "Please forgive me," he said. "I never intended to appear unconcerned." his eyes held on to Abigail's. "Steve had been missing for a brief spell," he shrugged. "I assumed they would turn up." Pete pointed across to Mark. "It was when Mark called me to say they hadn't when I became concerned."

— ▢ —

Abigail spent the afternoon re-counting her findings. She decided it would be best to leave out the drug connection and the Spanish police. Instead, Abigail explained her visit to the restaurant and all about Steve's proposal. Also explaining about the newspaper adverts she had placed.

"I can help pay for the adverts if you wish," Pete said as he sipped his tea, "Or we can return to Spain and renew the hunt?" he made an inquisitive look toward Abigail, "Unless you consider it's useless?" Pete's tanned complexion turned a coral pink when he realized how callous his last remark may have sounded. "I'm sorry," apologized Pete. "I didn't mean to be so negative."

"It's okay," Joyce reassured. "I thought the same about the adverts, but like Abi has pointed out. We need to be doing something."

He nodded in agreement and said. "I'm worried about my brother," he glanced around the room, "And Kirsty, of course."

Abigail smiled, "It's all right." she lay her palm upon Pete's knee. "It's fine." She felt a static crackle from their brief contact and couldn't explain why she found it sensuous. The connection tingled deeper and quivered in her tummy. *What are you doing?* She cringed inside as she berated herself. *Here you are — your friend is missing — and all you can think about is getting it on with some man you have only just met. You ought to be ashamed of yourself.* She jerked her hand away, as if burning her fingers upon an open flame. Perhaps when this is all over, she thought. *Jeez Abs, there you go again, you skank, stop being such a floozy.* The cedar tinge to her cheeks turned to red mahogany, dropping her eyes, but realized she was staring straight down towards his crotch. Abigail panicked and stood up all a fluster, she pretended to smooth out imaginary creases in her jeans before going to the small bay window. It was cooler by the window, but gave her a brief respite.

She stretched her arms above her head, then faked a yawn. She stifled it with the back of her hand. "I'm tired." This wasn't a lie. She felt drained, and yawned again. Talking between each gasping sigh, "I'm sorry… But I guess it is time… I went home… To bed."

"Oh, you poor dear. You look washed out," Ruth fussed as she gathered the teacups. "I was going to make more tea," smiling at Joyce. "But perhaps you should take yourself and Joyce home."

Joyce stood, "Yes, I should get home too." Unhooking her purse from the back of the chair, "Kirsty may have called the house phone, she knows I'm not great with my mobile."

Pete walked with Abigail toward the hallway. The same static charged within her chest. *He is the real reason you want to leave,* thought Abigail. *You need a cold shower.*

So as not to be heard; Pete whispered. He'd stepped in close, and the warmth of his breath made Abigail tremble. "I wished to avoid saying this in front of the others," he spoke

into Abigail's ear. "I preferred not to come across as pessimistic. In case it upsets them." He pointed towards the room they had just left.

Abigail gazed into his eyes. You must get out of here, Abs, she decided. But Pete held her gaze, as if knowing the effect he had upon her. "What?" Abigail looked away. "What is it you felt it would be better not to say in front of them?" She urged. Movement and voices from further inside made them conscious of the others.

"I wouldn't pin your hopes on the police," Pete answered. "It's only my opinion, but I don't think they take this sort of thing seriously." His face was grim. "I guess we may do better without their help."

Abigail was a little confused and responded, "So? What are you telling me?" Her brow creased into an immense chasm of concern. "Are you saying don't bother with the police?"

He smirked. "No — not at all. I didn't want you or them." Pointing back to the room they had left. "Getting any hopes up. You know how the police can be," he shrugged, "They always seem to get things wrong — these days."

"I must admit, I wasn't very thrilled with their attitude," she agreed. They reached the porch. "But it could help. We shouldn't just disregard them." She opened the door and stood inside the porch. Waiting for Joyce to say her goodbyes. "And like you said, Pete, it's only your opinion."

A Silly Fool

It had been days since Kirsty's failed escape. She stared at herself in the bathroom mirror and grimaced. Racoon eyes peered back at her. A scheme of smashing the mirror, to make a weapon from a jagged shard and force her way out; entered her mind. "Could you manage it?" Kirsty spoke aloud to her reflection. The answer appeared in those bloodshot, glazed orbs. *You're too weak*, she admitted. *Too dependent on the medicine. Too afraid.*

She ran the tap and splashed cool water on her face, making her hiss from the small fires that flared inside each cut. Not only that, but she felt the squirm of her cravings. "I can't carry on like this," and coughed. The cracks in her lips re-opened and provoked her to yelp. A darker thought penetrated her mind. Kirsty peered into the mirrored surface. *You could shatter it and finish this. Take your life with a slither of mirror glass. That would teach them.* She covered a towel around her fist to avoid cutting herself on broken mirror glass, but she dry laughed at the irony.

"Don't be so absurd," Kirsty chided. "If you're bothered about cutting your hand? How are you going to slash your wrists?"

She gave up and walked away and out of the bathroom. Slumping onto the bed's mattress and glancing toward the barred window. They would be here soon enough with the medicine. Not long to wait, she thought, and clawed at the crimson track marks on her right forearm. Kirsty knew she couldn't attempt an escape again. You must be smarter than this, she told herself, you're too reliant on them. "Come on. Think." She spat at the empty air. "No space for self-pity. You need another plan." She bought both arms up and gawked at the needle tracks. *You can fight this,* she responded to herself then repeated aloud, "You can break them."

— ☐ —

Baldomero had returned to Madrid and was now sitting at his desk, staring at his computer. He rubbed his eyes and felt the strain hammer against his skull. He'd been squinting into his screen for too long, wondering what could Brodie be hiding? Scratching his head, he leant back and smoothed his moustache. Next to the console was a newspaper. It showed the adverts placed by Abigail. He read over the scribbled notes he'd written when interviewing the English woman. He didn't suspect any involvement by this couple, but further thought they had been the victim of an extortion. This was the murdered couples' normal practice. The English couple, Kirsty and Steve's disappearance was unrelated to these savage crimes, or so Baldomero first supposed. But listening to Gonzalo's words echoing about his skull told him to look at the evidence from a different angle. The detective stood up, stretched his arms above his head as he yawned. *Perhaps Gonzalo's right.*

He divided each item of evidence, placing them into an order, then went over to the blank whiteboard fixed to his office wall. Using a marker pen, Baldomero drew an oval-shaped circle with a question mark at its centre. Returning to his piles of paperwork, the detective printed off large eight by eight-inch pictures of all the crime scenes.

Starting with the deceased woman discovered at the Manzanares river. Then the picture of Curly, and between these, he offset Sebastián Garcia and linked all three together with the dead English schoolgirl Kerry Wells. Heading this with a simple reference, "Linked by Toxicology." Including the case file of Joe Flanagan's drug possession into the mix. Between these, he added the picture and missing persons report of Kirsty and Steve. It was his guesswork, but placed them between Joe Flanagan's initial arrest and images of the dual murders. To this, he titled last known associates and attached the CCTV image of the pair. He also tied these to Brodie's Bar as an eventual destination, where the murder victims were last seen alive. Switching his concern to Marco Brancho. Likewise, he drew an arrow to each piece of evidence and marked it into the centre. Changing to a bright red marker pen, he then joined the arrows between each of the photographs and connected their links.

The murder in Madrid carried out by someone brutal like Marco, and an arrow pointed at him. The lab considered the death of the woman in the river as an overdose. But the individual had been dumped, by who? They were still to discover. Baldomero needed to return to the Medianoche Exótica dance club. The business, he felt certain, in some way linked to the dead woman. He recorded this at the side of her picture and made a large red question mark by the name. Standing back, he surveyed his handiwork. "Where do you fit into all this?" Baldomero asked the CCTV picture taken of Marco at the Bravo Murillo Metro station and marked another big question mark in red, next to Marco Branco's name.

Changing pens back to the original black, he formed another circle off to the left-hand side and set another copy of the crime scene pictures of Joe Flanagan and his girlfriend in its centre. He connected arrows from the murder victims' and fixed them with the CCTV picture of Kirsty and Steve. Then he pointed all at Brodie's Bar. "Why didn't I notice this before?" From Brodie's bar, he joined up the Salou CCTV picture of Marco. The images were of him entering Brodie's business, after all. From the Salou picture, he associated it back to the Metro CCTV picture. He gazed at the balloon diagram; its visual reference made things clear. Brodie's bar was significant in the Salou investigation, and Brodie needed to be brought in for questioning. Put the squeeze on him, as Gonzalo had called it. He returned to his computer and compiled an email to Chief Hernández with his suggestions. Baldomero turned back to the whiteboard and looked at the pictures of Marco. He could link the homicide case of Curly as Marco was the last known person seen with the deceased.

The drug dealer could be associated back to the Medianoche Exótica dance club and once again Marco Branco.

The words of Gonzalo still resounded in his head. *Listen to the victims,* it declared, *they all have a story to tell.* He knew he was talking to himself when he answered, but didn't care. "Looks like you're on to something. Al." Baldomero smoothed his moustache as he nodded agreement. "Brodie's bar has more to do with this. I've been focusing on the wrong stuff." Consternation filled him as he stared at the faces of Kirsty and Steve and said, "I don't assume you're involved in this murder." He tapped the pictures of Kirsty and Steve with the marker pen as he thought aloud. "So? Why have you disappeared?"

It was like a lightning bolt when the notion struck him. "Perhaps these two?" Baldomero again tapped the same picture on the board. "Perhaps they witnessed something they shouldn't have?" He looked at Kirsty and Steve, then at Marco. He pushed the pen into his mouth and gripped it with his teeth as if it were a cigar. "Perhaps you pair are the key?" Becoming curious as he stared at Kirsty and Steve's CCTV image. "This leaves one last question?" He murmured, then wrote. Who? Baldomero pondered. "Who the hell is behind this?"

— ▢ —

A metallic clunk from the closed bedroom door made Kirsty jump. She watched the door open and Chantelle enter. Kirsty rose from the bed, taking a defensive posture fit to oppose her intruder.

"Don't bother," said Chantelle as she stepped forward. "I'm not here for another argument. Celia has sent me to check up on you."

"Don't expect me to say sorry," Kirsty spat.

"Listen to you. You're an ungrateful bitch," Chantelle hissed at Kirsty. "I had to wash you when you puked and when you'd shit yourself." She saw Kirsty wither before her eyes and knew the girls' fight had dissolved with it.

"Anyway -You're wasting your time," she added, peering into Kirsty's injured face. "Even if you'd beaten me. Where did you think, you're running to?" Chantelle went back to the open bedroom door, then came back carrying a small purse, something comparable to a makeup pouch. Only the items this carried were more sinister. "You won't get away, and the sooner you accept it, the simpler life will be." Opening the bag and removing a ready-made syringe.

"Now." she said, waving the syringe about the air. "I hate these things. Needles, injecting. I detest it." Her words were scornful as she explained without looking at Kirsty, "I would prefer you to inject this yourself. It'll be so much easier."

Kirsty looked first at the syringe, then at Chantelle. "I will do it." She agreed. Holding out her hand, but halted before taking the syringe. "How do I know it's safe? That you've not done anything to it? Something that will poison me?"

"Huh," Chantelle snorted. "They would kill me dead, for sure, if I were to harm you again." She pointed to the open door as if someone lurked beyond its threshold. "Besides, I think we can help each other?"

"How so?" Kirsty asked.

"Well," Chantelle searched for the right words. "The way I see it — is like this." She placed the bag upon the bedside. "Like it or not. Fate has thrown us together. We're stuck with each other." She fixed Kirsty with a frigid stare. "I was you a few weeks ago, they took me off the Parisian streets." Her manner was ambivalent as she shared this information, "In many senses they did me a favour — I would no doubt have ended up dead."

Kirsty saw her chance to connect. "So? You know what I'm going through?" She was sympathetic but realized this could be her opportunity, a way to gain trust. A trust which she could exploit. "So? You understand why we must escape?"

"Ha." Chantelle scoffed. "Oh Honey, there isn't any escape," she replied with wretched cynicism. "Not for the likes of us," she resigned. "The only freedom we have is the stab of this needle." She held up the syringe. "So, you'd best get used to it."

"That can't be true," a defiant Kirsty said. "We have to get out and stop this happening to anyone else."

"Oh you..." Chantelle became derisive, "You're such a silly fool. The bastards who keep us here, they have men everywhere. If we run, they will find us and then kill us, or worse. When I say there isn't an escape, it's because there isn't. You're best off accepting that and allowing this sweet nectar." she jiggled the needle in front of Kirsty. "Allow this to be your freedom." Like I just said — I hate needles," holding up the syringe. She then asked, "You haven't ever serviced a client? Have you?"

Kirsty shook her head, "No, but if it's what I must do, then I will."

"Good to hear. But what if we looked out for each other? How about you help me with the injections, and I work with your clients?" She raised her eyebrows with a questioning stare. "We can watch out for each other. Make sure we don't... Well, you know?" She made a gesture with her hand, as if slicing her throat. "You know? In case one of us overdoses."

Kirsty nodded and thought for a moment. "But how do I know I can trust you?"

"Well. That's easy." Chantelle grinned without warmth. "You don't. But what have you got to lose?" She shrugged. "And it is better if someone has your back. Besides, I also have this." Chantelle held up a small vial of clear liquid. "It's Narc," She tutted at the confusion in Kirsty's face. "You never heard of Naloxone?" Chantelle shook her head. "It's like anti-dope. In case we overdose."

"How did you get that?" Kirsty reached for the antidote.

"Never mind how I got it," Chantelle said, snatching her hand aside. "I have my connections. So, are you in?"

"Yes," nodded Kirsty, "Yes. I'm in." She contemplated what this meant, then replied, "But you must wish to get away?"

Her defiance had come back, she wouldn't allow herself to roll over and play dead. She owed it to Steve to at least try to escape. Staring up at Chantelle, she added, "You can't stand there and tell me you enjoy this." Pointing around the room, but Chantelle understood she meant the club. "Look. What if we got free of the drugs? Being clear of them will help us get away." It filled her with naïve optimism. "I could help wean us off?"

"You're right. I hate it here," Chantelle confessed. "But they scare the hell out of me." She shuddered as if caught in an arctic blast. "But I like the dope. I can be free as a bird, free from everything. How am I going to get my shit if I don't work here?" Chantelle paced over to the window to peer through its opaque dust-smeared surface and down to the cobbled street below. She remained silent.

"I will do it on my own," Kirsty shrugged, "And as soon as I'm able to last without my medicine, I'm getting out of here. Forget I mentioned anything."

Huh, forget it? Ha? You're a joker? Chantelle thought. *And you won't be going anywhere. Not after I tell the Doc what your plan is, she smirked. The doc will soon put you in your place.* Looking over at Kirsty, she said, "Let me think about it. I'm scared in case we get caught. I know what'll happen to us." She smiled, but it was a fake smile. Done to relax Kirsty and it worked. "I will think it over, all right? But we need to determine the best way to do it."

At her feet on the threadbare carpet lay a hairbrush. Chantelle stooped to pick it up and brushed her hair. Looking at Kirsty, you haven't any idea. She grinned, *you're so gullible. Nothing but a silly, naïve fool.*

Wildfire

Emiliano Pérez scrutinized the report and made a negative shake of his head. "You haven't sufficient evidence," he declared, and lay the documents down on his desk. Removing his specs, the clerk glanced over to Baldomero.

The detective found Emiliano to be a pedantic annoyance. He was a desk warrior whose double chin and premature jowls showed him to be on a heart condition shortlist. It was regrettable that since Gonzalo's retirement, Baldomero had to use these official routes for obtaining search warrants. Emiliano, being the clerk of the magistrate issuing this warrant, was one of these routes.

"Come on?" Baldomero said, vexed and aggrieved by the rejection. "I have evidence to suspect a crime. That's enough. It must be?"

"The owner of this business is a significant investor in the capital and is someone I know very well; he would not threaten his reputation by being associated in the matters you're suggesting." Emiliano argued with judgemental disregard. "Your suspicion doesn't enter the matter. Your so-called evidence is pure conjecture and not factual."

"Yes, but…" he was incensed by the verdict. This would never have been the situation with Gonzalo. The element of unity and the trust between departments had evaporated upon his leaving. Just one of many adjustments I'm going to have to accept, he supposed. Firestorms raged in his cheeks. "… I'm sure we will discover the evidence at the Medianoche Exótica. All I require is a warrant to search, and I'll get you your evidence."

"My answer remains." Emiliano stated, keeping his manner direct. "There's no probable cause to grant you this warrant. Unless you can prove to the contrary or there's an immediate threat to life. I will not annoy the magistrate with this matter," He handed the file to Baldomero and sat back. Wisps of thinning black hair slid from covering a gleaming bald spot, and he pushed it into place with his fingers. "Concentrate your efforts on naming this body, so they can repatriate it with a family and allow it to be laid to rest."

— ☐ —

Abigail turned the key in the lock of her front door. She was at the end of an exhausting day and sighed when she kicked off her Chelsea boots in the hallway. Hanging up her dripping coat, she stepped towards the kitchen. A bedraggled Samson sat waiting by his food bowl. He meowed his displeasure at the rain they had both escaped. As if greeting her home, he meowed again. "Okay," she answered. "I have been out far too long." Samson purred and wrapped himself about her legs. "I can't have a minute's peace with you, eh?"

Abigail spied the wine glass upturned on the sink drainer. She allowed herself one glass of wine a week. Saturday nights were her usual habit whilst curled up on the sofa, watching what she termed slush TV. Re-runs of Made in Chelsea or the Kardashians' but lately languished in the newest series of Love Island which kept her entertained. It was her guilty pleasure and would pour a Chardonnay then relax. She would never have over one. Fear of her mother's sickness was always in the back of her mind. Abigail walked over to the fridge. *Do I break my rule?* Abigail wondered to herself as she leant against the fridge door. *Run a bath, Abs,* and decided against the drink.

— ☐ —

Abigail had soaked for almost an hour in waters which had once been hot enough to make her yelp. The now tepid tub, whose foam from the candy mountain bubble bar had long since melted, lapped her milk-chocolate skin. She found it impossible to relax. The developments over the previous few days were sandbags around her shoulders. *Perhaps you should've had that wine*, she considered.

From the bedroom, she heard her mobile ring.

A wishful Abigail hurried to answer it. *I hope it's Kirsty, the dozy cow, I bet she's waiting at the airport.*

The caller was unknown and Abigail answered, "Kirst? Is this you?" She gasped, "You're a silly cow. Where have you been?"

"Miss Simmons?" an authoritative voice spoke. "This is Sergeant Phillips."

Calming herself down, she sat on her quilted bed. Disappointment put lead to her words. "Hello, Sergeant. Sorry, I missed your calls. Have you any news?"

"I understand you have been to Spain. How was that? Have you found your friends?" Phillips asked.

"I came back late last night. Well, early morning. And no, I didn't find them." Abigail shuddered, her skin still damp and as she sat dripping water on the bed. She slid her arms into the softness of her pink bathrobe and responded, "I've been catching up with everything. How are you getting on?"

"Well. It isn't great news." he hesitated. "I have tried all the conventional channels of inquiries, with no success."

His tone was as dismal as the rain clouds, which aggravated the sky.

"What does this mean?" Abigail asked and perceived the conversation heading toward an unsatisfying outcome.

"Well, because your friends didn't come back to England, and there isn't any evidence of foul play. There isn't a lot more we can do," answered the sergeant, his tone matter-of-fact. "The C.P.S: that is the Crown Prosecution

Service has directed me to leave this to the Spanish Authorities."

"You're kidding me? Right?" Abigail shouted. "This is a joke? Right?" Anger flared. "This is outrageous. Preposterous even." She didn't indeed know what the word preposterous meant; it just sounded correct as it tumbled off her tongue.

Phillips waited until he was confident she was done. "Miss Simmons?"

"What?" she snapped.

"I preferred to inform you of this. I accept your irritations." He hesitated, considering his wording. "Believe me, I have tried to appeal against this result. The official view from the C.P.S is they don't have the resources to investigate something which may or may not have taken place on the continent, and I can no longer support it in any official capacity."

"Well, this is just fantastic. Thanks for nothing." Abigail was about to hang up.

"Wait — please... Miss Simmons." Phillips said, thinking he was already too late. "I cannot do anything on record. But I wished to reassure you, I am proceeding to investigate this case. I wish to help, so, please? Can we maintain our communication?" He exhaled a heavy sigh. "I will do as much as I am capable. I am sorry for this. I realize it wasn't the news you were after."

"Fine," Abigail replied. "Do whatever you can." Her tone mellowed. "Just help us find them. Please. It's all we ask."

— ☐ —

Abigail had no idea what had provoked her to ring Peter Douglas, and couldn't recall making the call. She was so annoyed by the Sergeant. So astounded; that she burst into tears and paced around her house then rang Peter. She couldn't indeed remember the exact conversation, when she had blurted through a shudder of sobs, "You were correct about the police."

Abigail hadn't bothered to dress before Peter arrived and now, as she stomped about her living room in only her pink bathrobe with him watching her, she was becoming mindful of how she looked. Her afro hair scraped back and secured in a bun. Without makeup to cover her tear-dampened cheeks. She must look in a frightful state. Shrugging off her embarrassments as she vented.

Pete watched as Abigail paced large circles about the lounge. "Try to calm down," he suggested. But, regretted it. Pete was a matador, brandishing his vivid red muleta and Abigail was the rampaging bull.

"Calm down?" Abigail glared at him. "Calm... down?" she spat the words. "You didn't just say that?" Tears of anger smouldered in her eyes. "How the hell do you expect me to calm down?"

Pete moved towards her, close enough to inhale the clean scent of the candy bar fragrance from her recent bath. He placed his grip on her shoulder.

She shrugged his hand away. *It isn't his fault, Abs,* she spoke to herself. To Pete, she responded, "Where are they?" she looked into his eyes. "Why hasn't she..." Abigail remembered Steve, "Why haven't they..."

Pete pulled her towards him; giving her little chance to react, he kissed her. The kiss was intense, molten, and passionate all at once.

— ☐ —

Surprise was Abigail's initial reaction. Confusion over her aroused sexual yearning, which swelled, was her second. And anger her third. She tore away, breathless and panting. Slapped him hard across his left cheek, but he stayed firm, his body taut against hers. She could feel the power of his biceps beneath his sweatshirt. Hear the hammering of her heart thunder inside. The passion ignited a wildfire of wanton lust. Primal urges rippled through her torso. The moistening warmth between her thighs ached to be gratified. She needed him more than anything. Her fingers dug into the thick locks of Pete's hair as she returned his kiss.

The power of their hunger was an unbroken colt, a powerful thoroughbred of unbridled desire. They broke, and she gasped when he tore free the robe to drink in her body. He marvelled at how the swell of her breasts rose and fell with each panted breath. Could see her pulse throb within her slender neck and observed how the cool air puckered each nipple, which stood erect, demanding attention. He sank his head and kissed her collar. Traced his tongue to further ignite her senses in a trail toward his target and nibbled sensitive flesh. She gasped, not wishing for him to stop as his mouth continued its campaign.

She tugged him toward her as she walked backward. Stopped by the coolness of the lounge wall when it pushed against her naked back. The enthusiasm and wetness of his kisses, as they glided over her skin, sent shivers tingling along her spine. Heat pulsed in her groin as Pete suckled and flicked his tongue over her sensitive buds. She ruffled her fingers through his hair.

Abigail tugged his sweatshirt. Pulling it up and over his head, then flung it aside. She clutched the openings of his shirt and tore it open. Buttons popping and flying in all directions. It was her turn to admire Pete's firm chest. She ran her fingers through the delicate hair which crowned his ribcage, drawing her manicured nails further down. Enjoying how the contours of his abdomen flinched beneath their gentle sharpness. She flattened her fingers upon the ridges of his toned muscles and thrust beneath his belt. A sigh escaped his lips as she grasped his hardness. Abigail's lust laden words gasped, "I need you inside me."

Pete felt Abigail's hand encircle his shaft. A thrill of anticipation made him return her gasp. He unbuckled his trousers and let them drop. His underwear lasted mere seconds. He lifted Abigail up, and she surrounded his buttocks with her legs. Pulling him towards her. Guiding the tip of his engorged manhood to her eager moistness. Feeling her excitement envelop him as he entered. Abigail's feet dug in as she pulled him deeper, making her gasp as she welcomed his length. Pete gave her a little time as she adjusted before her slick walls engulfed him whole. His tempo increased, driven on by Abigail's shouts.

Abigail writhed upon his rigid shaft as he filled her. She ground her hips and gyrated on his iron rod. Crying out her need as he thrust deep and moaned when he withdrew, only to renew her cries as he slammed into her once again. She didn't care about noise and flung her head back when she neared her climax. Abigail dug her nails into Pete's shoulders, vigorous enough to draw blood. She listened to Pete's grunts match her groans. Pulled him into her with her heels, and she rode this beast for all he was worth. Abigail was close. She could enjoy the pleasure building up within her, and sensed Pete was, too. Her passion increased. "Don't stop," she gasped as her climax rippled through her.

Pete felt the warmth of her grasp him. The wetness of her orgasm pulsed with each of his energetic thrusts, bringing him nearer to the edge. He felt the potent surge of his climax rise, then erupt with wave after wave of satisfaction. He grunted loud as it poured from him to leave him empty. His whole body tingled, and he went rigid while the ultimate throes of orgasm dissipated. Pete opened his eyes and stared into Abigail's dreamy expression. Pupils dilated and glazed. A wistful smile of gratification upon her lips. "Bedroom?" Pete gasped. Sweat beaded his brow and dampened his hair. He was breathless but not satiated. Abigail was just as breathless. She couldn't find any words, so pointed to the open lounge door and towards the stairs.

Dearest Abs

Abigail listened to the gentle whistle of Pete snoring next to her. She could feel the warmth from his body against hers and shuffled to cause a gap between them. The touching of skin exacerbated her feelings of selfishness and sense of betrayal toward her missing friends. *What the hell are you doing, Abs?* She asked herself. Guilt ate away like a parasite. *Why have you allowed this to happen?* She twisted to face away from him and scrunched into a foetal position. The duvet stayed with Pete and slithered off her shoulders. Her nakedness exposed to the blackness, and the bite of the room puckered her with goose flesh. Her phone display showed it was early morning, 4:30 am. They'd slipped into a sated slumber after sex. But for her, sleep hadn't lasted long before guilt came hammering on her door of regret.

Not that Pete was an inadequate lover. Far from it. Sex had been remarkable. It lacked any type of feeling other than their own carnal desires, and now a hollowness bored out of her stomach. The sexual gratification had been replaced, and she just felt dirty. *You're nothing but trash. Abs,* she decided. A solitary tear pooled at the corner of her eye, to puddle along the bridge of her nose. She sniffled as a tear dripped onto the pillow. *You couldn't control yourself,* she contended. *It just happened.* But she wasn't convinced. Her guilt so intense, it manifested itself into a loathsome creature which shrieked around her mind.

Abigail trembled beneath the chill. *You're a tramp, Abs, it is what you are.* She shook her head. *That's not true,* she argued with her guilt, *I didn't mean for this to happen. It just happened.*

Wake him up. Guilt chided, *tell him to leave.*

Okay, I will. Abigail decided, but lay statue still, silent but praying for the courage to wake him.

Go on then, Guilt taunted, *what are you waiting for?*

Slipping her legs over the edge of the bed, she sat and dangled her feet then pushed her toes into the thick piled carpet. Morning was breaking into the day, and Abigail sighed.

Making her jump, "Do you want me to leave?" Said Pete.

She could feel the heat of embarrassment flush her cheeks. Well, this is awkward. She cringed. "Err — no…" she lied. "No. Please, go back to sleep. "

Guilt's laughter echoed around her head. Its gleeful voice responded as it faded, *You're so pathetic.*

— ☐ —

They were watching each other across Abigail's kitchen table. She had dressed in a grey hoodie and matching sweatpants.

What do I say to him? Abigail worried. How do I tell him it was a mistake? Without hurting his feelings? Think Abs think.

They both spoke at the same moment.

"We shouldn't…" Abigail exclaimed.

"Why do I?" he interrupted.

They paused. Pete grinned and said. "Sorry. Go on. Ladies first."

"We shouldn't have…" Abigail replied with an embarrassed whisper, then bowed her head, too ashamed to look at him.

"Why do I feel as if I have done something wrong?" He exhaled and added, "I didn't come over last night for sex."

Abigail glanced up at him. Her cheeks wet from weeping, eyes puffy and bloodshot. She hadn't wanted him to say the word sex. As if by doing so, cemented her frivolous attitude over Kirsty and Steve's disappearance. Pull yourself together, Abs, she reprimanded. Stop being such a drama queen.

"I… We didn't." He stared at her. "We've done nothing wrong."

"Yes. But…" she started, became silent, at a loss for words.

"But what? We're both adults. I'm a few years older than you, and yes, perhaps I should have known better? But it isn't as if I took advantage of you." His tone rose, his face red and angry. "You desired me — just as much as I needed you."

He shunted the chair backward, then stood up and walked over to the sink to peer out of the window and into the wilderness of the overgrown rear garden. Incensed, he said, "If you wish me to leave? Just say?"

"No, please," she blurted. "I prefer not to be on my own. I'm just being ridiculous." She stared at him, "I'm sorry." She apologized, "I didn't mean to hurt your feelings." Standing up, she went to him. Placed both hands upon his shoulders. "Listen." Smiling as she peered into his piercing sapphire eyes, and was almost lost within them. "Last night was spectacular." She laughed and wiped tears from her face. "The best I have ever had. Honest."

She turned away. Desperate to maintain control. "I'm not just saying it, to make you feel better."

The tension slipped from Pete as he said, "So? You don't want me to go?"

"Of course, I don't. But." She moved back towards the table and dropped her gaze. The short distance helped strengthen her resolve. "Last night was a one-off. It mustn't happen again." She glanced up and smirked. "Well, at least not until after we have found Kirsty and Steve. Is that okay?"

"Yes, okay." he nodded. "What now?"

"Well. As we're up. I'm running a shower before I start today's search for Kirsty and Steve." She noticed the playful glimmer in Pete's eyes and tutted, "Jeez, have you not listened to anything I have said?" Shaking her head, Abigail chuckled, "I'm going… On my own."

— ☐ —

Showered. Abigail had dressed in knee ripped jeans and a bird print blouse. She was about to apply makeup when she noted the quietness of the house. Only flute whispers from the morning breeze broke the silence. *That's odd.* Abigail shrugged as she strode onto the landing. Calling out, "All okay, down there?" Pete didn't respond. The skin on her neck prickled, sending shivers down her spine. "Pete?" Abigail cried, again, "Pete? Are you still here?" Only the whistling wind came back.

Weird, Abigail thought as the hair on her sleeveless arms stood to attention. *You're freaking yourself out, you idiot.* She went down the stairs. "Stop fooling about. Pete?" Going down into the silence of the downstairs. "Get a grip, Abs." She scolded. "What's got into you?"

A swift rush of ginger fur thudded onto the floor, and Abigail let out a high-pitched squeal as Sammy scooted past her. Leaning against the stair bannisters, she shrieked, "You're a stupid cow." She criticized, "What are you getting so freaked out about."

Pete had left, but on the kitchen table lay a scrawled note.

"Well, that's a 'Dear John,' message if there ever was," she declared with a grunt.

Pete's note read:

(Dearest Abs,

Thank-you for an excellent night, but I have had to go. A few problems have emerged at work that I need to address. I am sorry to leave; I realize how this must look. Call or text me later.

Pete.

"Huh," Abigail grunted. "Coward — couldn't even tell me to my face." She couldn't help but feel used. "Seems to me like he took what he wanted and ran for the hills."

— □ —

Corruption and dishonesty had been a profitable road, well-trodden by Emiliano Pérez. His career had granted him a lifestyle of luxury adorned with exquisite food, extravagant clothes and bought women. He relished its benefits and the office it had secured him so far.

"This won't be forgotten, Emiliano," announced a grateful Mr Blue Eyes. "I have a couple of girls on their way to help convey our thanks." He laughed, "I know you admire a brunette, so this pair should be appropriate."

"There's no need," grinned an appreciative Emiliano, "Whatever would my wife say?"

"Well, I'm certain she's going to appreciate the diamond encrusted, 24 carat, gold necklace and the matching earrings; which are on their way to her," a laudatory Blue Eyes said. "Of course, I have delivered them in your name."

"You're too much. I'm positive she will be overjoyed," proclaimed Emiliano. "I will, of course, take excellent care of the girls when they arrive."

"Tell me more about this, detective?" Blue Eyes asked, becoming serious. "Just what is he after with my business?"

"He expects he will uncover evidence to incriminate you in a transgression. Believes he can draw a link to Stefania," explained Emiliano. "I have read over his case notes. He's talented and his evidence is on track, but doesn't yet realize what he's got."

"Is this something I need to be troubled about?" queried Blue Eyes. "I have Brodie, who is panicking and demands to be dealt with. Can this officer, be bought, or do I send Marco to see this detective and Brodie?"

"I have handled him," the egotistical Emiliano answered. "I have him bound up in so many legalities he won't be able to get anywhere near the place."

"I won't overlook this, and will give my compliments to my Russian counterparts," Blue Eyes praised. "Keep me updated."

"Leave it with me." Finished Emiliano.

— ☐ —

It had been a discouraging sort of day for Abigail, waiting to discover if Pete would ring. He didn't, and she now toyed with the idea to text him. Would texting him make me seem too keen? She wondered and decided against the idea. Taking her mind off him, Abigail attempted to call Detective Baldomero. He, too, wasn't returning her calls, and she gave up and phoned the newspaper to inquire about the adverts but, so far, they had gathered little interest.

She drummed her nails against the glass coffee table and rang Joyce. *Perhaps Kirsty is home?* Abigail hoped, as the ringtone buzzed in her ear. "Hi, Joyce. Any news?"

"Hello, Abigail." Joyce answered with a dispirited sigh. "I was going to ask the same question."

The previous night's activities twisted her gut into knots, but she shoved the guilt away and said. "I spoke to the police officer, Phillips, last night."

"Yes. I know. I have this minute, got off the phone with the Sergeant." admitted Joyce, anger edged her words.

"I would have called you, last night," Abigail explained. "I didn't wish to disturb you and waited till now." She felt awful for lying, but the truth made her feel even worse. "It's why I am calling you, now."

"I cannot accept why they can't or won't at least look into it," sobbed Joyce.

"I have been ringing around, to see if anything has turned up," Answered Abigail, then inquired, "Has Pete called you today?"

"No. No, Pete hasn't. Why?" replied Joyce. "Was he expected to?"

"No. I just assumed — I just thought he might have called, that was all." Abigail blurted.

"Do you have any other news?" Joyce asked.

"I'm afraid not. But I am awaiting a call from Detective Baldomero."

"Oh. Okay. And you?" Joyce quizzed. "Has Pete been in touch with you?"

Abigail's face blazed a fresh autumn glow. She wrapped up the call and answered, "No." She lied, "Not since last night."

The Shuffling Old Doctor

Doctor Drulovic gripped a fistful of Chantelle's dark hair and wrenched her head backwards. His vitriolic words were a steam vent hiss, "What did you say, slut?" As if Chantelle were nothing but rags, he forced her across the bed.

Her bagpipe breaths became ragged gasps. *What's got into him, he's in a ham-handed mood today,* she thought, *nastier than normal.* He came at her again. His slow shuffle was comical, but Chantelle knew better than to laugh.

"I said, Rosa's planning another escape." She squealed before Drulovic's brittle fingers encircled her throat. Her bagpipe whoop turned to a piccolo whistle as he squeezed. Christ, she feared, peering through a muslin cloth of greyness, and her vision ebbed toward the blackness. He's going to kill me, Chantelle thought, and her frenzied fingers clawed at his grasp. He had her pinned down and continued to crush. Her eyes fluttered then closed, her face changed to a blue-grey colour, and she teetered the precipice of consciousness. He released his grip, and she let out a seal yap that snatched at the air to fill Chantelle's depleted lungs. She slumped into a foetal position, whooping in more gulps like a drowning fish.

Drulovic sidled away. *It had been too tempting to kill her, he thought.* "Explain to me what she's been doing?" He asked, "Celia was sure the girl is using." He reached for his old medical bag, "she said. The two of you." He pointed at Chantelle. "You are helping each other?"

She screamed inside her head over the pain of her crushed throat. Her rising chest juddered with spasms, and she could not answer him.

"So, have you?" Drulovic moved towards her. He longed for the strength to tug back on her hair. But his ageing limbs, having spent what little stamina he possessed, now betrayed him. In his mind's eye, he punched her, smashed in Chantelle's cheekbones, and pulped the cartilage of her nose. In truth, he could only support his frail, old body against the small dresser. His voice lashed with viciousness. "What do you mean, she is trying to cut down her drugs? Have you been assisting her?"

"I wouldn't..." she was fearful of him now and cowered on the bed. "I daren't... I knew what you would do to me. To us." Chantelle spluttered, "Honest, why would I have told you — if I was encouraging her?" She wrapped her emaciated arms around her head and whimpered. "What do I have to gain?"

Drulovic returned to his bag and reached inside. She is right, he admitted. "You wish to help me? Then you bring her to this room, I can sort all this mess out." Having cooked up a syringe earlier, ready for Chantelle. It was stronger than Chantelle's usual dose, and should be enough to give her a nice little buzz.

Having removed the syringe from the bag, he placed it on the small bedside cabinet. Then took out the Taser gun, which he carried whenever he requested to inflict extra suffering. Its violet sparks snapped at the air and flashed within his eyes when he pulled the trigger. Faint wisps of smoke, accompanied by burnt ozone, drifted up from off the device. Drulovic's chuckle matched that of the rattle snake chatter caused by the Taser.

— ☐ —

It was in Kirsty's personality to want to help someone in need. So, when Chantelle bulldozed into the room with black lines of tree root tears and a cravat of violet finger-marks. Kirsty's impulse was to catch the woman as she collapsed into her arms.

"Christ," Kirsty said as she checked the bruising around Chantelle's throat, "What the? Who the?" Kirsty stammered.

"Please.", her unfortunate guest sobbed. "He wouldn't pay me. I told him he hadn't a choice." Chantelle's chest juddered. "He beat me. Then took what he'd come for. I believed he was going to kill me."

"Who?" a horrified Kirsty asked. "Where is he now?" She pushed Chantelle away, wanting to check on her, but the girls' legs buckled, and Kirsty needed to support her. "Have you told, Jonas?"

"You… You're the first person I have found since it happened." Chantelle's sob turned into a whimper. She rubbed a hand over her snot smeared face. "Please? Just come with me. I need a hit, please," she pleaded. "He may still be in my room. I can't go alone," Chantelle lied. "I need something to settle me down." she shook her head. "There's no way I can do it myself."

"Shouldn't we bring help first?" Kirsty asked, "He may be in your room."

"He's gone." Chantelle contradicted herself. Then begged, "Come on. Please? I need my fix."

"But?" Kirsty appeared puzzled. "I thought you said he may still be there? In your room?"

Chantelle hissed with venom, "Look." Her face crimson. "I have to get my fix, and if you will not help, I'll do it on my own." She became acrimonious and lumbered off. *Come on, you stupid cow. Take the bait,* Chantelle grinned to herself. *Not a poor performance,* she determined as they headed back towards her bedroom.

— ☐ —

Drulovic prepared himself. Taser held in one hand and a syringe in the other. He moved into the bathroom to hide and didn't have to wait long when voices echoed along the corridor. Drulovic smirked to himself.

Kirsty had struggled to argue. She appealed for them to at least inform Celia. But Chantelle ignored her.

"Anyway. If we tell that old whore," Chantelle counter-argued, she will make me pay the loss, even if it wasn't my fault. They entered the bedroom, and she guessed Drulovic was lurking in the bathroom. Walking over to the opposite side of the bed, Chantelle lured Kirsty further into their trap.

Kirsty gave little regard to the half-open door as she listened to Chantelle's excuses. Placed on top of the small bedside table was a familiar looking medical bag. It was the tattered leather bag the frightening doctor always carried with him.

That's strange, she puzzled, *what's his bag doing here?* She glanced at Chantelle. But her back was facing towards Kirsty. A creak from the floorboard and the shuffle of footsteps alerted Kirsty to the hidden danger. She realized they weren't alone and span on the spot to face Drulovic whose wheezing voice hissed serpent's words when he expressed.

"Well played, Chantelle." He applauded. His derisive tone showed contempt. For Kirsty's benefit, just so she understood the deception, the doctor proceeded. "I knew you wouldn't let me down." Drulovic's stare was as sharp as the needle on the syringe, which glinted in the meagre light as he brandished it about in his grip. "So?" He barked. "You believe you can wean yourself off the drugs?" His lizard tongue glided over his pencil thin lips. "You think you can spoil all my work. Ha." He pulsed the Taser in his other hand. "You think you're going to escape?" He made a disapproving shake of his head. "You, ridiculous girl," Drulovic said with a patronizing snarl and moved closer. "If I had my way, I'd kill you and be finished with it."

Kirsty's brain needed only a few seconds to catch up. The conniving little tramp, Kirsty thought; the pieces of her puzzled confusion clicked into place. Unable to determine who she was angrier with. She wasn't certain she was more annoyed at Chantelle's treachery or her own foolishness. "You, stupid slut." Kirsty screamed at Chantelle, but she realized it wasn't all her fault. At her periphery, Drulovic moved toward her. *Well, if it is watching out for yourself, I need to do?* Kirsty determined. *Then, that's what I'll do.* And like the spooked gazelle under the leopard's prowling stare, she bolted.

— ☐ —

Celia had been lurching from each room, checking on each of the girls. When she neared Chantelle's bedroom, to hear the rumble of Drulovic and the shriek from her, Rosa. Celia wondered: *What the hell is he doing with her now?* She stood in the open doorway and was confronted with Kirsty, having dodged Drulovic's shuffling advance. Watching as Kirsty side-stepped to the left and hopped up onto the bed. Celia's English Rosa rounded a rough semi-circle to avoid Drulovic's thrust and jumped past him, heading straight toward the door blocked by Celia.

Drulovic hadn't seen Celia. He was concentrating on his quarry, who could outmanoeuvre him. "You won't escape," he seethed as Kirsty rushed toward the doorway. "Stop her," he hollered when he spotted Celia.

Kirsty dodged him a second time, but felt the hairs rise on the back of her neck as the cackle of the Taser played castanets near to her skin. She stared toward where she was running and realized someone blocked her path. Kirsty ran straight into the wide arms of Celia.

"What…?" Celia looked first at Kirsty, then at Chantelle, and ended at Drulovic. "What is going on?"

"Plee…" Kirsty began to, but the bolt from the Taser slammed into her collar bone made her dance a sporadic seizure.

Drulovic pushed the Taser into the nape of Kirsty's neck. Pressing the trigger and sent 50,000 volts exploding throughout her body.

Kirsty gave up all motor skills, as her arms shook, and her back arched whilst her teeth rattled so hard inside her skull she suspected they would shatter. An involuntary gargle, "Uuuurgh," resounded from out of her tight pursed lips, and she relinquished control of her bladder just before her knees crumpled.

Drulovic waited for Kirsty's limbs to stop flapping like fragments of torn cotton caught in a storm gale. She remained still, and he reached for her limp forearm, grasped her hard to force veins to appear and in a single move his expert hands guided the needle into the first blueish venous line which emerged. Injecting the entire syringe of heroin into Kirsty.

Panting from his exertions, Drulovic staggered back before regaining his footing. Then, kicking Kirsty's incapacitated form, he roared, "Sort this mess out," and shuffled past Celia.

Kirsty felt herself absorbed into the carpeted floor as she slipped through the realms of consciousness and rushed toward the welcoming, frigid clutches of death.

PART 3

Overdose

Kirsty rushed toward a tide of blackness. Alone and adrift, a lone vessel buoyant upon a vast slick inkiness. The subconscious realm poured across her and sucked Kirsty down into its dank, frigid abyss.

"We're losing her," the timorous Celia shouted

Kirsty's chest swelled a fraction.

Celia's grim words instructed Chantelle, "Run to my office — call for help."

Kirsty's face was chalk-grey, her lips a hypoxic blue.

Sobriety washed over Celia like the tide beneath the full moon. She jabbed her fore and index fingers against Kirsty's throat to check for a pulse. It was there one minute and gone the next. A taunting irregular beat against her fingers, playing a vicious game of peekaboo. Celia glanced over at a frightened, wide-eyed Chantelle. "Get some help — you, stupid whore."

"But?" Chantelle became exculpatory as she stammered, "H… He said he would stop her from escaping." She was in a state of denial. This kept her glued to the spot. "This wasn't…" She pointed at Kirsty. "She isn't supposed to die." As if her words triggered something inside her, she rushed to the bedside cabinet. Inside its top drawer was her little zip-pouch. The one with her needles, tourniquet, and naloxone.

"She won't die if we can get her to the hospital," snapped Celia. She watched Chantelle collect the purse-like makeup bag and place it open by Kirsty's head. Glancing down at the empty syringes.

A disbelieving Celia shouted, "You, selfish cow." Frustrated and about to slap Chantelle, "We're close to losing this girl, and all you can think of is getting your next hit."

Bemused, Chantelle gasped, "No. It isn't like that." Her face glowed, a furnace fire blaze. "In the purse." She pointed to the makeup bag. "I have Naloxone." She shook the contents onto the bed and picked up the small vial. "I don't know how much to use."

"Give it to me." Celia didn't delay as she released Kirsty to snatch the antidote from Chantelle. "I saw Drulovic use this once, he injected 1ml." She glimpsed at Kirsty. Her chest hadn't risen for some time. "Make a syringe ready." Thrusting the medicine back to Chantelle. "We'll do her 2ml, the stronger dosage will work quicker." Celia hovered her palm a centimetre beneath Kirsty's nose. The moist warmth of breath wasn't there. Shit, she thought in panic, she's stopped breathing. Celia opened the mouth and tipped back her head to initiate rescue breaths. "Hurry, or we're going to lose her."

— ☐ —

"Settle down," a caustic Mr Blue Eyes said. Brodie's panicked call had angered him. Abigail's arrival at Brodie's bar and the inquiries by a retired examining magistrate, plus the local police, had made the Scotsman rattled. Mr Blue Eyes needed this contained. Meaning Brodie and whoever else was asking questions had to be silenced.

Brodie's brusque voice pierced his conclusions with a pneumatic hammering of profanities. "It's simple for you," retorted Brodie. "Sittin' in yer crakin', comfy affice. Ower thare, in englain." His volatile tone made him rasp, "You're nae th' yin wha haes git th' polis 'n' ithers, snooping aroond yer boozer."

Blue Eyes felt the volcano of his anger simmer through his blood. Its power was destructive, and he could feel control slipping. A once easily contained situation was about to erupt. *Damn you, Marco,* Blue Eyes thought as he squeezed his fingers to the bridge of his nose and tugged at his loose shirt collar. He breathed with slow, deliberate breaths and forced himself to hold together the fragmented pieces of his normal calm facade. Walking around the small coffee table which was centred in the quaint sitting room toward a curtain-shrouded bay window, he peered through the thin net of the semi-transparent draperies, *Brodie is turning into a liability.* He decided. *Marco was mistaken to have relied on him.*

"I'm nae stupid," Brodie shouted. "Ye expect me tae hawp Joe 'n' Hanna wur robbed?" He hesitated. "Ye think ah don't kno whit that lunatic, Marco, mist hae dane tae thaim?" His thunderous breathing gasped an organist's bellows of heated air, "Ah cuid hae tellt th' polis everything — juist ye mind that — bit ah kept me trap shut, didn't ah?" Brodie yelled. "'n' noo thare is this advert in th' paper," he snarled. "Sae, whit ur we aff tae dae, eh?" The sound of a drink being gulped interrupted his rant. "Ye said everything wid be fine," he snorted. "Weel everything isn't bloody fine. Is it?"

"Will you shut up and let me think." an irritated Mr Blue Eyes said, his words stern as he spoke. "I already know about the advert."

Drulovic had called him earlier in the day after discovering the newspaper advert. It was in a tabloid laid open for all to see on Celia's desk. She must have noticed the advert, too. Drulovic explained about Kirsty's recent troubles. Perhaps it had been a mistake to have kept her alive, Blue Eyes thought. Perhaps I should have executed her with that treacherous boyfriend of hers.

Blue Eyes was forthright when he declared, "Marco will deal with it."

"Sae, whit?" Brodie's harsh tone was slurred. "He is juist yin mair giant lump o' psycho."

Brodie is drunk, concluded Blue Eyes, *and his panicking is an irritation.*

"And I'll tell ya another thing," Brodie went on. "Ah can't afford tae hae polis snooping aroond mah boozer. It's ill fur business."

Mr Blue Eyes took a ceramic figure from off the window-sill. A Nao design of two white swans. Their elegant necks intertwined into the shape of a love heart. The Scotsman's tirade had become tedious. Blue Eyes imagined he held his grip around Brodie's throat and squeezed his hand with a vice-like crush. The intricacies of the swan figurine shattered into a trillion shards. A noise of gentle wind chimes jangled as fragments of the ornament fell to the floor. Sharp needles of china stabbed pain into his fingers. Speckles of blood wept from his skin. Mr Blue Eyes plucked out a clump of tissue from a pack on the coffee table and scrunched it to blot the blood. *Brodie is too much of a headache to discount*, he concluded. "I'll get it sorted, don't worry," he instructed, and cut the call.

Mr Blue Eyes looked out of the bay window. Somewhere further inside the house came the noises of a television. A televised cricket match and the commentator giving his match analysis. Blue Eyes listened as the lone man shouted abuse at the TV. Other sounds caught his awareness. A softer and further distant clink, like pebbles rattling upon glass, the chink of washing up crockery.

One of the inhabitants in the house was washing the dishes while the other watched the television. A soft feminine hum as the woman of the household sang gave Blue Eyes confidence. He could call Marco with no disruptions. Mr Blue eyes hit the speed dial.

Marco's acerbic tones answered on the second ring. "Yes."

Staring out of the Bay window, "We've got complications," Blue Eyes said. "Brodie's panicking." As if to give credence to his comments, the breeze outside whipped Rose petals from their blossoms spinning them in small tornadic gusts of floral confetti.

"I'm at the warehouse in Tarragona, cleaning up," said Marco. "What do you want done?"

Blue eyes lifted the net curtain from the window and peeped out, "I think you need to take care of him." The street beyond the glass appeared quiet. Only the piano fingers of a willow played a concerto against the roof of his car parked out front. "Has Drulovic called you?"

"No," Marco barked, "What's the problem?"

"I have underestimated the girl's family and her friends," Blue Eyes confessed. "There is an advert in the newspaper. It's searching for the girl and Steve."

"What does it matter?" Marco growled, "Has Drulovic seen the advert?"

Every so often, Marco's failure to appreciate or comprehend a situation was annoying. *It wasn't his fault*, Blue Eyes supposed. The lack of emotion made Marco the perfect killer.

"Of course, it matters–and yes, Drulovic has looked at it," Blue Eyes sighed. "Celia has mentioned nothing. It is a little disturbing." This thought infuriated him. "Brodie has also seen it." Remembering how frightened the Scotsman sounded, "He's a liability, a loose end."

The noises from the kitchen in the house had ceased, and Blue Eyes could hear a conversation in the adjoining room.

"You know how I hate loose ends. Marco." *This is his fault anyway,* Blue Eyes thought, "I told you it wasn't a brilliant plan to involve Brodie."

"What do you require me to do?" Marco asked, but already realized the answer.

"Go to his bar and shut him up." Blue Eyes instructed.

"Do you need me to kill him?" Excitement edged Marco's tone. Thrilled at the prospect of a fresh kill, "What about the capital he owes?"

Blue Eyes sighed. Marco always needed simple instructions. He couldn't read between the lines to interpret hidden messages. It was another result of his psychological instability. Sometimes, Marco, you can be tiresome, thought Blue Eyes as he squeezed his thumb and forefinger of his injured hand onto his closed eyelids.

"I realize, Brodie owes us money, yes it will be a shame to give up the revenue." Blue Eyes sucked at the air. It hissed when he breathed. "We have limited choices. Make certain you silence him. Yes, Marco, that means kill him."

A sound of someone shuffling in the hallway, the scuff of feet stepping over carpet, attracted his attention.

"Like I pointed out, Drulovic found the advert on Celia's desk."

"If that old slut, has shown the newspaper to the girl — we will need to do something about it," Marco suggested.

"I agree," Blue Eyes said, nodding his head. "I have a few loose ends of my own to deal with."

Movement came at the periphery of his vision; he was no longer alone.

"It's your call, but I think it's time you got your wish."

The faintest creak of loose floorboards squeaked when trodden. The uncanny feeling of being watched.

"If it's necessary — kill the stupid old bitch," Blue Eyes instructed.

"And the girl? What shall I do with her?" Marco asked.

Mr Blue Eyes, aware he was no longer alone, grinned at the paralysing fear exhibited in the woman's face. Unsure of how much of the conversation his new audience had heard. "Yes. Kill the girl as well," he affirmed. "We can soon replace her."

The woman who stared wide-eyed at him gasped, and Mr Blue Eyes's sinister smile widened.

"I will travel to Spain when I'm finished here."

He ended the call and shifted his attention to his unfortunate onlooker.

— ⬜ —

Below lay the frailty of her own mortal body. Kirsty watched an anxious Celia, who blew life into her lungs. *Strange?* Kirsty thought. The freight train of images flickered from every angle. She moved among this maelstrom and came to be part of the fine dust particles trapped within spectral towers of sunshine. Celia, Chantelle, and the club all evaporated into the ether as the zoetrope of memories slowed down. Soon, shapes morphed together and formed a fresh place. One which Kirsty recognized.

A room where she now stared into the strained features of her mother. Her mom's face was granite, cold and fraught with anguish. Tears streaked down her cheeks. Damp splotches dripped on the teddy-bear grasped within her hands. Kirsty recognized Sleepy Bear. The bear had always been with her. Through thick and thin, the good times and the bad. And now Sleepy Bear lay, clutched, in the hands of her sobbing mother.

"Don't cry, Mum," Kirsty shouted, but her words couldn't be heard, and her voice became absorbed in this celestial domain, "I'm here." Then, all too soon, the room faded. Kirsty, once again, found herself isolated on the oil-slick of blackness. "What's happening?" Her pain came back, "Please — let me stay." She implored. A hammer strike slammed her chest. Kirsty sank lower. "I wish to stay, — please."

Another hammer strike pummelled her rib cage, and she inhaled liquor tainted breath as it forced into her. Puffing out her cheeks to rush down her throat. The hammer strike belted her again as thunderous war drums pulsed inside her skull. Kirsty listened to the stricken cry of Celia.

"She's breathing," Celia shouted, "She's coming back."

Kirsty sucked a yawping breath. Arctic rivers rushed through her veins and caused her to shudder.

"Looks like the Naloxone is working," Chantelle said, and glanced over Celia's shoulder into the bleary, unfocussed eyes of Kirsty.

"Get some water," Celia panted. She swiped, with her forearm, the perspiration from her brow. "It was touch and go for a minute," Celia smiled as recognition flooded into Kirsty's face, "I thought we were going to lose you." She slumped her bulk down on the bed's edge. The strain of rescue breaths and chest compressions were making her wheeze. Kirsty's skin was corpse cold, but her cheek flinched from the warmth of Celia's hands. "We will have to keep a close eye on her," Celia said as Chantelle returned with a cup of water. "And, we had better make more Naloxone ready. Rosa may need another dose before she's out of danger."

Kirsty groaned from the flames of each scorched breath. She coughed a dry, raspy cough and hissed in pain from her bruised ribs. Hands as stable as a Parkinson's sufferer, she grasped for the drink of water held by Celia.

"Sshh." Celia said and stroked the back of Kirsty's shoulder. "Take it slow, my Rosa."

"What happened?" Kirsty wheezed before attempting the water again.

"You had too much medication," Chantelle said.

An onrush of memory struck with sledgehammer force. Kirsty's eyes narrowed into pinpoint daggers. "You stupid…"

"Enough," Celia snapped. "Leave us." she gestured to Chantelle toward the door.

Chantelle knew better than to argue and scuttled out of the room.

"Listen to me, Rosa." Celia spoke with a hushed whisper. "I have something to give you. An advert from a newspaper. Someone is looking for you."

"Who?" Kirsty gasped, "Show me…"

Celia pushed a finger to Kirsty's mouth, "Shhh." She was penitent when she continued, "You must regain your strength, then come to my office," leaning down next to Kirsty's ear. "Understand this," she said with seriousness, "First I need to take care of the doctor." She stroked Kirsty's hair. "I cannot let them kill another of my girls. Tell no-one, and I will help you escape."

The Reapers Trio

"Come in and close the door," her killer commanded.

Fear made her obey him, and she moved as instructed. "I… I… I," she stammered.

He covered the short distance between the bay window and the doorway with two enormous strides and stopped in front of her. She didn't have the chance to speak, and before her screams pierced the room. Mr Blue Eyes placed his solid grasp upon her open mouth.

"Shhh," he hushed with hypnotic charm, the seduction of a cobra. "You shouldn't eavesdrop," he declared, his manner condescending. The woman's moist breath stung the lacerations on his palm, but he held firm. She tensed as he pressed his hand harder, forming a seal over her lips. "It's dangerous to listen in on people," he smirked as he squeezed down on her nose, "It will get you into trouble." Mr Blue Eyes chuckled and watched her comprehend what was taking place. It drove her old brown eyes large with dread.

Twisting her head, she sought to tear away from his clasp, but couldn't. He followed her backwards until he had her against the frigid surface of the door. His grip became an airtight seal. Her cheeks bulged, then deflated, expanded again, but the spent air became ineffective. Fire burned in her lungs as she struggled to evict this used air. Freight trains ran so loud through her skull and her vision swam. Bright stars exploded with the intensified pressure behind her eyes to widen them further.

She was up on her tiptoes. Strength drained like a burst dam, and the aged woman faded as she tugged at the palm which clamped her mouth. Body convulsing in spasms against her aggressor. Her feet were clear of the floor, twitching as if performing an Irish jig between the killer's legs. With the last remnants of determination, she sought to reach up, but her leaden hands flopped at her sides like a puppet whose strings had been cut. A cannonade of heartbeats hammered within the cauldron of her chest. Its noise deafening and her lungs screamed their torment.

At first, she feared the encroaching fog, which lurked at the periphery of vision. But the blackness which gathered numbed all her misery. The blaze in her lungs decreased. A voice tempted her further inside. Its words, full of kindness and exuded trust. Encouraging her to let go, and she wished to. She needn't resist any more. Everything would be perfect if she could just release her tenuous grip on life. The Reaper's icy clutch encircled her mortality, and she embraced it with contented acceptance.

— ☐ —

Celia was in torment. It seemed as if her body was the epicentre of a tectonic shift, as she suffered violent shivers. After Drulovic had caused the near fatal overdose of her beautiful English Rosa, Celia had been determined to remain sober. She drew the bottle to her lips and sipped what Celia believed was a slight medicinal nip from the vodka. The bottle's rim danced across her nicotine teeth as her limbs felt the aftershocks of her inner battle. Closing her eyes to prevent the frenzied yearning to slug large glugs of fiery liquid.

Turning her concerns to Kirsty. *Enough is enough,* Celia agreed. *I cannot stand by and allow another girl to spiral down into Drulovic's sick depravity. It's time I defended them.*

A phantom voice of Stefania echoed through the room. "What's your plan?" It asked.

Celia realized Stefania was a figment of her drink deprived imaginations. An apparition of guilt wasn't unprecedented for Celia as she pursued her sobriety.

"You're pathetic," Stefania taunted. "First me and now this new girl. How long do you expect her to last?"

Celia lit a cigarette and blew a plume of bluish smoke, listening as her despondent words stuttered, "You realize they will kill me — don't you?"

Reading Celia's craving, the sound of Stefania chided, "Get yourself drunk. Lose yourself inside that bottle." The voice giggled a melancholic laugh, "If you hadn't been so sloshed — I might yet be alive, and it might have been me you had taken care of."

An ocean of regret washed over Celia in a rip tide of grief. "What can I do?" Celia demanded.

"Well? Isn't Drulovic already here? Isn't Chantelle with him?" Stefania's words rasped. "He relishes being tied up and wants to be struck." Stefania's remarks were savage, loaded with malignant intent. "It makes him more excited for when it is his turn. Pain fuels his desire to induce suffering to your girls."

"And what should I do?" But Celia already knew this answer.

In a matter-of-fact tone Stefania replied. "Kill him, of course." The malicious voice cackled. "If you are going to help the new girl escape? Then first you must be rid of him."

"You're certain. You're right?" Celia agreed and closed her eyes. Pulling more smoke from her cigarette. "Okay." She gave a resigned sigh, "I will take care of him."

Standing up on Bambi legs, Celia grasped the bottle of vodka, staggered from the office, and headed towards the stairs.

— □ —

Mr Blue Eyes watched the old woman's life ebb away and, like the last of the sun's warmth which dwindled from the day as it slunk below the horizon; she left this mortal realm. He released his grip and waited for her blood crazed pupils to present their vacant stare. A whooshing noise of stagnant air, fragranced with egg cress sandwiches, exhausted from her corpse. Blue Eyes carried her body and settled it in an armchair.

He listened to the sports commentator coming from the TV in the next room. Speed was of the essence, and he entered the area where the woman's companion sat.

Her spouse was in a recliner with his back to the open doorway, watching a televised game of cricket.

"Go on, you bumbling idiot," the husband exclaimed.

And, at first, Mr Blue Eyes thought he was speaking to him, but then understood the remarks to be aimed at the television.

"Howzat?" boomed the husband with exuberant delight. "Oh, come on, umpire," his joy turned to disappointment, and the old man complained when the umpire failed to agree. "It was leg first," he growled. "He is out. Are you blind, the ball struck his leg? Bloody bunch of cheats."

The announcer was speaking again, as they showed slow-motion replays. It was the distraction Mr Blue Eyes needed. He slipped undetected behind the man of the house. Unaware of Mr Blue Eyes, who attacked at rattlesnake speed and smashed the ridge of his hand, knife edge, into the older man's larynx. A gargle of violence erupted as tracheal cartilage crushed and his windpipe shattered.

The husband's frenzied fingers went to his throat as he rasped and choked. Mr Blue Eyes pressed his assault and grasped him beneath the chin and tugged backwards. The force lifted the man up and clear of his seat. The sharp jerk twist, brief but voracious, made the bones in the neck give a sickening snap as the vertebrae was broken and the husband's arms gave a sporadic twitch as they dropped to his sides in welcome to the Reaper's abrupt arrival.

Mr Blue Eyes lowered him down into the chair. The head of his victim slouched at a grotesque angle. Blood seeped from blue-tinged lips. The man's neck exhibited a mottled purplish scarf of bruising.

A shout of "Howzat," came from the television, and this time the umpire raised his arm. Signalling to the batsman that, like the deceased man in the chair, his luck had just run out.

— ☐ —

Wearing a high-cut leather corset trimmed with small metal spikes beneath open breast cups, Chantelle watched Celia stagger toward her. Chantelle's breasts were a stark contrast against the studded black leather bodice. Her forearms were wrapped in long PVC opera styled gloves and in her hand was an eight-inch square black paddle. Her legs gleamed in thigh-high PVC boots, which sported a six-inch shiny chrome heel, and she stood high above Celia. Blood-red lipstick made her appear provocative, while the dark shades of indigo eyeshadow and elongated eyeliner gave her an imperious air of vampirism.

This had little effect on Celia, who overlooked the girl's attire as she pursed her lips with her forefinger. "Sshh," she shushed, and whispered, "Where is he?"

Chantelle knew who she meant. "In there," she replied, equalling Celia's whisper, "On my bed," and thumbed over her shoulder, "What's going on?"

"Leave us," Celia ordered.

"I can't," Chantelle argued. "I've already stripped him and tied him to my bed. You know how he loves to be punished first."

Spittle shot from Celia's lips as she growled, "I don't care what state you have him in. Just go."

"But if you make him angry," Chantelle stood at the door's threshold, a half-hearted attempt to block out Celia. "It will provoke him to be vicious. I have been the receiver of his wrath when he's livid." She could see her pleading had limited effect. "He'll hurt me," she argued. "And won't allow me my dope."

The tempered glass of Celia's composure snapped, and she slapped Chantelle hard. The jolt and the echoed yelp resounded throughout the corridor. Celia snatched a fistful of Chantelle's braided hair and yanked backward. Pulling Chantelle into the hallway, she hurled her against the wall. "When I order you to leave," Celia hissed, "I don't expect you to argue." more frothy spittle sprayed, "You need to learn who's in charge. Now get out of my sight."

Celia stepped into the room. Closing the bedroom door and twisting the key in its lock.

— ☐ —

Drulovic was nude and lying face down, star-shaped, prone upon Chantelle's bed. Age had plundered the elasticity from his skin, making the flesh of his depleted wineskin buttocks, sag. The blackness of the silken sash cord stood out against his ochre tainted skin. The rope bound each of his wrists to the leading edges of the bed, and similar bindings fastened his feet to the opposite ends. A leather hooded mask encased his head and in his mouth was a solid, cherry red, rubber ball gag.

Celia stepped further into the lamp-lit room and snickered. "You shouldn't have harmed my Rosa." Her words spoken in a gentle whisper. Enjoying the panic when Drulovic realized it wasn't Chantelle with him any longer.

Celia's foot struck Drulovic's medicine bag, which toppled to scatter its contents across the floor. Straight away, she was attracted to the Taser, which had bounced onto the floor.

"Go on, pick it up," uttered the phantasm voice of Stefania.

She peered down at the Taser, then stooped to grasp it. Standing straight, she held it aloft as if lifting a winning trophy. A sadistic grin broadened Celia's face when she squeezed the trigger. A crackle of stroboscopic light flickered the area a lilac hue. The clamour made Drulovic freeze, for he knew what brutal instrument made that sound.

The doctor screamed into the bulbous rubber, which constrained his mouth. The room became silent.

Celia pressed it a second time, and once again the place was awake with sparks clattering violet. She released the button and silence reigned. She allowed the prongs of the Taser to drag across his weathered flesh. Down his bare spine, which jerked beneath her hand. She slipped the gun between his legs. Pushed up into the tender flesh of his groin before exploding 50,000 volts through his genitalia.

Drulovic's body danced like a 1960s hippy on acid. Arms and legs shook with uncontrollable convulsions. She stepped away and with bitter words said, "This isn't very nice — is it?" It was a ghoulish laugh which rattled from Celia, and she paraded around his sorrowful form. A harshness came into her speech, "That was for, Stefania."

A stinking yellow stain leached into the white-sheeted mattress. "Look at the mess, you're creating," she growled at him and charged another burst from the Taser. This time pushing against his outer thigh before firing.

Drulovic's body juddered with more contractions. His tongue bashed against the muzzle. Tried to dislodge its obstruction. Panic made him hyperventilate, and Drulovic gasped for a breath which wouldn't come.

Celia watched as Drulovic choked. You deserve this and more, she decided, and buzzed him a third time.

"And that was for almost killing my Rosa."

A vice gripped his rib cage and turned into an elephant, which squatted its crushing weight between his shoulders. The agony was brief but immense and the ensuing blackness which brought the Reaper to him, was bitter relief.

Celia waited for his electrified limbs to come still. Pushing her fingers against his throat, she couldn't feel any pulse, but, to be certain, Celia pressed against his wrist. Nothing drummed inside his skin, and he'd changed to a greyish colour. Kneeling at his side, Celia laid her head upon Drulovic's back and held an ear hard against his skin. The stillness of his silenced heart spoke volumes to Celia. Drulovic was dead.

A Call for Help

"First, I thank you for getting in touch, inspector. I don't doubt you're as busy over in England as we are here in Madrid." Said the appreciative Detective Baldomero.

"Yes, we're up to our necks in it. I won't bore you with details, but the usual staff issues, etcetera, etcetera." Inspector Collins responded. She was brusque in asking, "I understand you're after information concerning a recent case?"

"Yes, if that's OK." Baldomero replied and continued. "You dealt with the death of a young girl, Miss Kerry Wells. Her remains turned up on a local canal. The adolescent's death certificate recorded an opioid analgesic overdose."

"That's correct," Collins affirmed. "But I forwarded you this information via email. Did you not receive it?"

"I did." He admitted, "but I have a few further queries and was counting on you to shed some light on one or two points for me."

"I can try. But it may require you to go through the official channels. I'm sure your superiors want everything correct." Collins said.

"Yes, you're right. It's not like the old days, when we could just pick up the phone and one officer would help another. Now, it must be ironclad." Baldomero explained, "All the requests have been filed, and are awaiting sanction. There shouldn't be any issues. I'm trying to get a head start beyond all the red tape."

"What is it you need, Detective?" She asked.

"Well, the toxicology report is a perfect match to a Jane Doe we retrieved from the Manzanares river. Not only that, but it matches another overdose fatality we have on record. You would be excused if you thought all were from the same corpse and not three separate inquiries. I can't resolve how a girl in England has overdosed on what turns out to be the same dope."

"That seems curious and too improbable to be a fluke," Collins admitted. "If you can forward me what you have, I will look into it."

"I'm glad to share and collaborate our resources if you're willing to add a little more information," Baldomero Said.

"I will need to run this by my superiors. After all, from their point of view, the Kerry Wells case has been deemed death by misadventure and is now closed." Collins advised. "If there is substantial proof to the contrary, I'll have to show it to my bosses and reopen the investigation. I can then combine our shared resources." She finished, "If my boss seems satisfied with your evidence. I can hurry things along, but until I have the green light, there isn't a lot I can do."

"I understand," Baldomero agreed. "I will email you the information I have. Thank-you for your cooperation."

— ☐ —

Celia woke in a bewildered heap, slouched against the opposite wall facing Chantelle's bed. An empty vodka bottle lay at her side. That explains the jackhammer belting into my brain, she thought and squinted her eyes into the gloom. Moving her legs provoked hot rods of pins and needles to stab into her limbs. The shroud of drunkenness lifted and an ocean of foreboding swept upon her.

"No... no... no," she repeated with a frantic splutter. Pushing herself up from the floor as the recollection of the preceding night cleaved into her fears.

Celia panicked. "What are you planning to do now?" she stared at the carcass of Drulovic on the bed. How can I get rid of him? She wondered and became riveted by the cold talons of dread. "Slow down," she murmured, struggling to soothe her concerns. "Just breathe and think." A penny whistle of air squeaked when it surged in and out of her nostrils. "I need a smoke," she said matter-of-fact. "And a drink. That'll settle me, and then I can figure this out." She continued as if Drulovic were still alive. "You're not going anywhere — are you?" Celia became better composed. "First, I have my Rosa to help." She walked to the door and unlocked it. "I will return to sort you later," and went from the room, shutting him inside.

— ☐ —

Marco saw the dregs of customers saunter out of Brodie's bar before he neared the back of the building. Staff were active with their night-time close-down procedures and didn't notice him arrive. The door to Brodie's office was a gaping cavity of shadow, and as the club owner bid goodnight to his personnel. Marco evaporated into its blackness.

Listening as the Scotsman moved, shutting doors, jangling keys into locks and closing the business for the night. Marco sat and waited.

When Brodie entered, he turned on the office light and didn't appear shocked when it revealed Marco. He didn't speak, but walked to the far side of his desk and slumped into the chair behind it. He gripped a bottle of bourbon and gulped down the liquor, gasping from its harsh heat, but unsated, Brodie glugged another.

"You're 'ere tae murdurr me- urr ye then?" Brodie slurred. He hadn't appeared drunk, but his speech was thick as he chewed out each word. "I haven't spoken tae a'body. Nae that it matters tae you."

Marco's grin became fierce and his crypt quiet silence unnerved the Scotsman.

"Why did ye murdurr Joe 'n' Hanna?" Brodie asked as he slugged more bourbon. Wiping his hand across his mouth producing a wet smack sound, he said, "I made a promise tae them." The bottle sloshed when he thumped it down upon the desk. He equalled Marco's crazed stare with a bloodshot one of his own.

"I didn't have that enjoyment." Marco's weighted words expressed genuine regret. "I would have devoted hours to gain a trophy from them." He watched Brodie's face as he removed the mummified facial husk of Curly, which dangled like a medallion about his neck.

Brodie recoiled with revulsion, "You're sick — ye realize that don't ye — yi"ll need hulp, ye twisted maniac,"

Marco went on, "Mr Blue Eyes disposed of your associates." He was enjoying the effect Curly had. "He doesn't want loose ends, so, they had to go." Marco grinned. "My companion here," He pointed to the withered husk, "He needs company. He informs me he is lonesome, and you're going to make the ideal comrade."

An odd metallic taste tainted Brodie's mouth, as if he were sucking an antique copper coin. Thor's hammer boomed against his ribcage. "I cuid hae tellt th' polis everything." The alcohol had given him indigestion. It's molten rivers burned his throat. The cannonade of panic belted inside his skull. "I didn't, nevertheless, did I?" He gasped each word, "I... Kept... Mah... trap... Shut... Lik'... Ah promised... Yer." Perspiration ran tropical torrents to drip from his brow. He glugged another gulp of the bourbon to swill away the taste. Struggled to control his breathless gasps. Wished for the liquor to saturate the fire which overwhelmed him, but it only added to his anguish. "I... Did... As... Ye... Asked, ah... Didn't... Arg."

Brodie hugged his right fist up to his shoulder as an electric eel coiled along his arm. Sharp needle points made a claw of his hand. Bolts of lightning struck between his breastbone and seized a behemoth's grasp around his rib cage. Brodie became frozen by death's cadaverous clutch, and a cold cramp squeezed his dying heart. A sense of relief passed over him, realizing it wouldn't be Marco who took his life. A gargle slipped into a last gasp before the Scotsman slumped toward oblivion.

Disappointed to be denied his kill, Marco watched as the Scotsman struggled. He had no interest in preventing Brodie's death, and there would be no hospital trip. Instead, Marco sat and looked upon him with macabre fascination. Like the kid who admires a spider wrapping its prey within its silken cocoon of death. Marco watched Brodie succumb to the perpetual darkness. He rose and peered into the dead man's stare then shrugged.

An hour later, parked in his Range Rover outside the warehouse in Tarragona, Marco studied the newspaper advert.

"Look at this," Marco held it up and showed it to the blackened husk of Curly who he'd returned to the rear-view mirror.

Marco slammed his fist on the dash. "Well, it looks like we're travelling to Madrid in the morning."

"What trophy shall I collect from the old slut?" Marco asked and glanced at Curly as if waiting for an answer. Marco grinned. "Yes, I think so too," responding to a voice only audible to him, "I will take the skin from her saggy tits." He chuckled, "And the girl?" he peered up at Curly and responded with ghoulish delight. "Perfect," His grin widened, "I will cut out her eyes, but only after I deal with that old hag Celia. They will both become our new trophies."

Abigail held the phone against her left ear as she listened to its insistent ring, and she made a dissatisfied tut when the call went through to the electronic voice from the answer machine. She hung up without leaving a message, having recorded several throughout the day.

"Still no answer?" Asked a disconcerted Pete.

"Nothing," replied Abigail. She gave a worried shake of her head. "It's the sixth time I have tried today. It's not like them."

"All seemed fine when I saw them last night." He smiled, then shrugged. "I visited Ruth and Mark late yesterday. Just for an update, but they didn't know a great deal." Pete pointed to the extra box of paperwork which he had brought with him, "That's how I got this."

"And?" Abigail asked and she slumped against her small sofa, "How did they seem?"

He looked at her, sat cross-legged on the floor, using the settee as a backrest, with her exposed knees peeking out of her ripped skinny jeans. With a flippant shrug, he answered, "Like I said, all seemed fine."

Kneeling on the floor with the mound of paperwork in front of him. "The answer is here," Pete assured, "I'm certain of it. We just need to continue looking."

After searching through Steve's bedroom, Pete had found a black plastic box filled with documents. A memory box of sorts but, so far, nothing of relevance had been discovered.

"So where is it?" Abigail barked. Then, before Pete could object, she tipped the box upside-down and emptied it among the pile. "This information you're so confident we're going to find? Eh? Where is it then?"

"I don't know Abs," he sighed, "But it must be here. Perhaps something has caused them to run off." He picked up the plastic container to put everything back when he noticed something at the bottom. He removed a brown envelope and held it up for Abigail to see. An official letter with a crested emblem printed at the top left-hand corner.

"What's that?" Abigail asked with genuine intrigue.

Pete turned it over in his fingers, failing to hide his puzzled expression. The marker read McLaren and Daughter — Wills, Estates and Probate Solicitors. He recognized the name. "These were the same people who dealt with our parent's estate," Pete said as he studied the envelope.

"It's post-dated the week before they went to Spain." He smiled at Abigail who glanced at the unopened letter. "You want me to open it — don't you?"

"No," Abigail's protests were unconvincing, "Don't be absurd," she dropped her gaze. "Well? What do you consider it to be?"

"I don't expect we need to be geniuses to work that out." Pete put the envelope on the pile of paperwork. "I would guess it's Steve's will."

"But?" she paused. "Isn't he too young to have made out a will?"

"Mom and Dad had substantial life insurance. All of it was left for Steve. They," Pete pointed to the crest upon the envelope, "Placed it in a trust fund until he reached 21. I imagine it has matured into a considerable amount of money by now," he explained. "Also, with the loss of our parents when my brother was so little. It's driven him to be mindful of the unforeseen. So, no. I don't think Steve is too young to have made out a will."

"Shouldn't we open it and find out?" Abigail asked.

"I want to, but," Pete shrugged, searching for the correct words, "Isn't it a bad omen? Isn't it suggesting what both of us fear?"

"Well, we may have to talk about it." Abigail's mood was icy. "Something dreadful may have taken place. We just don't know." She picked up a handful of Steve's hospital wage slips. All in neat bundles, bound with an elastic band. "Seeing how Steve liked to…" she realized how tactless this may seem and changed her wording. "Knowing how, Steve likes to keep everything tidy. He might have placed something in that envelope to give us a clue."

Thirty minutes later, and holding Steve's official last will and testament, with Abigail telling him to calm down, Pete stomped around like a spoilt child.

"Calm down…" he spat, "Why the hell should I calm down?"

Confused, Abigail wondered why on earth was he so worked up? The contents of the brown envelope had bothered him, but why? She was as astonished as him to learn Kirsty was the lone beneficiary of Steve's inheritance. "Look, I'm positive you and Steve can sort this out once we have found them."

"What on earth is he thinking," Pete responded with a vehement growl. "How foolish is he to make some stupid tart…" Pete fell silent when he remembered his audience.

"Go on?" she said, incensed by his remarks. "You were saying?" Abigail glowered at him. She bunched her fists at her side. It was all she could do to keep from slapping Pete hard across his face. Voice raised, her words acidic, she turned on him. "So, Kirsty is just some tart, is she? Eh? Is that what you think?"

Pete failed to stop his mouth from getting the better of him and couldn't disguise his harsh tone. "Well? This is a motive.

"How…" the avalanche of obscenities wishing to escape became a bottleneck trapped in her throat. Annoyed, she gasped the air, speechless for a moment. "How dare you," she managed to say. "You — you — complete arsehole."

"Well, money causes people to do many things…"
The fire which slashed across his face was instantaneous, as
the palm of Abigail's hand slapped him hard. He glared at
her as a crimson handprint bloomed on his cheek. Pete's
demeanour changed, "Honey." He began, but Abigail cut him
off.

"Don't you dare, 'Honey' me," she screamed, jabbing
an aggressive finger toward him. "You, patronizing —
arrogant pig," Hell's fury raged, and she hissed through
clenched teeth, "I ain't yours or anyone else's — honey."

Pete moved to hold her, but it was a mistake and
Abigail let both hands fly. He was too close to fend off the
onslaught, and another hard slap seared his cheek. He
resisted the impulse to reciprocate and backed off.

"You're upset…" He declared, but his demeaning
tone lacked sincerity as he bought up his palms.

"No shit. You — disrespectful prick."

"I think… I should leave," Pete resigned.

Arctic cold, Abigail responded, "Well, that's
something we can both agree upon."

"For what it's worth — I'm sorry." Pete apologized.

— ☐ —

A men's grey fleece sweatpants and a similar hoodie
drowned Kirsty. The wizard sleeve arms of the oversized
hoodie dangled, whilst the bottoms of the trousers bunched
about her feet. She sat watching the old crone, who opened
her desk drawer to take out a new packet of Lucky Strikes.
Kirsty noticed how Celia's hands shook when the older
woman slugged an enormous mouthful of vodka. She's more
shaken than normal, Kirsty thought, and was blunt in asking,
"So?"

Celia pushed a newspaper in front of her. "You need
to read this." A harsh crackle hissed as she dragged on her

cigarette. "I should've shown you this sooner," smoke gushed dragon style from her nostrils, "I guess — I'm sorry." She stated, her abashed demeanour hidden behind a shrouded haze, "I didn't realize Drulovic's intentions." Wet lips sucked another lungful of nicotine infused smog, "He won't kill any more of my girls. Not now."

Kirsty didn't altogether know what Celia meant by her last statement, but swept it aside as she took hold of the paper. A half page sized black and white advert and even before Kirsty had read the caption along the bottom of the picture, she recognized herself in the photograph. Shock made her snort, and Kirsty held the publication in skittish hands and granted it a closer inspection. "How?" glancing over with a querying look at Celia. "Why?" The jolt of the advert was a sledgehammer to the gut, and the strength diminished from her limbs.

Grief became a wide chasm of sorrow when Kirsty peered into Steve's joyful face. Emotions of guilt, fear, and anger coursed their heated torrents upon her cheeks, and as the pages blotted up her tears, Kirsty re-read the words. She'd been so wrapped up in this vile realm of lies, so dominated by all this deceit, that it had never occurred to her, she could be missed. Nor had Kirsty deemed it possible someone would come searching for them.

Hope thawed her frigid heart, and Kirsty's elation grew, fed by the knowledge of someone out there was looking for them. Kirsty read the piece over and over. Words put there by Abigail, sweet, reliable Abigail.

"I must call her… please?" pleaded Kirsty.

Celia stared at the cluttered desktop. As if the right response lay between the detritus of stale cigarette nubs and the three heroin filled syringes nestled against the ancient Bakelite telephone. Celia glared at the needles. Their vile contents had provoked so much anguish, then her gaze wandered to the phone's once age dulled black exterior. She jabbed an arthritic finger toward it. "Make it quick — before I change my mind."

Guilt had been a vampire on Abigail's conscience. It had left her drained as she worried about Pete and how matters had concluded between them the previous evening. He hadn't merited the response she'd given. Abigail agreed. She felt dreadful for being such a bitch. You should call him, she considered, and say what? She shrugged and peered down at the tea bag she had strained to death in the mug of boiled water and conceded, I will try him later and apologize.

Abigail carried her drink into the front room when, in the kitchen, her mobile rang. *That's him,* she thought. Placing the cup down, she hurried to answer her phone. The number wasn't Pete's or one she recognized. It had the same international code as the one she had been given to call Detective Baldomero and Abigail expected to hear Baldomero's voice. Instead, only a strange silence greeted her.

Damn it — I've missed it, she cussed. Then the slightest flutter of a gasp broke from the handset.

"Hello," Abigail said again. "Who is this — hello?" Silence, except for a delicate sob. Excitement rose. Abigail just knew the caller was Kirsty, wished it to be her, prayed it to be. "Who is this?" A sharp nervousness etched in her voice. She bit her bottom lip and listened. "I'm not good with practical jokes — I know someone's there — I hear your breathing." Only silence rewarded her. "I'm putting the phone down now."

A quiet, almost indistinguishable voice answered, "It's me, Abs." Kirsty's low sobbing cry became louder, "It's me — I'm — I'm here, Abs, I'm alive."

Hot streams ran upon Abigail's face, tears of joy, of relief. "Kirsty?" Abigail screamed, "My God, where have you been?" She gasped, "We've been searching everywhere for you. Where are you?"

"I'm still in Spain. At a club in Madrid," Kirsty's words were running out too quick. "I am near a train station.

Every so often I hear the trains — that's all I know." her voice broke, "They're forcing me to do such awful things — please, bring help."

Abigail, shocked at the anguish in Kirsty's comments, felt a torrent of sorrow pour from her friend's manner. "Say again, Kirst– I didn't understand. What are you telling me?"

"I found an old flyer advertising the Medianoche Exótica club," Kirsty blurted and continued. "I don't even know if I'm at this place. It's the only information I have." Kirsty's tone took on a more urgent fashion, "Please Abi — please help me."

Abigail couldn't grasp the pace at which this was developing. "What — you have, err — you're where? Kirsty, this isn't making sense. Where are you?"

Kirsty repeated, "The Medianoche Exótica..."

As if the earth had erupted and released demonic hounds of hell upon the world, a roar rushed down the phone. Such abhorrent hatred almost made Abigail drop the handset. She brought it a few inches away from her ear, as a sound like plastic being scrunched into the earpiece. The crackle of static preceded several clicks, then cut off.

A Viperous Blow

Earlier in the day Detective Baldomero had been given a breakthrough by Doctor Luciana De León. She'd phoned him that morning to share her discoveries and present a name for the deceased girl they had taken out from the river.

"What answers do you have for me, Doc?" inquired Baldomero.

"Since I didn't have a DNA record on file for this woman or any fingerprint data in our system. I've needed to trace backwards," said De León.

"Are you telling me she isn't a street girl?" replied the detective, striving to repress his scepticism. "I'd have put money on her being a working girl."

"And you'd be correct in your suspicions," agreed De León. "We have not processed her through our legal system. And she wasn't always a street girl."

"So, what are you telling me?"

"I'm saying she led a different lifestyle in her home country. She was from Romania. Because of lividity and decay, we missed this in our original assessment of the cadaver. But on her left buttock is a tattoo. It illustrates a crown beneath blue eyes balanced upon what, I presumed, was the crescent moon. Under microscope observation, it is a sickle. Like the one at the top corner of the former soviet flag. It's symbolic, establishing a mark of ownership with associations with ex KGB and Russian mafia."

"I see, and how did she finish up in Madrid?"

"The skin growth over the tattoo plus the fading of ink suggests it's been on her; I'd say about five years or more. I started studying her remains for other identifiable additions or markings to her body. I detected a left side internal radial distal reconstruction."

"Radial distal?" queried the bewildered detective.

"A repair to the bones of the wrist, a plate secured in place with screws. A common enough injury, but the type more fitting to that of a gymnast or a similar sporting or dancing vocation. The regenerated bone growth around the reconstruction shows this to have taken place in her mid to late teens."

"So how does this lead to her name?" Baldomero asked.

"The plate bears a serial number. Something I'm able to track back to when the surgery took place. This serial number is just a batch code but is sufficient, thanks to a colleague of mine, to trace. I determine the age at the point of death to be between 33 and 35 years, and the operation around 17 years old. In the time frame we are looking at there were only two radial distal fixations using this matching serial. These were in Bucharest, Romania. One on a male patient leaving the other on our female, which I have established an identification against early dental records to be those of the woman in my deep freeze."

"As usual, Doc, you never fail to amaze me. So, what's her name?"

"Loan Stefania Florescu." Said De León. "I'm certain that's our woman from the river. Once a talented athlete and part of her national development team. Until the accident which not only crushed her wrist but destroyed her confidence and dreams. Afterward, she came a dancer and finished up working as a street girl under the control of the Russian mafia, hence her tattoo."

Astounded by her information, Baldomero said, "How have you found this out?"

"I mentioned I had help from a colleague of mine. He's an authority in sporting injuries and one of the leading consultants in his field. His knowledge is unquestionable, and there isn't anything he cannot turn up. With his intelligence, I discovered all this information to enable an identification. One thing we learned is she never went by her first name; but always preferred Stefania, Stefania Florescu."

— ☐ —

The drive from Tarragona to Madrid had been tiresome, but as Marco entered the club and headed toward Celia's office, his senses became energized by the noise of the female voices coming from within. With narrowed eyes, he squinted through the crack in the ajar door. The girl he'd come to kill, sat with her back to him, facing Celia. She gripped the phone to her ear and conversed with someone and was oblivious of his presence. He nudged open the door.

A horrified Celia had turned into a statue of granite, frozen with fear. The glass she'd gripped slipped from her grasp to turn into wind-chimes of shattering shards.

Marco exploded into the office just as the glass splintered on the floor. A freight train roar burst from his lungs and he shot across the room, a tornado of violence with Kirsty in its path. He snatched clumps of her hair, and dragged Kirsty up and out of her chair. His sledgehammer fist connected onto her left cheek and drove the blow home. Kirsty stumbled a rag-doll dance as she collided, then skidded across the desk.

She crumpled between consciousness and blackout and battled against the unconscious abyss, which threatened to overwhelm her. Falling to the floor together with the three heroin filled syringes, cigarette butt's and other detritus which had strewn the desktop. One syringe bounced away, lost, but its two companions stayed within her reach.

Marco stooped to pick up the Bakelite phone and tore the curved handset from its cradle. Nostrils flared as his rage poured forth. A grin of malice became a sneer of hatred when he shifted toward Celia.

— ☐ —

"Kirsty," an anxious Abigail screamed at her phone, filled with a strong sense of foreboding, as she pushed it back against her ear. "Kirsty — Kirsty?" She repeated, "Are you there? Can you hear me?" Something dreadful had taken place, Abigail knew and couldn't help the fearful tremble which shook her hands. "Hold on, Kirst — I'm gonna get help." Abigail pin-balled against the walls of her downstairs hallway as she scrambled along in her panic. Leaping up the stairs, two at a time, and stumbled about halfway up, she let out a yelp of pain when she skinned her knee against the carpet. Abigail grappled with the rail of the banister and dragged herself upward toward her bedroom.

A cacophony of thunder splintered inside her skull. Her chest rattled hot coals as her heart thrummed at her ribs. Fear took charge, and she became disheartened upon realizing nothing could be done. I'm too far away to be of any use, she despaired. "Think, Abs — why have you run up here?" She yelled out in frustration, "What has brought you up here?"

Stopping at the side of her bed, she searched around, wishing for an epiphany. Any solution to enlighten her, but it didn't take place, and she dropped upon the mattress in a demoralized heap before crying out into her empty room. "I'm sorry, Kirst. I… I… I just don't know what to do?" she sobbed salt rivers from monsoon tears which dripped off her face.

On the floor by Abigail's bare feet lay the bag she'd used on her travels to Spain. She swooped on it and lifted it onto the bed, recalling the small two by three-inch laminated business card stuffed inside the suitcase's front compartment. The police insignia stood out in bold font and read, Policia Nacional with the name of Detective Baldomero and his contact number. *Perhaps he's the one person who can help,* a frantic Abigail thought, *but you must move fast.*

— ▢ —

The phone handset swung back and forth as Marco stepped over Kirsty's incapacitated heap. To him, she was nothing more than a writhing mass of human waste. He kept his next target, Celia, frozen by fear. Marco's movements were deliberate and slow. He twisted the cord of the handset around the clenched fist of his right hand to form a makeshift ligature.

Celia attempted to speak but it was a silent gesture as the words became trapped. She peered deep into his eyes and realized his were the last eyes she would look upon.

Placing a finger up to his lips, Marco said, "Sshh."

She longed for escape, but her limbs wouldn't respond. Run — get away. Her panic-driven brain screamed, but his gaze held her rigid. On jellied legs, she lingered for death. Feeble whimpers trembled from her, and she jumped each time Marco stepped forward. As if death itself had washed over her; Marco's putrid breath carried the stink of decay. Celia shrank beneath his monstrous glare and attempted to meld herself into the timber of the cabinet she'd become pressed against.

Marco stopped mere inches from her. His nose almost brushing hers. She could see the fires of eternal damnation which blazed within his eyes.

Despite his size, Marco moved as fluid as water and forced the ligature tight against Celia's throat. The wire cut into the delicate flesh and crushed her airway. She made a rasping gargle, the same noise as a water vortex into a plughole. She raised her leaden arms to fend him off, but he was too powerful. Panic clanged inside her skull. She dug at the ligature, but realized it was futile. Her arms dangled down against her sides and she yielded to the advancing greyness which fluttered her vision.

Marco did something unexpected as he leant forward. Pushing his face close to Celia's, allowing his breath to warm her skin. His tongue traced a viscous, silvery trail of saliva across her left cheek.

Mopping away tears as he savoured their saltiness and watched the flickering candlelight of life drain out from Celia's eyes.

Marco released the old woman as she plummeted toward death. Then he turned toward Kirsty.

— ☐ —

"Buenos noches hablas con el Detective Baldomero," he answered.

Abigail interrupted, "Hello, can you speak in English? Is this Baldomero — Detective Baldomero?" She caught her breath before continuing. "Please — you must help," she said with grave concern, "You're the only one who can." She swallowed air with a gasp. "Please," Abigail gasped a second time, "I spoke to you about my missing friends — Do you remember me?" She was at the edge of her hysteria, which gave a shrillness to her speech.

"It's my friend Kirsty — she — she's in trouble," Abigail sobbed. "Kirsty called me, please hurry."

Using her pause for breath as his cue to speak, Baldomero said, "Can you slow down? I remember who you are. This is Detective Baldomero — how can I help?"

Abigail became urgent, at the same time stuffing clothes inside her travel bag as she declared, "Kirsty called me — but something happened."

Remaining calm, "Okay," Baldomero said, "Did Kirsty say where she is?"

"Kirsty said she's forced to work in a club, the Medianoche Exótica." Abigail replied with an impatient harshness to her tone. "She rang me — only five minutes ago," Abigail glimpsed her reflection. Face pallid, like over creamed coffee, and worried eyes which deceived her youth to add ten years onto her grim expression.

"Listen — this is important," advised the detective, "I must put you on hold..." He halted as Abigail argued, "... Miss Simmons, it's just for a short while. Please don't panic. I'm not hanging up."

Before she could protest, the phone fell silent. Even the gale outside had abated, as if it, too, was holding its breath, awaiting his return. The detective startled her when he broke through the silence.

"Miss Simmons..." He spoke, "Abigail? Are you still there?"

"Yes, I'm here — please, we have to hurry?"

His voice authoritative, but calm, as he said. "We know the club you speak of— It's the only one within the Bravo Murrilo area. I have instructed officers to enter and search this business. They're on route now. I will follow them and be in there within the next fifteen to twenty minutes," He wound up the call, adding, "Stay near your phone — I'll ring you as soon as I have more."

— ▢ —

Pain burst white-hot embers across Kirsty's face. She gagged on a copper taste as she came back from the black void of unconsciousness. The fog of confusion lifted into a buzz of hornets trapped inside her ears.

She became like the myriad of roaches she had seen scurrying about the dance floors and, on elbow and knee, scrabbled toward the yawning mouth beneath the desk, wishing to seek refuge. Unsure why she had taken them with her, but she carried the syringes, which had fallen close when Kirsty had been thrown across the tabletop. Now she dragged them along with herself across the floor toward her haven. Each shuffle sent canon volleys throughout her face and bile up her throat. The desk space almost hid her, but a seismic shockwave rippled when a sledgehammer force slammed into her spine. Marco stomped his colossal, booted foot into the small of her back and halted her retreat. Gripping Kirsty by the ankles, he wrenched her body backwards. Twisting her over toward his left as he lifted, driving her leg down toward the floor. This made Kirsty spin mid-air before landing, stunned, upon her back. He pounced upon her and crushed the wind from her abdomen. Spittle dripped from off his chin as if he were a rabid dog, and he growled. "Now you're mine."

But Marco didn't foresee Kirsty's attack until she had struck. He thought she was weak, that she was feeble, but how wrong he'd been. These weren't the eyes of a defenceless creature he stared into, but the intense, venomous eyes of a strike primed snake.

Survival instinct aided Kirsty's recovery and as she remained beneath him, Kirsty summoned her last reserves of strength until the final moments. Knowing this would be her sole chance and conscious, the only reward for failure would be death. The heroin filled syringes held in her grasp were now her venom, which she directed toward the exposed veins pulsing at the side of Marco's neck. She took aim and struck her viperous blow.

The needles pierced Marco's jugular vein and pumped him full of dope. There wasn't a steady rise towards utopia for Marco. No pleasurable rush to enlightenment. The fatal dose coursed into his heart and pulsed throughout his entire system. Powerless to prevent the cold tendrils which slivered around his spine as he struggled to fight death's frigid grip. Toxic shock sent Marco toward death's ever-welcoming embrace. A series of small seizures rattled him with dying breaths until one last whistle vacated his lifeless body. He became as solid as the trunk of a fallen oak, which timbered forward and pinned Kirsty beneath his dead bulk.

The crushing weight of Marco bore down upon her, where she remained quiet and still. Music played as the onrushing void descended. A warbling noise Kirsty had

heard before and now, before the dark cloak of
unconsciousness took her. Kirsty understood. It wasn't music
she could hear, but the distinctive two-tone warble of police
sirens.

— ◻ —

The rain returned, descending in sheets which chased
Pete from the car to Abigail's front door. "How awful is the
weather?" He stated when he entered.

"It's dreadful," she answered, then helped Pete
remove his sopping jacket. "I'll hang this on the radiator."

Pete looked at the bag. "Planning a trip?" he asked,
with a questioning glance as he accompanied her inside.
"What's the news? Have you discovered anything?"

Ten minutes after speaking with Baldomero Abigail
had called Pete. Neither of them had spoken about the
previous night's argument but now they ignored it as if it had
ever happened.

She answered him. "Not a thing which is driving me
nuts," Abigail sighed. "But, as soon as I know what's
happening, I plan to travel to Spain."

Pete allowed her to lead the way as she spoke.

"Kirsty called me," Abigail said. "She's being held —
forced to work as some sort of slave."

"Did she say where?" Pete asked, "And, what about
Steve?"

"Sorry, but she didn't get the chance to explain."
Abigail shuddered." Her mobile rang before she could
elaborate further, and Abigail was quick to answer. "Hello —
is this…"

"We found her," Baldomero said. "She's alive and on
route to the hospital."

Wolf in Sheep's Clothing

Abigail peered through the aircraft's oval window toward the indigo skyline as the aeroplane started its final approach toward Madrid's Barajas airport. The rising sun having sliced into the blackness of night, pouring in warmth of coral and amber tones. She had attempted to snooze, but it hadn't come, for apprehension had held her far from sleep's languid shores.

Pete sat to her right, snoring, contented, with a tranquil expression on his face. He is the reason you are on this flight, appreciated Abigail, grant him his sleep. After all, Pete had organized this private jet. A bump from the aircraft brought them back to realism. The plane made another rumbling judder and touched down on the runway.

The preceding few days had been a whirlwind of action, and Abigail felt the impending hours wouldn't be any different. *At least Pete is with me*, she thought as they disembarked the modest, six-seater Learjet. Nerves turned her legs into rubber and tied knots in Abigail's belly. The closer she got to see Kirsty, the higher her anxiety rose. *Please, God? Please let Kirsty be okay*, Abigail prayed as she looked back at the sleek, white, and grey Lear jet with an enormous golden crown emblem along its side above the blue eye logo of the S.F.A. Corporation. She turned and followed Pete as they entered the airport to head towards a hire car firm.

"We could take a taxi — I know," Pete offered, pointing to the taxi company "But, this will be quicker — it'll be better that way."

She nodded her agreement then stated, "I don't care how I travel — just as long as we get to the hospital."

— ▢ —

Hypnotic waves of sedation thrummed with a harmonious percussion as Kirsty's pulse throbbed within her sub-conscious mind.

Thub-ub. Darkness. Thub-ub, thub-ub. Quiet and soothing blackness.

Thub-ub, thub-ub, thub-ub.

A steady be-beep, be-beep rhythm matched the tidal ebbing. Perhaps this is death? Considered Kirsty.

Thub-ub, thub-ub.

Be-beep, be-beep.

The beeping sound attracted her attention. No longer comforting but saturated with apprehension and someplace else, far within the deepest recess of her mind, a lantern of light pulsed. A phosphorescent flood which washed through the darkness.

Thub-ub, be-beep. Thub-ub, be-beep. Faster. Thub-ub, be-beep. Faster still. Thub-ub, be-beep, be-beep cantering hooves galloping.

Swaths of warmth permeated her coolness as the intense explosions of light blazed behind her eyes. The cinematic memories cascaded, the images of Steve's ravaged body as his murder re-played through her nightmares. The blue-eyed spectre turned into a wraith of her mind, with a phantasm of vileness.

"I know you," her inner voice yelled as Kirsty recoiled from their approach. But like moths to a flame, it attracted this blue-eyed spectre toward her, abhorrent and full of malice. It shrieked with a haunted sigh, "Sshh, my sweet darling, it's all okay, it's over now."

In Abigail's opinion, the foyer of the hospital's reception bore little resemblance to any hospital she had been in before. The pale blue of its corridors and the bright white fluorescent lighting in the suspended ceiling reflected against the polished terrazzo floor to feed its sterile ambience. The hallway was silent and made Abigail conscious of her horse clip-clopping footsteps when they walked towards the reception booth. Two clerks busied themselves, and neither glanced up at Abigail nor Pete until Pete knocked hard upon the solid surface of the countertop.

"Excuse me — do you speak English?" Abigail asked.

The receptionists looked at one another before answering. "I know a little," one of them said, "I can try to help?"

"My friend," Abigail showed a picture of Kirsty. "They brought her here last night — can you tell me if a…" She was interrupted by the familiar tone of Detective Baldomero.

She turned on, hearing his voice.

"Abigail?" Baldomero called, "Ah yes, it is you — and you've a companion with you?" He was staring at Pete.

Offering his hand, "Hello," Pete said. "I'm Pete,— Steve Douglas's brother."

"Ah, I see…" the detective's demeanour changed from inquisitive to apologetic. "I'm sorry, but there's still no sign of Steve. But please be assured we're doing everything to find him." Baldomero informed before adding. "You're familiar. Have we met before?"

"I don't think so. I'm pretty sure I would remember." Pete replied, but he became vague and dropped his gaze.

"I am pretty good with faces. It comes with the territory," was Baldomero's candid response. He shrugged,

"Oh well; it will come to me." His stance shifted to face Abigail, "Thank you for coming."

"Please — tell me? Is Kirsty? — is she alive?" Abigail blurted.

"She is, and she's stable." Baldomero paused. Another man approached. "This is Gonzalo," the detective announced, "He's supporting me with this case."

Abigail smiled as Gonzalo nodded his hello. "I don't mean to sound rude but, can I go to her?" her uneasiness growing as she stared at both Baldomero and Gonzalo. "Please — when can I visit her?"

"Try to remain calm," suggested Pete. "We'll get to her soon enough?" he slid his arm around her shoulder. "Is it feasible?" Pete asked.

"If you follow me," Baldomero said, and pointed towards the lifts. "I will take you to the doctor."

On the first floor Baldomero ushered them into an empty office, "If you wait in here — I'll find the physician taking care of Kirsty."

Abigail wasn't sure who Pete was trying to reassure when he spoke, "I'm certain she'll be fine."

"I'm scared to death," Abigail sobbed. "What's happened to her? They're not telling us a thing." She felt a need to be held and threw her arms around him. They parted when the door opened and in walked a leathery-faced doctor, followed by the detective.

Without waiting for introductions, Abigail asked, "How is she?"

He introduced himself anyway, "I'm Doctor Kadakia," he sat down opposite and pointed to two grey-plastic chairs. They accepted the hint.

"The patient -your friend — has suffered damage to her skull, face and neck," Kadakia informed, talking over Abigail's judder of a sob. "Your friend's condition is stable," he affirmed, fiddling with the stethoscope draped around his collar. "And is responding well to treatment."

"Okay," Abigail nodded and rubbed her eyes with the palm of her hands, "So when can I see her?"

"In normal cases, I'd restrict visiting to direct family," Kadakia explained. "But, because of this situation — I'll forgo the usual rules and allow you to visit." He didn't smile, but stayed stern and detached. "Although most of her bruises are quite severe, she will heal; leaving her with a few scars." He shoved his hand through his lustrous silver hair, "But, it isn't the personal injuries which concern me."

Abigail listened in silence and allowed the doctor to speak.

"The patient received both physical and psychological damage," Kadakia continued while Abigail dabbed tears from her face. "You may have to prepare yourself," He noticed Abigail's vacant face, "When she came too, she attacked me and another of the surgeons. She was so aggressive, we had limited choice but to sedate her."

Shocked, Abigail held her hand up to her mouth. "Oh my God," she glanced at Pete, "What's happened to her?"

"Your friend has been beaten…"

"What monster could have done this?" Abigail gasped. "Dear God — what has Kirsty been through?" unchecked, tears flowed. "I've heard enough — doctor," she snapped with an acerbic manner, "When can I see her?"

"I am preparing you, so the injuries do not startle you," Kadakia said, "To help you realize the swelling this has caused. What I am struggling to convey is…"

"I may not recognize her. Is that it? Doc?" she interrupted, "Who or what bastard could have managed this?"

It was Detective Baldomero who explained, "When my officers found Kirsty — she was beneath the body of her assailant. This man turns out to have received a fatal dose. I'm still waiting for toxicology to come back, but I suspect heroin or a similar opioid."

Pete closed his eyes and pressed his fingers into their lids. He was the first to talk. "When you say fatal — do you mean this person — he's dead? Right?"

"That's correct," Baldomero affirmed. "His death — we're uncertain how, but it looks that Kirsty killed him." He looked at Pete's reaction, and something seemed off. He couldn't quite pin it down. "We came upon the corpse of a second woman in the same room. She appears to have been battered to death — mutilated beyond recognition. Again, it isn't confirmed, but I believe the individual who attacked Kirsty, to be the offender." He watched Abigail flinch when he spoke of the term battered to death, then noticed Pete's empty-eyed, unemotional face, "My best guess — is the man attacked both women, but somehow Kirsty got the better of him. We also discovered the body of another man — we recognize him, as he used to be a doctor. Looks like he suffered a seizure, but the coroner's report will let us know more."

Pete's tone was distant, monotonous, and detached. "That poor girl."

It seemed only Baldomero picked up on it, and he watched Pete with increasing wariness as Pete's demeanour lacked any warmth and a suspicious Baldomero studied him. We have met before; I know we have. I have known of psychopaths to express more sorrow than you are showing me now. Something is off about you. Suddenly, a tap at the door cut short his thoughts, and a nurse entered.

After chatting with Kadakia, she left the room. The doctor stared at Abigail and announced, "It appears Kirsty is awake,"

"Take me to her." She responded and stood up, "Please — I need to see her."

Purplish bruises swelled her face. Her battered body bore the medals from her aggressor's anger as violet blotches against her chalk skin. The swelling of her cheeks forced Kirsty's jaw shut, whilst finger marks collared her throat with a mottled blue neckerchief of violence. From her mouth stretched a white plastic endotracheal intubation tubing. A ventilator pumped its rhythmic thub-ub, thub-ub. While an echo-cardiograph's insistent be-beep, be-beep pinged into Kirsty's ear.

A nurse studied Kirsty's vitals when Kirsty attempted to move, but she couldn't. Straps around her wrists and ankles secured her to the bed. Kirsty wanted to scream out, but couldn't. Why can't I open my mouth? She panicked. Her tongue rubbed against something solid and a strong metal taste filled her senses. Or was it blood? Kirsty couldn't be certain.

Kirsty flinched when she felt warm but delicate hands upon her. They held her wrist and checked her pulse. More movement and someone pushed the lid of her right eye open, then needles of light stabbed with blinding force. Kirsty snapped her eyelid lid shut after the undesirable intrusion and blinked in rapid succession. A flaming sunset haze which fogged her vision cleared, and Kirsty noticed the sterile smell of the hospital room.

A doctor clad in blue hospital scrubs had entered the area and, from Kirsty's vantage point, he appeared almost freak-show tall. His mannerisms exuded a competence which only doctors carry. Confidence, yes, but he had more than that. An endearing tenderness and empathy which spilled from him. Kirsty wasn't convinced, she mistrusted him because of the way Drulovic had treated her.

"Hello, again," the doctor said before shifting to talk with the nurse. He pointed to the tubing. "I expect that can be taken out." Returning his concern to Kirsty, he revealed, "My name is Doctor Kadakia." He scribbled his observations down on a chart at the side of the bed. "You're in the hospital. Can you recall? Do you know what has happened to you?" He glanced down. "Sorry about these." He placed his hand on the restraints. "They're a safety measure because of the fight you gave yesterday."

Kirsty couldn't blink away from the penlight, which the doctor flicked over her eye.

"You have friends waiting to see you." Kadakia announced and peered over his shoulder toward the door. "I will let them in once I have checked you over." He picked up a full plastic syringe and plugged it into the cannula jutting out from Kirsty's left wrist. "I will give you something for the discomfort. It will make you feel a little drowsy. Let me know if your pain becomes worse." Kadakia pushed the plunger down upon the syringe. "Your visitors can't stay long. You're not strong enough and need to rest."

— ▢ —

Kirsty's appearance was that of an emaciated old woman, and Abigail was aghast as she gawked at this unrecognizable person who carried little resemblance to her once vibrant friend. Her pallid skin was both sallow and marbled with angry purple bruising. Her hair, once a silken strawberry blond, now as lacklustre as old straw. Kirsty's left eye, an over ripened plum, swollen closed and dark purple. Her other, as indigo as twilight but not so inflamed, allowing her to see out through a coral encrusted slit.

Was this the correct person? Abigail wondered, "Are you positive this is Kirsty?" she murmured, disbelieving this was her friend. She shifted to face Baldomero who'd stayed close. "It looks nothing like her."

"We tried to brace you for this." Baldomero said, solemnly, and shook his head, "But, I suppose nobody can prepare you."

Gonzalo added, "It is a good job we found her when we did."

Pete watched Kirsty lying on the hospital bed. He recognized this was her and remained silent.

In her quest for answers, Abigail asked no-one in particular, "Who? Who would carry out something like this? Why would someone do a thing like this?"

Neither Pete nor the detective offered an answer.

— ☐ —

Movement in Kirsty's blurred periphery drew her attention. Shapes swam in and out of focus as she observed people enter the room. The familiar voice of Abigail echoed into her dreams and made Kirsty's heart pound.

She listened to Abigail's compassionate words that whispered, "My God — you, poor darling?" Felt the genial warmth of her friend's touch thaw her chilled skin.

"We've been looking everywhere for you," said Abigail, as she placed her hand on Kirsty's shoulder. "Kirsty — it's me."

Abigail's delicate features fell into view, and Kirsty wanted to turn towards her. Attempted to fling her arms up, needed to hug and be hugged by her friend. Then the image of someone else caused her to come to an abrupt stop, and her fear returned.

Kirsty became confused and questioned herself, is my mind playing some sick, twisted trick? Fear turned into terror. *He can't be here.* Hyperventilating, she gasped in dread as she stared into the brilliant blue eyes of this wolf in sheep's clothing.

I recognize you. Kirsty's brain clanged as a thousand bell towers rang inside her skull. *You can't hide from me.* Her sinister thoughts screamed; *I see who you are.*

She bit into the plastic of the tubing. "Nnn — nnn — nnn," Kirsty grunted. Her eyes fixated upon the menacing blue spheres of Steve's killer, who now approached the bed.

Kirsty willed herself to move. She ignored her suffering as she battled against the restraints. A persistent be-beep, be-beep echoed fast, too fast. *Why — why are you with him? Why? He's a monster?* Her fear-driven thoughts spiralled. *Abs? Why — why him? Why this savage beast?* She longed to scream, wished to call out, demanded to warn her friend of the danger. But she couldn't. Deep inside, the steam piston hammered against her chest.

Doctor Kadakia stepped in. "Step back, something's wrong," he pushed Abigail aside.

"Kirsty…" she screamed as Abigail watched her friend convulse.

Kirsty's half-open eye remained fixed on Mr Blue Eyes. I know who you are. Her inner voice shattered her skull.

Pete sneered as his bright blue eyes twinkled. His contempt oozed, and his soothing words mocked. "Sshh — My Sweet Darling — it's all okay, it's over now."

A Broken Swan

Sergeant Philips looked through the window of his little Ford Fiesta at an aircraft as it sliced its path through the grey filth of the cotton ball clouds. Opposite him danced the overhanging limbs of a weeping willow. Its branches chattered at the squall, which blew litter along the gutters of Silver Street. More rain moving in, he supposed with a shrug.

He glanced over to the file, which lay open in his passenger seat. Documents from Inspector Collins and her officer 572 report, plus intel he had gained. The opening page was a colour photograph of Peter Kilkenny, whose cold and calculating eyes stared up at the Sergeant. He was the brother to Steven Kilkenny who after their parents' demise had been adopted by Ruth and Mark Douglas. Steven had taken their second name to become Steven Douglas.

The last known whereabouts of Peter was the visit to his brother's adoptive parents' home, outside which Phillips had parked. He sighed his hesitation to step into the dismal day and closed the folder. Taking the keys from the car's ignition, Phillips stepped out into the gale.

— ☐ —

The doorbell chimed out Beethoven's fifth symphony, but it produced him no reply. The Sergeant pushed the bell, and Beethoven played once again. No-one appeared. Phillips gave four loud thuds with his hand upon the door, vigorous enough to vibrate the framework. Then he pressed the chime for the third time but conceded his defeat and turned to leave.

From over the fence came a frail voice of an elderly woman. "Pardon me," she said, but the snatching wind stole her words. She called again, but failed to make Phillips hear as he walked away. "Excuse me — officer?" Waving her arms, "Yoo-hoo. Excuuuuse Me?"

He had arrived at his car and was about to clamber inside when he spotted the crooked framed woman perched upon a cane in one hand and waving at him with her other. She lived in the neighbouring house.

"Morning," he said as he neared.

"Don't stand out there, you'll catch your death." She responded and gestured for him to follow her inside.

Toast crumbed at the edges of her mouth and was dusted down the front of her pale blue blouse patterned with tiny yellow daisies. This she wore inside out, and a flap hung loose from her grey polyester trousers. She radiated a genuine friendliness and slight naivety, found in the young and the elderly. Phillips couldn't help to notice her brown moccasin slippers on the wrong feet. A sadness swallowed his heart because she reminded him of when his mother had first been diagnosed with dementia.

"They're in." she was forthright and stated, "Ruth and Mark." Pointing towards their property. "They're home. Haven't been out for a couple of days." The vivid red cheeks on the woman's face emptied of colour. "Is everything all right?"

"Yes, Madam," answered Phillips. "You mention Mr and Mrs Douglas are in?" he peered back toward the house. "How can you be certain?"

"They always tell me when they're going out," she smiled. "They look after me, they are splendid people." Her face slackened with sorrow. "I must be such a bother," she murmured. "I can't get out anymore — not since my Arthur left me." She blessed herself by touching her shoulders and forehead, "God rest him." Her eyes glazed, and she forgot about the Sergeant. When her attention returned, she said,

"Whenever Ruth or Mark travel to the shops — they ask if I require anything. Have never let me down. That's how I know they haven't been out today. Wait, it is Thursday, isn't it? Oh blast, I'm in such a muddle these days."

You're losing her, he realized and interrupted. "And they haven't been out?" Phillips asked. "Perhaps they were in a rush this morning, or they have forgotten," he suggested. "People can forget."

"No — officer. You see?" And she pointed to a vacant spot on the beige carpet in the porch's corner. "There isn't any red top." She said.

"Red-top?" Philips quizzed.

"Milk," she chuckled, "There isn't any red-top milk." Her hazel eyes narrowed, and she looked confused, as if unfamiliar with her surroundings. Her gaze fixed upon the police officer, and calmness reasserted itself. "In the past eight years — since my Arthur passed — God rest him," she blessed herself again. "They have never, once, failed to pick up my milk." This appeared to be a fact she seemed most proud of. "Even when Mr Smoothie visited the other day — they still brought some round."

"Mr Smoothie?" quizzed the Sergeant.

"Yes," she answered as she flattened out the creases of her daisy patterned blouse. A gust of wind rushed in from outside to ruffle the sparse locks of her greyish white hair. "Some high-flier from the city. All fancy pants in his expensive car." She fixed the Sergeant with a knowing stare. "He didn't fool me," she scoffed. "I took one look at him and told myself, 'Martha, he's a bad sort, that one.' It's what I said to myself," concern etched onto her face. "I'm becoming concerned — officer. About Ruth and Mark." Pointing again at their residence. "They'd have been over to see me by now. But nothing?" She pointed at her front window. "I should know — I have little else to do these days — other than sit staring out of that blessed window." Martha now spoke with confidence. "Nobody has been or gone from Ruth and Mark's house. Not since Mr Smoothie last visited."

"Would they have left you a key?" asked Sergeant Philips.

"There is no need for me to have a spare key — Silly." Martha chuckled again, "I would only lose it." Pointing toward the hanging baskets of trailing petunia, whirling in the breeze as they hung on the veranda of Ruth and Mark's house. "In the basket — the one on the left side of the porch. They placed the key just inside the pot." She pointed a warning finger at Phillips. "You make certain you wipe your feet, you hear. Ruth will not be happy if you ruin her carpets."

— ☐ —

Before retrieving the spare key, Sergeant Phillips approached Ruth and Mark's front door for the second time and rang the doorbell. Then he knelt to peep through their letterbox. This was when the distinctive pungent smell made him stop. An odour which triggered the alarm bells to clang around inside his head. A strong gagging smell of gas which came from the letterbox. He hadn't detected the gas earlier, but assumed the turbulent conditions had held it at bay.

His heart thundered as he thought, gas leak, and backed his way off the porch. He scanned the immediate area around the dwelling, searching for the cupboard to where the gas meter would be kept. It wasn't out front. On the right, a slim side-entry lead towards the rear gardens. A wrought-iron gate secured it closed, but no padlock to keep it locked. Just on the other part of the doorway was a small white plastic door sitting flat against the bricks of Ruth and Mark's house. Inside this door sat the gas meter and isolation valve. A notice printed in a broad red font read: In the event of a leak, turn this handle to its off position and call the emergency number above. Phillips turned off the gas, then hurried along the narrow pathway and out onto the rear paved veranda. The smell of gas was much stronger out here. Sergeant Philips found the back door bolted. Next, he peeped through a set of patio doors near to his left, but the cream-coloured curtains obscured his view. At first, he saw nothing out of the ordinary but, on closer investigation, and between the slimmest of gaps in the curtains. Phillips studied the soft cushioned fabric of a single seat sofa. Flopped over the sofa's edge was an arm. The rest of the body was out of sight, but, Phillips could tell from the swollen purplish fingers, the owner of this limb had perished.

Okay, think, Sergeant Phillips instructed himself, his police training taking over. "You need to evacuate all the homes," he told himself. "And you had better call in the fire brigade and the gas board. You're going to need help."

— ☐ —

Sergeant Philips combed his fingers through the thinning strands of hair covering his scalp and squinted out through the broad windows. He observed two wagtails, who flew a skittish dance across the parkland. He remained, with the evacuees of Silver Street, awaiting the all-clear to be announced.

A drone of voices from disrupted families who all studied him. Phillips knew he was the focus of their conversations, but found the looks of silent admiration disconcerting. Several had praised him for his wise reactions. Some went as far to say he was a hero. I'm no hero, Phillips thought. I was in the right place — at the right time. Anybody else would have acted the same. He made a casual shrug. It's just another day at the office.

A voice warbled from his radio and yanked him out of his reflections. "Serge, are you receiving? Over," the radio buzzed.

Unclipping the handset, "Phillips here. Go ahead, Bill."

"The Chief fire officer has given the all-clear, claims you're damn lucky," Bill's voice crackled in the handset. "The chief has reported two fatalities — says you better get to the house. Over."

Phillips closed his eyes and knew they would be Ruth and Mark Douglas. "Roger that. I'm on my way — over and out." he headed to the exit when the radio crackled again.

"Forensics are on the way," squawked Bill, "Collins is on route too and instructed she'll meet you at the scene."

— ☐ —

Police tape cordoned off the road with bright yellow barriers restricting entry to car or pedestrian. The distorted words, "Police line do not cross," had been stretched in the gale. Police officer Eddy stood guarding this part of the roadway and tipped the corner of his helmet toward Sergeant Phillips through way of acknowledgement.

"All okay, constable?" Phillips shouted as he ducked beneath the wind buzzed tape.

"Yes, Sir," came Eddy's reply.

In the distance, at the bottom end of the street, was the silhouetted shape of Bill Macey. Phillips radioed to him, "All okay down your side, Bill?"

"Everything normal — the usual media circus arriving, but nothing I can't handle — Sir."

Phillips instructed, "We may have an all-clear from the fire service, but nobody enters — unless authorized. Over and out."

"Roger that — Sarge," returned Bill.

Phillips approached one of two fire trucks, and a fire chief stood towards its back end, busy organizing the scene. The white helmet showed this was the officer in charge. She stared over at Phillips. "So you must be Sergeant Phillips?" the Chief said with a quizzical manner. "How you didn't wipe out this whole street, is beyond me?" shaking her head and pointed toward the house, "You have a crime scene inside — we have done our best to protect contamination, but we needed to make sure the building is safe to enter."

"And is it?" Phillips asked, "Is it safe?"

"You did the right thing — switching the gas supply off. That was the correct call," approved the chief with a nod. Chief slipped off her helmet, tucking it under an arm. "Yes — the emergency gas crew has established it's now safe. We found the oven in the kitchen switched on. But I think you should have a look, Sergeant."

Phillips looked up at the house, then asked, "How bad is it?"

"Well. I'm no doctor," stated the matter-of-fact Chief. "But I have seen enough road accidents to identify when someone suffers a broken neck." She harnessed the helmet back on, "You had better come with me — there's something I need to show you."

Walking up the path, they entered the porch, "Everybody in this street owes their lives to that electric meter." Chief said, pointing to an electricity card meter beneath the fuse board inside the hallway. "The electricity switched itself off in the early hours of this morning — if not for that, then boom." The chief used her hands to imitate an explosion. "We're lucky we didn't lose the entire road."

— ☐ —

Inside, Phillips moved into the front room to where Ruth's body lay sprawled over the settee, as if asleep. Her sallow cheeks, a mix of white-violet and her lips indigo-blue, the only noticeable signs of death. Ruth appeared to be resting. Perhaps she'd been dozing when the gas had filled the room. Phillips would wait for the coroner to inspect the carcass and left her in peace. Further into the house, he went into the back room. A gust rushed in from the wide patio doors to waft a slight bouquet of death toward him.

The chair which Philips had spied when looking through the narrow crack in the curtains earlier that morning. The TV screen's obsidian reflection became an art gallery of Mark's gruesome image. He bore the suggestions of a struggle. An ooze of dried blood ran from the corner of Mark's lip to drip a brownish-red stain on the carpet. Mark's eyes drooped half closed, his cheeks a deep violet. Bloat swelled Mark's face. However, the myriad of blow flies and other critters who were death's natural companions had been suppressed because of the gas.

"In here, Sergeant, in the kitchen," the fire chief announced. "I need to show you the oven."

The compressed kitchen had a table which took up most of the space in the middle of the room. A broken lamp placed at the table's centre, and at first, Phillips didn't grasp what he was staring at.

"Look closer at the lamp — the bulb in particular," the chief said.

"It's ruined?" Phillips commented.

Philips's eyes followed the lamp-lead down and noticed this to be plugged into a timer-switch. The same type of timer that Sergeant Phillips always recommended residents use when attending his regular neighbourhood watch meetings. Looking back at the chief, "And you have removed nothing from this kitchen — since you entered?"

"Like I said, Sergeant. Once I understood, we were dealing with a crime scene, we did our best to preserve it. We isolated the cooker to make it safe, but haven't moved the lamp." Confirmed the Chief, "The families in this street need to be grateful that these residents were on a pay as you go electric meter. The meter ran out of credit during the night." She looked around the area and shook her head, "If not for that…" Chief left the sentence unfinished. "There wouldn't have been anything left of this place." She waved her hands around the room. "You would have rubble as evidence to work through."

Movement from the front door attracted their attention and Phillips recognized the voice of Inspector Collins when she called through to them.

"I'm in the kitchen, Ma-am," Phillips responded, "Keep walking straight," he shifted back to the fire chief and added, "Thanks for your help, I will let you carry on."

— ☐ —

"Sergeant," stated an authoritarian Inspector Collins, "Chief," she addressed with a blunt, tight-lipped expression. She scrutinized the eight by twelve-foot kitchen. The cupboards were light oak with Formica worktops of imitation granite. She noted the milky-grey dishwater in the sink and clean drip-dried dishes placed upon the drainer.

A white gas oven stood next to the adjoining wall. Someone had depressed the dials for its cooking rings into their open position. Its oven door propped open with a chair, and the oven dial also adjusted to release the gas flow. The automatic ignition, a safety feature on the cooker, had been wrecked. Collins turned her attention to the table and the lamp upon it. She leant forward for a better inspection, studying the shattered bulb and its exposed filament. "Well, you don't see this every day," she said. Retrieving a pen from the inside pocket of her jacket and following it down toward the timer. She made a mental note of the time, which had been set at 4:30 am. The timer's clock had stopped working at 3:45 am. Collins whistled, "This could have been a serious wake-up call."

"It's been a lucky escape," said Philips, his comments blunt. "Not so for the Douglas's. I suspect they were gone long before the gas would have taken them."

"Where are they?" Collins asked,

"Mrs Douglas is in the front room," Phillips explained. "The husband is in the back room — neck broken."

Nothing appeared to be improper with Ruth Douglas. The net curtains which draped across the room's small bay window drew Inspector Collins's scrutiny. A collection of six ornaments were in place upon the windowsill. Five white swan figurines, all in various postures, placed neat and intact. However, the sixth white swan lay shattered; its tall neck and wing were lying next to it.

Detective Collins bent forward for a closer examination and scrutinized this broken figure. It scattered several fragments on the sill. Beneath the window's ledge lay further fragmented shards on the lilac Axminster carpet.

"This is odd?" she said, puzzled, and examined the splintered stump of the swan's missing neck. Her nose almost brushing the porcelain ornament where the slightest remnant of blood stained the now jagged neck. "There is a light bead of what looks to be dried blood — it must be from whoever smashed it. Get forensics on this straight away."

"Yes, ma-am," responded Phillips.

As if on cue, Bill Macey's voice crackled from the radio. "Forensics are here, Sarge, and the coroner. Shall I send them to you? Over."

"Go ahead, thanks, Bill. Over and out."

Out of Options

Doctor Kadakia insisted both Abigail and Pete leave and allow Kirsty the chance to rest. Detective Baldomero helped the pair organize two suites at an adjacent guest house. A bland hotel of a cramped three-storey, rust-red brick construction. This looked out on the many small flats in a poor commercial side street called Calle de Màrquez.

It was mid-afternoon, and the day had been an exhausting one. Abigail's eyes felt raw and stung when she blinked. "After what Kirsty has been through," Abigail said with a hapless whisper, "I shouldn't whine but, I feel like death."

Twisting a bobble into her hair, she scraped the tight ringlets back from her face and fixed it into a rough bun. They mounted the hotel's three concrete steps. "It's not the Savoy, but it will do." Pete shrugged as he shoved open a huge plate glass entrance. "How was Joyce?" he asked and held the door wide allowing her to go in before him. "I'm presuming it was Joyce who you called back there?" Pete thumbed over his shoulder as he pointed back toward the hospital.

As soon as she could upon leaving, Abigail made the phone call to Joyce. Giving her the news that they had found Kirsty.

"Y… Yes," she stammered, her thoughts elsewhere. "Joyce took it as predicted." Abigail replied with an anxious expression. "We didn't talk for long. I will ring her again later. After I freshen up." They entered the hotel foyer and were embraced by an unmistakable funk of cannabis. Abigail wrinkled up her nose and quipped, "Well — we'll be okay if we wish to get wasted."

After booking into their accommodation and following the hotel's crimson-eyed, weed infused concierge up one flight of stairs, they stood outside the doors of two separate bedrooms. The attendant opened both before handing over the key cards and left Abigail and Pete in peace.

The rooms were back-to-back with a symmetrical layout. A slim three-foot wide entrance hall led into the room's central area. A separate bed pushed beneath a steel barred window and a dilapidated looking pine wardrobe. The paint blistered doorway halfway down the entrance corridor hid a basic bathroom.

Turning to Pete, Abigail declared, "I'm beat," giving an elaborate yawn as she stretched her arms above her. "If it's okay with you, and before we head back to Kirsty. I'm going to run a bath."

"Yeah, that's fine," Pete responded. "I plan to get rid of this." He held up his light suitcase. "And then? I may go for a walk." He shrugged. His eyes became watery as he played to Abigail's tenderness, "I need to create some sort of sense out of this."

Captivated by his concern, Abigail fell for Pete's charade. She pulled him close and hugged into him. "We'll catch these bastards," her words impassioned as she made this promise. "The ones who have done this. We'll make them pay."

Pete's emotion slid away as he looked over her shoulder. His lips curled into a sneer as his thoughts became sinister. *Kirsty will not live long enough.* He grinned as he held Abigail's embrace. *And you?* He hugged Abigail a little tighter. *Huh, well, you're just another slut whom I can sell to my Russian friends.*

— □ —

Detective Baldomero had returned to the Medianoche Exótica. He strolled the same cobbled street towards the entrance as he'd wandered in his earlier case to determine Stefania Florescu's identification. Back then, there wasn't an official cordon in place, nor was there a significant police presence. Music had played into the night, and party revellers danced beneath the club's neon signed frontage. Now all was silent, and as Baldomero turned to glance back along the route, the flashback hit. The recollection made him falter a couple of strides. It gripped him in the fierce clutch of dread as he recalled the man he had barged into at his original visit when leaving this business. "I knew I'd seen you before," the detective shouted with indignation. "I said I would remember you."

His outburst had attracted attention from a police official standing guard. Baldomero ignored the odd way the officer scrutinized him and scurried back along the pavement to his car. He needed to get back to the hospital. He had to warn Abigail.

Baldomero wished he'd acted upon his gut instinct. Most people would have been horrified when listening to the ordeal their friend had been through, especially if they still had a family member missing. But Pete's attitude hadn't appeared to be one of concern for Kirsty or fear about the safety of his brother. Not like Abigail, who'd been distraught. There had been something about Peter's eyes, and he hadn't reacted in a way Baldomero would have expected. Instead, they held a distant, emotionless, and glazed expression. This absence of compassion had first raised his distrust, and now he recalled where he had met Peter before; Baldomero was further convinced Abigail's male companion shouldn't be trusted.

To confirm suspicion, an Interpol alert email beeped from his phone, which he'd held out to call Abigail. His display showed Inspector Collins had linked him to this alert, and Baldomero knew this would be relevant. First, it provided an advisory warning about Peter Kilkenny who had become someone of considerable interest to the British serious organized crime department. Baldomero scanned through the following attachments, found the file of officer 572 of particular significance. Remembering how the couple in Salou had been executed in such a clinical attack, which fitted the view the assailant had previous military training. Kilkenny or Officer 572, as the document specified, revealed about his past special forces' involvement. The detective had little doubt Peter Kilkenny was the suspect they hunted.

On route back to the hospital, Baldomero rang Abigail's mobile, but it rang out without response. He would make certain Gonzalo could protect Kirsty, and he could locate Abigail then apprehend Kilkenny before he was too late.

— ☐ —

Pete went to visit the hotel receptionist and picked up an extra two key-cards for both his and Abigail's rooms. After obtaining the requested spare keys, he strode out of the inn and down the front steps. "What the hell happened?" Incensed by the turn of events, Pete spoke to nothing besides the warm evening breeze. He snarled, "How did she kill Marco?"

A group of youths walked past, throwing him a cautious sideways glance. Pete ignored them and proceeded down the street toward a fast-food restaurant further ahead. Becoming enraged, "I just don't get how? How can she have done it?" Anger overwhelmed him like a firestorm raging through a tinder dry canyon.

"Well, it doesn't matter if you find out or not — she killed Marco and that's that."

Pete reached the restaurant's entrance but found his appetite had passed, and he went on strolling down the pavement. Before he even realized, Pete was outside the hospital. Kirsty had recognized him, that much he had learned from the look on her face. At this moment, doctors overlooked her mumbled rants. They considered it to be that of a woman balancing over the precipice of the deranged. But the truth would materialize, and time was fast running out. It wouldn't be long before they would take notice and understand her crazed ramblings to be true. He had to get rid of her.

"What about Steve's cash?" Pete hissed, reeling on the spot. "If Kirsty is to inherit Steve's capital, then I need to make certain she can't receive it. The money is mine."

In the parking lot Pete halted and took a step back when he spotted the detective and Gonzalo. Their backs were toward him and stooped over the boot of the police car. "I won't get close enough to Kirsty." Pete said with disappointed frustration. "Looks like I'll have to return later."

— ☐ —

Before he arrived at the hospital, Baldomero called inspector Collins. She informed him of the deaths of Steve Douglas's foster parents and the need to apprehend Peter Kilkenny for questioning. Kilkenny was considered dangerous and not to be under-estimated. So, it was with trepidation that Baldomero drove into the hospital car park and met a bewildered Gonzalo.

"What's going on Nick?" asked the confused Gonzalo.

"There isn't time to explain," answered Baldomero, his manner brusque as he stepped out of the car and went straight to the boot and snatched it open. "I knew something wasn't right with him," he unlocked the weapons compartment.

That's when Gonzalo grabbed his shoulder. "Nick?" concern evident in his voice. "What is it? Tell me?"

"Okay – listen," Baldomero said, his words as brisk as his actions. "I remembered where I have met him."

"Met who Nick?" Gonzalo quizzed the abstruse detective. "You're not making a lot of sense."

"Kilkenny, Peter Kilkenny – he owns, amongst other businesses, the Medianoche Exótica. He is wanted by the British for questioning over murders in England." He took a breath whilst his friend digested what he'd just said. "He is military trained; Kilkenny is ex-special forces. Don't you see? He is the one responsible for all this. It's all falling into place.

Gonzalo began to say, "Then that means Abig..." but the detective cut him off.

"It means Abigail is in serious trouble. And we need to put things in place to make sure Kirsty is out of danger too." He slammed his hands hard into the open lid of the car. "Peter Kilkenny is our main suspect."

Baldomero reached inside and took out his service pistol. Its cold metal grip pressed hard into his hand. His fingers trembled as they encircled this instrument of death.

"You had better wear this," said Gonzalo and held out a Kevlar body armoured vest. "You can't be too careful."

Holding the pistol in his right hand, Baldomero released its ammo clip into his left. The metallic click focused his attention as he checked the guns magazine. Loaded to capacity. He made it safe then placed the weapon by the side of its case, turning to Gonzalo, "I only have the one pistol and one vest."

"There are plenty of officers here with weapons. I'll be safe enough. But it's you I am worried about," answered Gonzalo.

Baldomero stripped his shirt as he put the Kevlar vest beneath it. "Thanks," he said when Gonzalo passed him the pistol. "I'll go after Kilkenny. Don't worry. It'll be okay." But Baldomero remembered the warning Collins had given. The edge in the detective's voice sounded far from convincing. He looked at Gonzalo and changing the subject, said, "Keep an eye on Kirsty."

Pete had a compulsion to kill and he knew it wouldn't go away without being sated. *It's a shame*, thought Pete, *but if I can't get in to finish Kirsty, then Abigail will have to do.* He began the walk back to the hotel, allowing the heat of his earlier anger to return.

"You must regain control," Pete said to himself. "What's done – is done," he shrugged. "You will kill Kirsty before anyone believes her."

Pete pushed through the door to the hotel. His thoughts turning to Abigail and his lust for violence brewed. *If I'm quick, then Abigail will be easy prey.* Pete sneered a grin and approached Abigail's bedroom door. Pressing his ear flat against its cold wooden surface he listened. His own rapid breathing galloped inside his head. The journey back from the hospital and his eagerness to reach the hotel. Together with his quick ascent of the stairs, were all having an effect. Taking deep steadier breaths, he waited for the hammer inside his skull to soften. Pete listened to the gentle splashing sound of bath water. *Perfect*, Pete's grin was full of malice. He presented the spare key card, twisted the door handle, and crept inside.

— ☐ —

The tepid water of Abigail's bath tickled the underside of her chin as it lapped around her neck. Exhaustion having claimed her, she'd drifted into a deep but dreamless sleep until the lily of the valley scented bath water had rushed up her nostrils. She bolted upright in a fit of wheezing coughs that sent ripples to lap over the tub's edge.

"You, stupid cow," Abigail spluttered, "You're going to drown yourself, you – silly sod." The walls of the white tiled bathroom gave an acoustic echo to her voice. The reverberated sound bounced back twice as loud.

From outside the bathroom door a clicking noise drew her attention. Startled, what was that? Abigail wondered, an uncanny sense of fear welled up inside her, in silence she sat and strained hard to listen. Wishing her ears to hear. *Should I call out?* Abigail deliberated. *Perhaps it's room service? Oh, Abs. This is ridiculous. Why are you such a scaredy-cat? The noise is from next door, it will be Pete back from his walk.* She felt foolish, and scolded, "Stop being so pathetic, Abs."

A series of loud bangs knocked her bedroom door which startled Abigail further and made her yelp out in surprise.

— ☐ —

Pete listened to the sounds coming from inside the bathroom. He went further into the bedroom. *I need something to tie her up,* pulling the telephone cable out from its wall socket he tore it out from the back. *This'll do,* he grinned.

"Is someone there?" Abigail called.

His grin vanished and he felt every bit the proverbial rabbit caught in the glare of a car's headlamp and froze. A sigh of relief escaped him when he realised she was talking to herself. His eyes darted around every corner and searched the bedroom. The clothes she had been wearing were strewn across a brown mattress. He picked up her blouse and scrunched it into a ball then held it against his face. He savoured her scent, a mix of deodorant tainted body odour which excited his primal desires.

A vibrating hum came from Abigail's mobile which buzzed upon the floor. Watching the black rectangular object chatter against the carpet he lifted his foot ready to stomp the smartphone into oblivion. *Wait- not yet,* he decided, his foot hovering inches above the device. *If you smash it, the noise will alert her.*

That's when someone banged on the bedroom door and almost stopped his heart.

— ☐ —

Bang – bang- bang.

It came again with equal urgency.

Bang – bang – bang. Again, but louder.

Pete watched the door shake within the frame. From inside the bathroom came Abigail's surprised scream and Pete was already on the move. He paced around the small space inside the bedroom. Again, someone thumped the hotel room door. Pete's heart leapt a thousand beats per second. *Well, this is an unexpected situation you've got yourself in, he admitted.* But fuelled by desperation and galvanised by panic he looked towards the door. The thin strip of light from underneath was blocked, he could tell the hammerings were not that of the hotel concierge. Glancing over at the bars on the bedroom window. *You're not getting out that way. What do I do now? I'm trapped. Cornered, like a rat.* Pete's eyes darted this way and that. He searched for a hiding place. Shit. Pete's foot hit the broken telephone, so he picked it up. *Not much time. Now, what – shit – shit. Come on, think?* Movement from the bathroom. "Shit," he cussed under his breath. He was out of options and out of luck. *Aargh nowhere to go,* he screamed in silence.

A voice called out as the door hammered, "Abigail?"

Bang – bang – bang.

Pete recognised the detective and rolled his eyes with despair. Under his breath he said, "Great. This is all I need."

"Abigail?" Baldomero called again.

Bang- bang – bang.

"Abigail – are you there? – this is Detective Baldomero."

Pete stepped backwards into the bedroom and almost tumbled over the corner of the bed. An idea sprung to mind. He lifted the mattress to check the space beneath it. The bed low to the floor, too low. Nowhere to hide. The scrape of a latch on the bathroom door. His back struck something solid, which creaked as if encouraging him inside. Spinning on the spot, Pete stifled the impulse to cheer, "Yes." Instead, he tore open the doors of the wardrobe and plunged into its confines, closing the door with himself inside.

"Shit," Pete whispered in a breathless panic. "Too close — Pete — too damn close."

Vanished

Kirsty clawed through the inkiness of her sedated sleep and woke to discover the tracheal tubing removed. The straps which had once secured her to the bed were no longer in place, and she could move with a little more relief. She drew her hand up to the inflammation of her face and danced delicate fingers around her left cheek. The swelling had diminished enough to oblige her to squint and open her eye in full on her right side. Kirsty stared into an alien realm of kaleidoscopic crimson swirls. The fluorescent glare, from razorblade lighting, hurt enough to make Kirsty wince before her vision settled and blurred images cleared. She attempted sitting up, but her washing machine head made her wretch and almost vomit as movement became awash with napalm's fury, which charged a galloping torrent of anguish.

A nurse came into the room. "Detener," she said, admonishing as she moved to Kirsty's aide, "Detener. Debes quedarte quieto." Looking into the world of turmoil that radiated from Kirsty's semi-open eyes. She pleaded with Spanish accented English, "Stop — you must remain still."

"Please — I have to sit up," Kirsty argued, but her words became incomprehensible.

"I will get the doctor," the nurse informed and scurried away.

Kadakia entered the room, "Please — you must lie down," he added, "Please allow me to check you over."

Kirsty slurred, "Pleash," she responded, "I neeth to wan Abssss."

Kadakia wasn't confident Kirsty would not attack him again as he pulled the cotton bed sheets up to cover her legs. "You didn't require the machines, and I removed the restraints. You're not here against your will." He examined her face. "I have given you something to reduce the swelling, which seems to have helped." He spoke with compassion and held on to her hand as he declared. "We'll do everything we can to make you comfortable. Once you're fit enough, you can go home. But, for now, you must rest and regain your strength."

Kirsty listened to his comments, but her mind yelled, *you need to get out of here, Abigail needs you.*

— ☐ —

Gonzalo headed into the hospital. *Nick's right*, he admitted, *someone should remain at the ward in case Peter Kilkenny shows up. The building was immense, with many entrances. It would be an effort to keep secure. Only he and Baldomero knew the danger Kilkenny posed, and it would be easy for a man like him to enter.*

None of the police officers reported anything unusual when Gonzalo briefed each of the four standing inside the reception foyer. He headed to Kirsty's room and walked down the long corridor. He checked in with Doctor Kadakia, who was carrying out his rounds.

"How's the patient?" Gonzalo asked, concerned but direct.

"Tougher than she looks." The physician answered. "She is off the ventilator."

"That's excellent," nodded Gonzalo, "Is she up for a visitor?"

"I would prefer her to rest," Kadakia said with a shake of his head.

"I understand." Gonzalo moved a little closer and dropped his voice. "I just need to ask a few questions. We believe the individual answerable for Kirsty's abduction is the same guy who was here earlier today. The fellow who's with her friend Abigail." He studied the doctor, believing his remarks would have an effect. When they didn't, he added, "I wanted to get confirmation from Kirsty?"

"Because of the swelling in her face and throat, she can't communicate well. Plus the medication we have her on." Explained the physician. "I don't think she would make an expert witness to confirm anything. I'm sorry, but I must insist you wait until tomorrow. My patient needs her rest."

— ☐ —

Kirsty waited until she was alone before making her move. She tore the cannula from her left wrist and tossed it aside before placing her hands palm flat on the bed at either side of her hips, then shoved up. A barrage of pain shot a trillion stars behind her eyes. Battling her dizziness, she pushed harder and shifted herself into a seating position. The room spun a merry-go-round of colour. *How the hell can you help Abigail?* She worried. But the spinning top inside her skull eased. *I must get out,* she ordered herself.

Kirsty pulled herself forward and wriggled her torso until her feet dangled toward the floor. *Now comes the fun part,* she determined, hands flat against the mattress, advancing until her feet reached the frigid floor. Putting more pressure on her legs she supressed a scream as she hauled herself to a crooked standing position. Unable to straighten, she hobbled, an old crone shuffle. Like a reluctant child refusing to leave the play area, her left leg dragged behind her as she moved forwards. Each small stumble caused the next stagger to become a little smoother.

Kirsty willed herself over to the doorway, where she recovered before slipping open the door and treading out of the room. Kirsty hobbled away from Gonzalo, who had been conversing with the doctor. She was stooped and used the wall as support, expecting to be confronted, but it didn't happen. Kirsty staggered with each jerked step; she gained in determination. Reaching the dogleg in the passageway part way down the corridor, and walked out of view. Ahead, facing her, were the silver doors of the lift, which slid open as she neared. Two people wandered past, ignoring her as they went by. Kirsty seized the moment and strode through the closing lift doors into a squared mirrored box and leant against the inner rail.

— □ —

Gonzalo had looked at the hunched woman who shuffled barefoot further down the corridor. Her dishevelled appearance made him guess he was observing an elderly woman, whom he soon disregarded. He strolled towards the closed door of Kirsty's room and nudged it open. To his dismay, he realized the bed in which Kirsty had once lain now sat empty.

Kadakia let out a sigh of relief as he watched the patient stabilize. "Okay, nurse — I think we have this under control." He said, mopping perspiration from off his brow, then stared across to the nurse and saw Gonzalo standing in the open doorway.

Kadakia mistook Gonzalo's alarmed look as one of concern for the case that had just been treated and proclaimed, "He gave us a little scare," pointing to the man lying down on the bed, "but I'm confident he'll be okay."

"Where is she, doctor?" Gonzalo said, his manner blunt, his remarks almost biting at the physician.

"Where's who?" Kadakia asked, bewildered by the unexpected panic.

"The young woman?" snapped the acerbic Gonzalo. "Where's Kirsty?"

The medic replied, "She's next door, but like I said…"

Gonzalo's abrupt response cut him off. "She isn't there." He pointed toward the unoccupied room. "It's empty."

"I don't understand." He said. "She can't have just vanished."

"Well, she isn't in there?" Gonzalo was becoming disconcerted and losing patience.

"But she can't have got up and strolled out?" the doctor argued. "Her injuries were extreme. If the patient could support herself, I doubt she could walk faster than a shuffle."

"When did you last see her?" Gonzalo asked.

"About fifteen minutes before we talked in the hallway.

Fifteen minutes doesn't allow a lot of time, Gonzalo thought. *I don't expect Peter Kilkenny could have got to Kirsty without being spotted. So? Where has she gone?* Then he recalled the huddled woman shuffling down the corridor, and he understood. *She must have been Kirsty.*

— ☐ —

Kirsty shuffled herself from the lift and entered the hospital's reception foyer. Each step, like treading in a minefield, with the occasional wrong move, shooting lightning bolts of agony up through her lower back. The impact caused her to gasp and linger until the tide of pain ebbed away. The reception area, now a hive of movement, with hordes of individuals moving in every direction. No one took notice of a decrepit, hospital gowned girl, who became lost between their numbers. Next to a disabled toilet stood a Zimmer frame. Kirsty concluded her need to save Abigail from the murderous clutches of Pete, justified commandeering the walking frame. She clattered through the foyer with a click-clacked noise as she moved around the perimeter towards the exit. Reaching the reception area before the way out, someone bumped into her. Although the jolt was slight, it sent seismic spasms throughout her slender frame. She staggered towards the right. The frame almost slid from her grasp and provoked her to grab out for the counter to gain support.

Behind the booth, an assistant had been busy performing clerical tasks. Using scissors to cut out portions of paperwork. She failed to see Kirsty now gasping for breath, leaning against the surface. The fellow who'd bumped Kirsty ignored her as well and spoke to the attendant. The receptionist put the scissors she had been holding on the counter-top in front of Kirsty. They mirrored the glint from the brilliant lighting, as if beckoning Kirsty to pick them up. The blades were 8-inches and finished at a point. She grabbed them without hesitation, then eased herself and the Zimmer away to blend into insignificance towards the wide glass doors of the entrance.

Clueless of Abigail and Pete's whereabouts, Kirsty hissed in pain. "I have to find Abigail," and grunted, "I have to save her from him." Inching forwards, she made gradual progress onto the pedestrianized path between the parked cars. "I have to stop him."

Hidden Surprise

The cannon thump of his heart thundered, so intense, Pete felt it would reveal him. He squinted through the slimmest sliver between the wardrobe doors and watched as Detective Baldomero walked toward his hiding place. Pete held his breath and didn't dare move until the detective slipped out of his view.

Abigail followed in behind Baldomero. Her naked shoulders glistened, water beaded coconut skin, which was tantalizing to Pete as she stood mere inches from his shelter. Abigail and the police officer were clueless about him hiding behind the closet's pine doors. A towel cloaked Abigail's nakedness wrapped tight beneath her armpits to end high above her knees. Her lithe thighs became exposed and teased Pete further as he turned into a spectator to Baldomero's apologies.

"I am sorry to trouble you — Miss Simmons." asserted the abashed Baldomero.

Abigail cut him off. "Is everything okay?" she asked, embarrassed and collecting fresh underwear, jeans, and a T-shirt. "I will be right back; I'm just going to put on some clothes." Abigail declared, holding up the garments to show her plan, and retired to the bathroom. "Is Kirsty okay?"

Waiting until Abigail had returned, now dressed, she scrunched her hair dry with the towel as she entered.

"Last I learned, Kirsty isn't any different." Baldomero stated before inquiring. "Is Peter here? Is he in the hotel?"

"I don't know. Why?" she challenged as she wriggled her feet into a pair of sandals.

He pointed to the bed and said, "I think you'd better sit down?"

— ☐ —

The wardrobe plunged into twilight darkness when blocked by the shadow of Baldomero who stood in front of it. Pete was cramping up, and his hiding place produced a groan as he shifted position. The noise caused him to freeze. Perspiration ran pearls from his brow that trickled down his cheek before dripping off his chin. Pete didn't dare move a second time, and again held his breath when sunlight slashed through the doors once more. The detective, who had been leaning against the closet, moved elsewhere. Pete realized his earlier movement had granted him a better angle of the room. He noticed the firearm strapped above the officer's left hip. *He hadn't been carrying a gun earlier,* Pete recalled. *Something's changed,* and he listened as the police officer spoke.

"Where is Mr Kilkenny?" Baldomero asked, his tone brusque.

"Pete's gone out for a walk," answered Abigail, a little unsettled. "You're scaring me, Detective — what's this about?"

Pete realized he held the element of surprise; the tables had now shifted in his favour. A smirk curved his lip. The situation is laughable. Pete shook his head in disbelief. *How ironic,* he reflected, *this is farcical, as if this is happening to me.* He risked a restrained chuckle as he surveyed his surroundings. A vague smell of pine, scented by old mothballs, tickled his nostrils as he snorted a breath. *All the money I have... And with all the lunatics I know,* he gave a disbelieving head shake. *Yet here I am, trapped inside this closet, like a kid playing hide-and-seek.* The sear of embarrassment scalded his face.

Pete welcomed the element of surprise and waited for his moment to strike. Patience is the key, he agreed. *An opportunity will present itself.* He nodded at the thought. At significant risk, he altered his position again to relieve the cramp biting into his calf muscles. The detective's solid form moved into view.

Pete looked for a weakness. Something he could employ to get the upper hand. Although surprise was a helpful ally, it wasn't the killer strike he called for, and there was no way to tell how Abigail might behave. She could freeze, she might run, he couldn't be certain. Abigail could assist Baldomero, so Pete searched every inch of the detective. A blow to the detective's tree-trunk throat wouldn't be successful, and the failed attack would lose Pete his edge. He looked lower and noted the unclipped holster clasp didn't secure the pistol, understanding the gun would slip out with ease and Pete saw what he needed to do.

"Perfect," he smirked.

— ☐ —

Abigail sat cross-legged, her flip-flop sandals she now wore slung from one foot as she perched on the corner of the bed. She observed, with increasing unease, an agitated Baldomero pace back and forth between the window and the wardrobe. He appeared restless. She spotted the gun, and this made Abigail anxious, having never been up close to someone who was armed before, causing her to be nervous. For the second time, she inquired, "Is everything okay with Kirsty?"

Baldomero stopped. He turned to Abigail, leaving his back to the closet. "Kirsty is the same," he responded, "Nothing has changed from earlier."

"So?" Abigail asked, her eyebrows creased and wrinkled deep furrows upon her forehead. "You seem tense — Detective, it's a little disconcerting."

"I've received intelligence concerning Mr Kilkenny...Peter," Baldomero answered. "How closely do you know him?" He leant against the wardrobe, which creaked under his weight.

Abigail scratched her head as she thought about his question. "Well — I met him the day I arrived back home after my initial visit," she glanced up at him. "When I came to search for Kirsty and Steve," frustrated by the seriousness of his tone. "You can't think Pete has anything to do with this?" she scoffed. "He's Kirsty's boyfriend's — He's Steve's brother."

Baldomero's silence spoke volumes while he listened to Abigail.

"Steve never spoke about him — and I can only go by what I have seen, but Pete seems a nice guy. Perhaps a little secretive, but nice enough. Why? What's this about?"

"So, you hadn't known Peter before Kirsty and Steve's disappearance?" Baldomero moved away from the wardrobe. "You are unaware of Peter's businesses?"

Abigail retorted, "Why would I be interested in his business when we have only just met?"

"Earlier — after you left the hospital — I went back to the Medianoche Exótica, where we found Kirsty. I recognized Peter Kilkenny; I realized I had seen him before. It was when I returned to the club that I remembered. I have in recent weeks been to the same place investigating a separate case. It was during this visit that my and Peter's paths first crossed. When I recalled this, I spoke to an Inspector Collins. She works for the British police and has been investigating Peter — for some time."

The surprise on Abigail's face appeared to be genuine as the detective went on.

"I suspect Peter is the man responsible for Kirsty's kidnapping." He watched Abigail give an uncertain shake of her head. "We're yet to find Steven Douglas, I won't lie to you, Miss Simmons — the longer time goes on, the less chance we have of a positive outcome."

The sharpness of his words inflamed her denial. "This is ludicrous," she argued with visible anger as she balled her hands into fists. She stood up, outraged at his suggestion. "Oh, come on, detective," she said, failing to hide the sharpness in her tone. "This is Pete you're talking about. He has been nothing but helpful — so supportive. If you don't believe me, then speak to Ruth. Ruth Douglas. That's Steve's mum. She'll vouch for him."

— ☐ —

Aghast, "What do you mean they're dead?" Abigail gasped. Tears ran hot streams down her cheeks. "They can't be dead. Pete was with them yesterday, and they were fi…" The realization dawned on her, and she wiped her face. She knew Baldomero was speaking the truth. "Oh God — how could I be so stupid?"

"I don't know the entire details," said Baldomero, "But, it appears to have been a gas leakage." He felt awkward. He always detested being the bearer of bad news. It was the one part of the job he'd never got used to.

"A gas leak?" Abigail glanced up at him, puzzled, "How — how is that possible?" She shook her head again. "So? Pete didn't kill them?" She gawked at him. "Was there an explosion?"

He stepped toward her and answered, "There wasn't a fire." He was in front of her and reached down to put his hand on Abigail's shoulder.

Inside the wardrobe, Pete listened. *Why wasn't the house destroyed?* He was angered and wondered what had gone wrong? *This is a problem. There should have been an explosion, and it should have wiped out any evidence.* His rage burned. *If I hadn't come over here with you,* he glared through the crack in the doors at Abigail. He braced his feet against the wooden back of his hiding place. It will soon be time. *You're going to pay for this.* His heart raced as adrenaline fuelled his anger. *If not for you?* He scowled at her, his nostrils flared, like a horse wild and unbroken. *I could have made sure all the evidence went up in flames. Now the police have a crime scene and my fingerprints are all over the place. Oh, I will have some fun with you.* He jabbed his finger as if pointing at her. *You will suffer for dragging me over here.*

Having listened to enough, Pete watched the detective edge closer to him, Baldomero faced away from his hideout and that's when Pete sprang into action.

— ☐ —

The doors splintered into a trillion shards as Pete erupted from inside the wardrobe. He crashed hard into Baldomero's back, a juggernaut of fury. Abigail's shriek was born more from shock than fright. Instant flight mode kicked in, sending her up onto the bed and stumbling backward. It all happened in a whirlwind of violence. A flurry of thrashing limbs which broke out into the cramped space. The unexpected impact slammed into the startled detective, whose knee buckled beneath him to tumble face forward into the mattress. He star-fished half on and half off the bed as he went down in an awkward slump, trapping his right arm beneath him.

Something popped in his shoulder, and white-fiery sparks shot blinding pain through Baldomero's back. The aggressor's fist hit into his vulnerable throat, and the detective slipped towards unconsciousness. He bit his tongue and choked upon the slick, metallic oiliness which oozed crimson fluid into his mouth. The battle almost lost, so he sought to stand up. The strength had vanished from his limbs. He reached for his gun instead, but couldn't unwrap his one arm while his free left arm grappled with the unknown assailant. He barked like an injured seal and sucked large gulps of air. The fuzziness that greyed his vision receded, his energy returned, just a little, but sufficient to recognize he wasn't yet beaten. His grunt was guttural as he pushed backward with all his power, seeking to increase leverage. Like an eel, he slithered from beneath his aggressor and in a mindless panic made a grab for his handgun. But the pistol had gone.

Pete leapt towards the Detective. Pressed his advantage and wouldn't allow Baldomero a chance to recover. He gripped his right arm around the detective's collar and thrust his left arm up under the police officer's shoulder, a half-nelson style grip. Applying pressure to the cartilage of the oesophagus, Pete squeezed. Baldomero knew Pete's purpose. Adrenaline dulled the pain as he floundered to break the viper's grip. It didn't work and was held firm. The detective squeezed a wrist up between Pete's clamping arm and averted his throat from being crushed. Almost all his strength had come back, and Baldomero could sense he was getting the upper hand. He forced his heels against the bed and drove his head backwards, and was rewarded with a satisfying wet thwack and crunch of bone. Pete's grasp weakened, and he cried out with an injured dog yelp.

Baldomero's fist glanced a blow across the temple, but Pete ducked beneath the flailing arm. He tripped and went down, landing in a stunned heap on the floor. His laboured breath bubbled claret from his broken nostrils, but he thrust himself up and turned, all in one motion. Making a rugby style tackle, he took Baldomero below the hips and they both fell upon the mattress. More luck than fortune, Pete placed his hand upon the gun, which he found rumpled in the bed linen. They separated for a final face-off. Baldomero readied his attack. Pete, despite squinting through tear streamed eyes, acted by instinct, and clicked the pistol off safe and raised the weapon in a single action. Pointed at Baldomero's chest and pulled the trigger.

Boom.

Fire sent the bullet point-blank into the detective's rib cage to send him cartwheeling backward.

— □ —

The gunshot filled Abigail's head with a mass of white noise. A static buzz deafened her as the flash of gunfire filled the room. She watched Baldomero gambol across the bed and end up on the floor by her feet. Face down, she saw Pete straddle over the police officer and steadied himself to carry out the kill.

Audible sounds mingled to jangle through Abigail's tinnitus. Someone screamed. A terrified, tortured screech, and she realized they came from herself. She watched Baldomero raise his head and looked her in the eyes.

"Run," Baldomero said.

Abigail lip-read the word and didn't need to be told twice. Galvanized into action, she spun and bolted to the door. Burst into the passage as a second gunshot exploded. She veered into, then bounced off the wall opposite. Stumbled and went down with a solid thump. Pain danced sprites of needle-pointed daggers along her spine. She didn't allow it to slow her and was up, clawing the walls in terror. Scrabbling either side, picking up momentum. Bolting toward the stairs, she threw herself down the first four. A third gunshot boomed. Heat zinged past her head. Close enough to feel her hair crackle and sniff the burnt cordite. Wood splinters from off the wooden banister showered her with shrapnel. A swarm of angered hornets kissed her face, and she covered her eyes. Jumping the last few steps, Abigail's sandaled feet slapped against the terrazzo floor, an echoing clip-clap, as she ran across the lobby.

— □ —

The hotel receptionist inspected the fat, cone-shaped joint. He'd just finished rolling it when the upstairs commotion disturbed the tranquil foyer. *Must be the couple who rented rooms earlier, arguing,* he speculated. He got up and went to close his office door, and that's when the first gunshot shattered his peace.

The reefer fell from his grip, bounced once upon the counter, and dropped to the floor. *That was a gunshot*. His head screamed. Someone above him shouted. One other person had been standing in the reception lobby, but vanished at the initial blast. Only the late-afternoon sunlight, which glared through the glazed entrance as the door swung closed. *It can't have been a gun*, he thought, but the second shot answered any doubt he might have had. The hotel receptionist stepped into the reception hall. A third shot showered splinters over the figure of a woman who jumped down the last few steps.

"Help, please," came the woman's frantic plea. "Ring the police — for Christ's sake," terror quaked her voice. "Get help," she shouted.

He didn't understand what she'd said, but reached for the phone, anyway. The fourth and final shot took him right between the eyes. His head jerked backwards at the same instant the coolness of death overwhelmed him.

Abigail came to a stop. Her scream wedged in her throat as scarlet sprayed the reception wall. The receptionist was dead before he'd hit the floor and slipped out of sight behind the counter. Abigail, powerless to fathom the viciousness of violence, stayed stock still. Too afraid to run for fear the next shot might take her. Pete was behind her in seconds and dug the pistol against her ribs. Heat from the weapon burnt through the cotton vest top she wore, and she attempted to tear away.

Pete held her tight. "Don't you move," he said, breathless from his recent exertions. "If you cry out, you will be dead like that detective."

Abigail believed him and drew her palms backward, like she had seen many times in the movies. She realized he would kill her if she gave him a reason, and attempted to twist to confront him. He clutched her harder and jabbed the gun farther into her ribs.

"I hope you liked my surprise," he chuckled, a wet hoarse sort of chuckle "It's time we visit Kirsty," then spat a gob of blood upon the floor as he guided her towards the exit.

"You bastard," she answered with a snarl, "I trusted you. How could you?"

Pete laughed, a harsh chattering like a crow's cackle, "I'm going to enjoy killing your friend."

They strolled out into the sun-bleached street. "Now walk."

They stepped together. He linked arms and kept the gun hidden, crammed into Abigail's side.

"Move," he ordered with a bark, and nudged the firearm with painful intent. "If you dare give me any trouble." He squeezed harder, "Understand?"

She acknowledged, "Please — don't do this…"

He thrust the pistol deeper and delivered a strong nudge forward.

"Okay," she conceded with more vigour, and went with him.

A Cold Sapphire Blueness

Gonzalo ran the length of the corridor. He dodged medical personnel and patients alike in his hunt for Kirsty. He rushed dancing the cha-cha slide around the dogleg further up the passage and peered at himself in the reflective elevator doors as he rushed toward them. *Come on — come on*, his panicked inner voice pleaded. His uneasiness increased as his finger jabbed at the call button several times.

He gave up when the elevator went past his floor without stopping. Gonzalo bolted into the exit staircase to the right of him. Descending the treads two at a time, he proceeded down to the ground floor reception. Gonzalo approached officer Mateo, one of the four officials who stood nearby. "The young woman?" he whooped. *God — I'm out of shape,* he admitted to himself, leaning over to rest his hands on his knees, quaffing at the air. "The girl," he stated more urgently, "The one we brought in? She's missing. Have you noticed her in this area?"

"No, Sir," replied Mateo, "But, I have only just started my rounds. I will check with the others." He unclipped his two-way radio. After several conversations on the radio Mateo returned his attention to Gonzalo and said, "She hasn't been identified — Sir."

"With the girl missing — I haven't had the chance to call this in, but Detective Baldomero has gone to the hotel across the street. He may be in danger. Call control and let them know what's happening? Organize backup to meet Nick?" Gonzalo waited while Mateo dealt with his requests before giving further instruction. "Now, inform the other officers — we need to search every room. First, I'll review the cameras." He pointed to a fisheye camera on the wall as he hurried off. Shouting over his shoulder. "I will be at the security office."

Tomǎs was the chief of the hospital security system, and he sat controlling the CCTV cameras. Gonzalo approached the office desk and said, "I require you to check the cameras."

"What are you searching for?" Asked Tomǎs as he clicked the buttons of the CCTV. The screen flashed blue before splitting into several smaller pictures, which displayed footage from all the specific camera locations.

"I need footage from that camera?" Gonzalo said, touching the screen to point out the camera by the elevator. "Can you pull that one up on a slow rewind?"

Tomǎs did as desired, and Gonzalo watched himself appear backwards from the staircase entrance. "Can this move any quicker?"

"I'm certain she went this way," Gonzalo said, but was doubting himself. "She must have taken the elevator?" Talking more to himself than to Tomǎs. Watching the seconds roll backwards and the minutes build up, Gonzalo was about to stop until the silver doors opened and the character, who he had earlier mistaken for an old woman, straggled into view.

"Okay." Gonzalo said and pointed to the screen. "I need to follow this woman. I must find out where she goes."

— ☐ —

"Just move." Pete drove the handgun into Abigail's armpit, and they crossed the street towards the hospital. Blood still bled from his nose, and he wore a mask of crimson. He was attracting undesirable attention from passers-by and pushed Abigail toward the fast-food restaurant he'd stopped at earlier. Entering the restroom area, he shoved Abigail into the disabled toilet. Pete held the gun in front of her. "Stand there and keep your mouth shut."

Pete washed his face and winced as he plugged tissue into his nostrils. He was already sporting racoon eyes and an angry plum sized lump swelled the left side of his head. "That bastard," Pete growled as he gawked at the mirror, "Well, he caught himself two slugs," he declared and brandished the pistol about in the air, "From this," he thumped it against his chest, "Ha–ha." He whooped, "Right there," pointing the gun. "I double tapped him. In his heart."

"Wha… what… what are you going to do to me?" a terrified Abigail whimpered. "Please…" She cowered beneath his fist when he grasped her shoulder.

"Shut your snivelling."

Although the rumble in his tone was low and guttural, it subdued Abigail into hopeless obedience. Fear unlike any she had felt before twisted her gut, and a bitter taste of bile soured the back of her mouth. "W… w… why?" She pleaded, dubious of his intent.

"Why?" Pete mocked with a ghoulish whine, mimicking her. "Why?" he repeated, only this time, his caustic growl had returned. Then his voice shifted into a whisper. He announced, "I took her dignity, you know." He smirked and insanity twinkled his eyes. "I stole her." Pete rubbed his groin, and a wistful look creased his face. He licked his lips and quivered his tongue in the air, serpent-like, "I made her mine."

Abigail knew what he meant and couldn't hold it back any longer. Her stomach cramped as bile decorated the floor. "How could you?" she snorted with an involuntary warble. "How could you do this?" Her eyes met his. It did not bother her about the drool dripping from her chin, and Abigail aimed her revulsion toward Pete when she answered him, "Why, Kirsty? And Steve?" Her voice had raised its pitch, "He's your brother." Tears stung their fresh tracks upon her cheeks. "How could you?"

Pete smirked at Abigail, as if she had suggested something incredulous. "Huh… Brother?" he growled. "They offered him everything. I could have been dead — for all it meant." he turned vitriolic and hollered into the air. "Mother and Father… They wouldn't even speak to me. Not after I joined up. You should be honoured to have a son serve for Queen and country. Just like Uncle Tommy during the Falklands." As if he were conducting an incoherent orchestra, Pete twirled the handgun at imagined spectres. He wasn't talking to Abigail anymore, but conversed with wraiths deep within his psyche. "Just because Tommy paid his ultimate sacrifice when HMS Coventry went down." He'd become detached from reality as he recalled the dispute he'd had with his parents and shouted at his imaginary phantoms in the air. "Dad should be honoured. I wished to be like Tommy. But you renounced me instead. Huh, you wrote me out of it all." His remarks dwindled to a hiss and grew full of venom. "You threw it all to him…" He growled loud again. "How was I expected to know you would come after me?" He whirled around and around. "Why did you follow me out, eh?" A sound came out of Pete, one more suited to the cackle of a hyena. He referred to Steve. "Why didn't you take him with you?" Pete continued, with more of a snarl in his tone. "Would have worked so well, Steve should have died in the collision too. I was just a kid. I didn't understand what to do with him." Pete shifted, became matter of fact, and shrugged, "Huh — and then, they were gone. The police report said it was an accident. But we all realize it was my fault, and you'd had your last laugh?"

Abigail saw Pete's normality unhinge. His mind withdrew away from her. She trod backwards. He didn't seem to acknowledge her shift. She continued with slow, deliberate steps back towards the door. His voice thundered like another gunshot, and she froze.

"I showed you — didn't I?" Pete bellowed, his words echoed into the small washroom as he whirled about, looking up at the ceiling. He arched backward and threw his head back then roared with laughter, "You believed you could close me out — didn't you? Thought you could give Steve everything that's mine? Hah." His taunting laugh tainted by hysteria. "I didn't need you?" Waving his arms in wide circles. "Look — look at what I…" he hammered an apish palm flat upon his chest, "… Look at what I've built." He snarled, "I didn't need you then, and I don't now."

Abigail continued to creep toward the exit. Her eyes locked on Pete. She reached her hand up, searching for the bolt.

Then, drifting in like an early morning mist, reality reasserted itself. Pete returned and pointed the gun up at Abigail's face. "And?" his stare held her rigid. "Just where do you think you're going?"

— □ —

It seemed to be an invisible force which drew Kirsty towards the far end of the car-park. She shuffled a snail's crawl, inch by excruciating inch, along the pedestrian walkway between parked cars. A tar-pit of fatigue sucked at her extremities, which made movement tedious and cumbersome. An almost precognitive sense for Abigail's safety swam through Kirsty's concerns. Fear swelled her heart as dread throbbed in her veins. With each stride, she hissed a silent prayer. *Please, God — one more step— just one.*

— □ —

Gonzalo had now identified Kirsty with two cameras. He trailed her progress through the reception area. He already knew where she was headed. After watching Kirsty catch her breath against the desk, he saw her exit the building. Gonzalo checked the time to show Kirsty having left the hospital seven minutes earlier.

— □ —

Pete grabbed Abigail by the arm and wedged the gun up into her armpit, then shoved her out of the restaurant. They reached the hospital and were at the bottom of the steps leading up to the carpark.

He nudged her with the pistol to move just as a scarecrow of a woman emerged at the top.

Dressed in a pastel blue, polka dotted hospital gown, and supporting herself with help of a Zimmer frame. Her swollen face resembled that of a gerbil and wasn't recognized by either Abigail or Pete, who hadn't expected Kirsty to be in the carpark. Neither of them realized this forlorn, broken-faced girl was her.

— ▢ —

Kirsty watched as Pete and Abigail climbed the steps. *What are you going to do now?* She urged herself, but didn't have an answer. *They didn't give you a second glance. They haven't recognized you. But what now? Now you've got here — what will you do?* Kirsty stumbled backward. Her head a mishmash of thought, unable to think. Then she remembered the scissors in her grip.

— ▢ —

Gonzalo slammed open the entrance doors and burst into the car-park. He could see Kirsty at the far edge, staring down the steps as if considering her descent. "What on earth are you doing?" He mumbled and raced along the pedestrianized walkway. He called out, "Kirsty?" But she didn't twist to look at him. "Kirsty — where are you going?"

— ▢ —

They were on the last but one step when Abigail heard someone shout Kirsty's name and, at the same instant, she recognized her friend. "No." She gasped, "Kirsty, run — you have to get away from him." But it was too late. She knew Kirsty couldn't run, plus there wasn't anywhere she could go.

Pete watched Gonzalo run between the parked cars. At the same moment, he pushed Abigail aside and lifted the gun.

Both Abigail and Kirsty reacted as one.

Abigail pulled Pete backwards to tumble him down the steps.

While Kirsty used the last of her energy to thrust the Zimmer Frame at her blue-eyed demon. This action unbalanced her, and she toppled forwards before continuing down in a tangle with Pete. The barrel of the gun belched fire, and a bullet zinged just millimetres past Kirsty's face. The trajectory missed its mark, but struck the onrushing Gonzalo to pitch him backward.

The aluminium Zimmer frame hit Pete to bounce off him with ease, but the dead weight of Kirsty surprised him. She fell and pushed forwards, pressing home her attack. The end of the scissors slid with minimal resistance into the flesh of Pete's torso as both he and Kirsty cartwheeled down the steps.

Pete sat hunched on all fours, unable to catch his breath. The angle of his lower arm screamed with pain from the compound brake he had suffered to his wrist. But it was the least of his problems. Panic yelled in his head, why can't I breathe? Hot rivers ran a scarlet pool beneath him. He attempted to stand but skidded on a dark viscose ooze. A frigid heaviness seeped strength from his limbs as he knelt in a maroon puddle of life's fluid. Pete stared at the strange figure of eight handles poking out from his ribs. Using his good hand, he clutched the object and yanked, but his blood slicked fingers slipped. A rasp of agonized laughter rattled from him and his arms slumped to his side and Pete looked into Kirsty's eyes.

She lay sprawled mere inches from him and held his stare and watched those cold sapphire eyes slide toward oblivion.

— ☐ —

A continuous pressure upon the lids of Baldomero's eyes seemed as if invisible thumbs kept them closed. Pain blinded his vision as the detective prised them open. A drunken fog dulled his thoughts. It faded from his mind as he grew more aware. The bleat of a siren shrilled his ears. A gentle rocking motion, which he first mistook for the effects of unconsciousness, but then turned into reality. He groaned a second time, louder, and went to sit up. Dizziness spilt into him, a whirlwind of nausea.

"Please try to remain still — Detective," came a somewhat ethereal tone. "You have been shot, and you're on the way to Centro hospital." The paramedic said, and her face morphed into view.

Cathedral bells played with skull-shattering clangs as specks of light, like fireflies on a velvet night, flared at the back of Baldomero's eyelids. Images of Pete's attack flashed. Gunshots echoed. He snapped his eyes wide. His throat, desert dry. "How bad is it?" he reacted with a frog-like croak. Talking intensified the scalding rivers which boiled fury within his chest.

"You're a lucky man," the Medic said, while checking Baldomero's stats. She placed a compassionate hand upon his shoulder and added, "Your vest saved your life." She pointed with a small penlight towards the body armour he had slipped on. "You have a serious contusion to the side of your head and were unconscious when we entered."

Baldomero once again tried to sit up but the medic's hands became more resistant. Gravity appeared to work against him as fatigue ebbed into every muscle.

"You have trauma to your rib cage." holding him firmer. "Please — detective — you must remain still. We're taking you to the emergency room," she echoed. "You may have internal injuries. We need to assess you — so, please remain calm."

Ignoring her plea, "The young woman?" Baldomero asked. "Is the girl okay?" Furnace bellows blew within his chest. He moved his arms with a slow, almost robotic movement and dragged his right hand across his torso. Pain ripped through him and cut off his breathing. The bell ringer inside the detective's skull clanged. Perspiration trickled from his brow as he wished for the spasm to pass. "Was there a girl?"

"I don't know," the medic answered. "Not as far as we're aware." She pointed toward her colleague, who was driving. "We needed to treat you." She was becoming concerned about Baldomero's stats. "Another man had also been shot, but we couldn't save him." She held up a syringe. "Like I said, you have been fortunate. Okay, that's enough talking. You need to rest. I am going to give you a sedative — it will help you relax and ease your pain."

— ☐ —

The bullet which Pete fired took Gonzalo high in the right shoulder. It ricocheted off and splintered the bone before exiting his scapula. A thousand scorpion stings throbbed across his chest. The jolt had lifted him off his feet, and he landed with a considerable thump flat on his back. Stars danced about his vision, almost fooling him into thinking his life was over. Only the pain which gripped him said otherwise. He clambered to his feet and leant upon the bonnet of a nearby Audi. Its gleaming white paintwork became blood smeared. The headiness dissipated, and his torment eased. Gonzalo staggered toward the steps.

He found Abigail helping Kirsty move away from Pete. If Kirsty hadn't acted as she had, the gun wouldn't have strayed from its mark. The outcome for Gonzalo, he didn't doubt, would have been his death. He owed his survival to the brave actions of Kirsty. He couldn't be more thankful, for he knew Kirsty had saved his life. Others had arrived now, medical personnel and security swamped the scene. They began work on Pete whilst Gonzalo slid down and sat on the top step. Kirsty looked up toward him and relief swelled into her features.

Goodnight My Sweet.

A morning breeze sang cherub song between the mid springtime cherry blossoms. Winter fought a last-ditch attempt to maintain its grip as an unseasonal, nor-westerly chill edged the springtime air. It prickled goosebumps across the flesh of Kirsty's arms. She folded them into herself and across the delicate material of her sleeveless blouse.

"Well? Darling?" she whispered with soft elegiac tones. Looking toward Steve's epitaph, "I hope you're proud of me?" A lasting reminder from her ordeal made Kirsty's speech slur with a lisp. Her R's sounded more like W's and altered the words darling into dawling, and proud came out as pwoud. A tear welled at the corner of her eye, and she blotted it away with a tissue. Kirsty always spoke to Steve when she visited him, and his silence didn't perturb her. In fact, she often found the peace reassuring.

After surviving her abduction and forced incarceration, Kirsty was an insomniac. Plagued by nightmares, all driven by a guilt so profound, she thought it would never ease. Sometimes during the bleak, bitter months of withdrawal, her self-loathing would only improve when she visited Steve. Kirsty's homage to him developed into an everyday routine of endless weeping. Little by little, her grief became part of her burden, which, with each visit to the cemetery, grew easier to bear.

These days, Kirsty's visits were less frequent. Perhaps twice, maybe three times per week, depending on how bleak the darkness inside her heart felt. Today was different. It was a special day. One which filled her with nervous apprehension, but the nerves were a good thing.

The ambrosial scents from the orchard were intoxicating as the light breeze snatched at the modest pink blooms. Petals danced as if fairy wings soared and swooped throughout an enchanted realm and produced a shrine to Steve's resting place. The peace of the graveyard was beautiful. Kirsty always mentioned this to Steve whenever they had visited before his death. Now 6:30 am ; the day was just coming alive. The sun's warm caress crept higher into the dawn, and the chill eased.

— ☐ —

It was approaching sixteen months since Steve's death. The tranquil solitude, which surrounded Steve's grave site, had never failed to purge Kirsty of those awful experiences. She imagined it was Steve who had restrained her from entering the hellish helter-skelter of relapse. Her mother together with Abigail helped in her feud against addiction. Kirsty no-longer-used any type of heroin substitute or felt the nagging urge for narcotic release, but the horrors still troubled her sleep. Kirsty had been diagnosed with suffering post-traumatic stress and assigned to Julie, her therapist. Julie held therapy sessions twice a week, and little by little Kirsty's confidence returned as the visions of blue orbs faded.

A tear rolled onto her cheek. Its heat stung, and again she dabbed it away. She had come to terms with Steve's death; it had taken her a long, long time, but she learned to live with the grief. Looking over towards the right of the plot; bitterness clutched her heart. The man answerable for all this suffering, all this misery was incarcerated inside a Spanish prison but it didn't make matters any less painful.

A grey squirrel hopped down from the cherry tree to make Kirsty gasp in delight. The squirrel perched himself upon the black marble headstone. A smile curved into the corner of Kirsty's mouth. "Hello, Mr Squirrel," she lisped. The creature cocked his head, first to the left, then to the right. He pushed his twitching nose into the air before turning his back, and off he scampered. She watched the squirrel dart between several headstones. The wind sighed and branches chattered. A shower of confetti blossom fell like rain. Kirsty's hair flipped up in this stronger gust, then streamed across her face. The squirrel peered back for one last time, rose on its haunches and cupped his snout with both front paws as if attempting to holler out. He made one last glance over his shoulder and vanished into the thicket of a hawthorn hedge. Kirsty could almost hear him call to her; she could have sworn the animal called the name Kirsty, but then, like the critter himself, it was gone.

— □ —

The S.F.A. Corporation had been the tip of the iceberg, and the publicized court appearances of Kirsty and Abigail were decisive in bringing down a European web of organized trafficking. Gangs who forced many victims into modern-day slavery. Once the inquiry into Peter Kilkenny's associates had concluded, it smashed open the doors to several firms with dealings in similar trades.

Using a generous contribution from the inheritance she had gained through Steve's estate, and, thanks to the generosity of Edna Williams who was the older sister of Ruth Douglas. Edna had inherited Ruth and Mark's estate after their tragic deaths. Upon hearing Kirsty's intentions, the older relative had given a substantial donation to help Kirsty. Kirsty aided by Abigail had set up an association devoted in the support of sexual enslavement victims. She was determined to provide a refuge for the unfortunate women still suffering. Her organization provided an asylum and relocation. A means to evade the organized gangs who targeted them.

She listened and savoured the orchestral twittering of springtime birdsong. The merry chirp of the skylark together with the whistling calls of a nearby song thrush. Both of which contended against the musical trill of a blackbird. The sun now warmed away the goose flesh upon her uncovered arms, and she hugged into her knees. Her peace was interrupted by a crunch of shale which signalled the approach of footsteps that halted by her side. Opening her eyes, Kirsty stared at Steve's resting place.

"We expected you would be here," came Abigail's voice. "Steve has a lovely spot. It's so peaceful." She sat down next to Kirsty. "You going to be okay, — Hun?" Abigail draped her arm around Kirsty's shoulder while they peered out across the cemetery.

"I miss him so much," Kirsty said as she leant her head into the welcoming comfort of Abigail's embrace. "Will it ever stop hurting?"

Abigail didn't answer. In moments like this, she found it best to remain silent. When she sensed it was appropriate to do so, she spoke, "Come on, it's time to go."

— □ —

Today, after months of hard work and preparation, they were launching the D.S.W. Centre. They had abbreviated the name down from The Douglas Shelter for Women. This offered two meanings. For Kirsty, it was a means of honouring Steve, and it made her feel he was always with her. For Abigail, it took on a more ironic significance. An insult towards Peter Kilkenny and the corporations involved with exploitation of woman who they forced into the sex industry. The D.S.W. Center also represented a place of hope and freedom, somewhere to rebuild the shattered lives of the many who sought their help.

"The press is going to be there," Abigail warned. "You fit for that?"

Both Kirsty and Abigail were to be interviewed by radio, TV, and local tabloids, a signal of the triumphal conclusion to their nightmare.

Pushing back on her palms and upward with her legs, Kirsty stood. She shuffled and reached down to help Abigail.

Holding on to both Abigail's hands, Kirsty stared into her friend's eyes and said, "Thank-you."

"Don't be soft." Abigail blushed; her cocoa skin turned deep mahogany. "You know you don't need to thank me. I'm pleased to do it."

"I didn't mean thanks for the support of launching the centre. Although I do thank-you for that, as well." Kirsty peered deep into her friend's chestnut eyes, as if searching within her soul.

Shaking her head and wrinkling up her face in protest, "I appreciate what you're thanking me for." Abigail gripped onto Kirsty's hands to provide consolation. Watching her image within the mill-pools of Kirsty's face, "You would have done the same for me if it had been the other way around. Besides, it's me who should thank you. You're the one who stopped him, you spared us both."

Kirsty didn't respond. Instead, she knelt, kissed her hand, and placed it on top of Steve's grave.

"Goodnight my sweet."

A Way Out of This Mess.

1999... Shērkhān Bandar, Afghanistan.

Anton Lenkov established the Solntsevskaya Bratva in 1989. Identified as the biggest and most influential crime syndicate of the Russian mafia. During the late 1980s, soviet forces began their disengagement from Afghanistan. The Bratva cartel created a trade route along the Impoverished Tajikistan border with Afghanistan. Responsible for the vast transfer of illicit heroin and opium. About 10 years of transportations had seen the growth of Anton Lenkov's legacy before his merciless assassination in 1997, outside his home in the Solntsevo District of Mosco. This organization and its reputation were taken over by Anton's sole heir, his son Dmitry Lenkov. It was 1999 when Pete started working for Dmitry as his chauffeur. The Russian hadn't made up his mind about the ex-British military man. Dmitry scrutinized his new driver.

Driving through the barren desert toward the Afghan border town of Shērkhān Bandar. A dry port at the border between Afghanistan and Tajikistan. Crossing from Kara-Dum Gora peaks some 7 kilometres north of their present position, the mountainous scenery yawned with opposing shadow as sunlight withered and bled the dusk sky into hues of an indigo glow. This journey through the Kunduz Province of Afghanistan had become unstable after the Taliban snatched control of the territory in 1996.Taliban patrols in non-standard tactical vehicles such as pickup trucks with mounted machine guns for its payload visited the Panj River. They would meet with Dmitry and require payment for secure movement of his product, but this was an unscheduled trip. A risk, Dmitry took on occasional intervals to smuggle an extra consignment out of the country. These were to be secured by his comrades based in Tajikistan.

Dust from the dry land parched his mouth, grating against his teeth. They journeyed inside the soviet made Gaz-66, a lightweight personal carrier, which grumbled along the jarring road. A trail plume followed in its wake. The vehicle was suited to this terrain and coped with the grit which ground into every crevice. Dmitry glanced down at his feet. Next to him in the footwell were two AK74 assault rifles. A reliable and low-maintenance 5.45-mm weapon which had a bigger aiming range than the more notorious Kalashnikov and was excellent for this region. The truck carried two other men who guarded their illicit cargo that would be loaded onto a boat to cross into Tajikistan. Lenkov peered out of his window and into the passenger side mirror. Something in the distance shimmered, a brief flare beneath the vanishing rays of a coral sun.

"You expecting company, boss?" said his inquisitive British comrade.

"You've seen them as well?" responded Lenkov, and pulled up both rifles. "There shouldn't be anybody here. That's why I chose this evening fo…"

A shatter of glass and a loud thud cut him off. The first rocket-propelled grenade hit through the windscreen and thumped into the middle seat between each of them. Pete stamped on the brake. Neither Dmitry nor Pete had the time to admire their luck as they gawked at the smouldering point of the dud missile.

"Out…" Pete hollered as he threw the door open.

Dmitry mirrored Pete and gambolled out. Hot needles jarred the bones of his shoulder when he crashed into the ground and bounced like tumbleweed across the desolate countryside. Then the second grenade hit broadside into the abandoned truck. The world became a fireball.

Dmitry felt the intense heat cocoon his limbs before the shockwave discarded him as if he were nothing but the last autumn leaf snatched away from its branch. A swarm of killer bee shrapnel tore at his clothes. Ravaged his skin. A taste of metal swamped his mouth and choked his throat. The stench of cordite, with burnt bacon, inhaled him. His flesh became engulfed in flame. He rolled in the dirt. Extinguished but smouldering, Dmitry lay on his back, peering into the darkening sky. He noticed the silence.

Dmitry rolled onto his front. His liquid vision swam. It confused him as he watched small geysers spout up from the ground. The explosion had knocked him senseless and he failed to recognize the danger from the bullets which danced about his flailing limbs. Then he saw him. The burqa clad assassin, who raised his machine gun. The approaching killer had steadied himself and took his aim. Weapon remained on its target. This is when the brown burqa cloth which circled the aggressor's head erupted into a crimson halo. In those split seconds in the time it took for the burqa man to crumple, Dmitry thought he witnessed the angel of death. Pete was at his side. Replying to his mute bewilderment. White noise hissed, a ringing calamity, as out of sync chapel bells broke the silence. Dmitry glared into the face of the blue-eyed companion, who shouted silent words into his face. He felt a tugging on his clothes and couldn't comprehend why he dragged him behind the cover of the smouldering vehicle he had once been sitting in. He stared into the eyes of wild blue oceans which drifted into view and realized he owed his survival to this man.

— ▢ —

Present day… Spain.

Above Alicante sat in the surrounding hills, is the notorious Fontcalent prison, the biggest and most dangerous penitentiary in the region. It was a place Geoffrey loathed visiting, but with this appointment, he delivered positive news. Peter Kilkenny was to be repatriated and authorized to serve out his sentence in a British jail.

Geoffrey studied the dishevelled unshaven man seated before him, a person who was a shadow of his former self. Pete's arctic pool eyes were devoid of emotion as the company's solicitor revealed his coming change. These recent months had been a hassle, and this slight flicker of success pleased Geoffrey when he reported back to his employer.

Pete's demeanour was as inanimate as a slab of granite. The imminent move served to excite his rage and provide the thirst for vengeance, which simmered upon a hotplate of fury.

— ☐ —

Six weeks later...

The sweatbox prison transport bus had fishtailed to a stop across the highway. Its tyres shredded from the stinger flung across the baking asphalt. Its occupants gawked out at the balaclava hooded figures. Three men in total. All clad in black combat uniform, as if they were a special forces outfit on an exercise.

Dmitry, who led the raiders, bought the AK74 up as he aimed the automatic rifle at the disabled vehicle. Three olive skinned faces gaped out at him, but they soon vanished from sight when he peppered a quick burst of gunfire into the side of the bus.

"Abrir..." (open up) Dmitry hollered in Russian accented Spanish.

"Abrir...abrir." He yelled again, this time sending another burst of bullets soaring into the air.

The doors hissed as they opened, and a Spanish prison guard threw out his weapon before he clambered down.

"No dispares," (don't shoot.) He yelled before stepping down from inside.

Dmitry shoved him aside and was about to climb into the bus, but halted when scared voices and a gunshot rang into the air. Pressing the muzzle into the temple of the guard, who he forced to kneel in the dirt and had now started jabbering in Spanish hands held in prayer pose as he rocked on his knees.

"diles que salgan," (tell them to come out) Dmitry spoke with a snarl.

More muttered Spanish came from the guard before they threw two more guns from the doorway and two more guards stepped down onto the sun blazed roadway.

Dmitry went in and went to the dishevelled man cramped inside a minuscule pen.

"Well, old friend," Dmitry spoke in Russian slanted English. He smirked at Pete when he slipped off his balaclava hood. "I think it's time we got you out of this mess."

To be continued…

About the Author: David Mayall.

David Mayall was born in 1972 in the rural village of
Wythall; situated near the outskirts of Birmingham in England.
Growing up in a middle-class happy home David is the youngest of
four brothers. David is a first-time author of the thriller/suspense
genre. Writing has always been David's passion, producing short
stories and poetry from his early teens. Most recently David's poetry
has featured within anthologies, Love is in the air volume 2, Perfect
Pets, and Limerick Legends produced through
www.forwardpoetry.co.uk . He also has poetry featured in the
anthology, Winter Wonderland, produced through United Press ltd.

David is the creator of a blog page, "David Mayall's Authors Spotlight." He spends his spare time actively helping to promote other authors from any genre. The page now has developed an increasing audience within the writing community. These pages, together with a selection of early poetry works and other helpful information can be found at David Mayall's WordPress site: writerdmayall.wordpress.com

Another of David's passions is Kickboxing where he helps coach classes and train fighters. David takes great pride in helping develop the children at the club who suffer with low confidence, ADHD and autism. David is the British bronze medal holder at the world kickboxing and karate union's British open.

David keeps a personal connection with a growing following on twitter and can be found via twitter: @writerdmayall

You can also look David up on Facebook @writerdmayall or Instagram @dmayallauthor

Printed in Great Britain
by Amazon

15594075R00164